GIVE ME YOUR HAND

MEGAN ABBOTT

GIVE ME YOUR HAND

PICADOR

First published 2018 by Little, Brown and Company,
Hachette Book Group, Inc., New York

First published in the UK 2018 by Picador
an imprint of Pan Macmillan
20 New Wharf Road, London N1 9RR
Associated companies throughout the world
www.panmacmillan.com

ISBN 978-1-5098-5568-1

1 3 5 7 9 8 6 4 2

A CIP catalogue record for this book is available from the British Library.

Printed and bound by CPI Group (UK) Ltd, Croydon, CR0 4YY

Visit **www.picador.com** to read more about all our books
and to buy them. You will also find features, author interviews and
news of any author events, and you can sign up for e-newsletters
so that you're always first to hear about our new releases.

For Jack Pendarvis

GIVE ME YOUR HAND

PROLOGUE

I guess I always knew, in some subterranean way, Diane and I would end up back together.

We are bound, ankle to ankle, a monstrous three-legged race.

Accidental accomplices. Wary conspirators.

Or Siamese twins, fused in some hidden place.

It's that powerful, this thing we share. A murky history, its narrative near impenetrable. We keep telling it to ourselves, noting its twists and turns, trying to make sense of it. And hiding it from everyone else.

Sometimes it feels like Diane is a corner of myself broken off and left to roam my body, floating through my blood.

On occasional nights, stumbling to the bathroom after a bad dream, a Diane dream, I avoid the mirror, averting my eyes, leaving the light off, some primitive part of my half-asleep brain certain that if I looked, she might be there. (*Cover your mirrors after dark,* my great-grandma used to say. *Or they trap the dreamer's wandering soul.*)

So, even though I haven't seen her in years, it isn't truly a surprise when Diane appears at the Severin Lab, my workplace, the building in which I spend most of my waking life. *Of all the labs in all the world, she had to walk into mine.* And everything begins again.

The strangest part is how little we actually know about each other. Not our birthdays, our favorite songs, who made our hearts beat faster, or didn't. We were friends, if Diane is friends with any-one, only for a few months and long ago.

But we do know the one thing no one else in the world knows about the other.

The only important thing.

I.

The world is blood-hot and personal.

—Sylvia Plath

THEN

This was twelve years ago. We were seventeen, Diane and me, and for the eight or nine months of our senior year, we shared an energy that crackled in both of us, a drive, a hunger, a singing ambition.

Then, one night, everything broke.

We were at my house, my mom's cramped, Lysol-laden house, thick with rescue animals, and absent all privacy. None of the doors fully shut, swollen wood in cheap frames, accordion doors off their tracks. But she told me anyway.

When it started, we were sitting at either end of my twin bed doing our *Hamlet* study questions, Diane with her meticulous handwriting and tidy nails, wearing one of her dozen soft-as-lamb sweaters—a girl so refined she could even get a holiday job at the perfume counter at the fancy department store. She always came here to study, even though the house she lived in with her grand-father was three times the size of ours.

Here we were, so tightly quartered we could hear my mom already creeping to bed, the *slith-slith* of her slippers.

Things felt off from the start. Each time I read out a question

("What is Hamlet's central crisis?"), Diane would look at me blankly. Each time, the same distracted look, stroking the locket around her neck as if it were a genie's bottle.

"Diane," I said, crossing my legs, the narrow mattress undulating with every move, scrunched pillows, spiral notebooks tilting, our cross-country letter jackets and itchy scarves swarmed around our legs, "is this about what happened in class today?"

Because something had happened: Ms. Cameron had asked Diane to read aloud Claudius's speech—the best in the whole play—but Diane, pale as Hamlet's ghost himself, refused to open her book, arms folded and eyes blinking. When she did finally submit, the words came slow as pine sap, as that cough syrup my mom used to give me that tasted like the inside of a dying tree. *Diane, Diane, are you okay?*

"Nothing happened," Diane insisted now, turning sideways, her long blond bangs hanging like a gilt chandelier over that beauty-queen face of hers. "You know, none of these characters are real."

It was hard to argue with that, and I wondered if we should just drop it. But there was something hovering behind Diane's eyes. Diane, who'd never shared a private thought with me that wasn't about chemistry or college scholarships or the fairness of the ionic-compound question on the last exam.

I admit it: I wanted to know.

"Kit," Diane said, gripping her little Signet *Hamlet* in her hand now, the gold Jesus ring from her grandfather gleaming, "did you mean what you said in class? About Claudius having no conscience?"

I could feel something happening, something heavy in the room, a heat shuddering off Diane, her neck pink and pink spots at her temples.

"Sure," I said. "He kills his own brother to get what he wants. Which means he just has no morals."

For a moment, neither of us said anything, the air in the room pressing our faces with thickish fingers. And what was that buzzing? The halogen bulb? The chugging old laptop the PTA gave all the students who couldn't afford computers? Or was it like that time I found Sadie, our scruffed-up lap cat, under the porch, covered in flies?

"Kit," she said, her voice quiet and even, "do you think it could happen in real life?"

"What?"

"For someone to have no conscience."

"Yes," I said so quickly I surprised myself. I believed it, utterly.

Diane didn't say anything, and her hand wrapped tight around that delicate locket, tugging it down, leaving a red ring on her long white neck.

"Diane," I said, "what is it?"

We sat a moment, the buzzing still buzzing and my feet nearly asleep from stillness.

"Did someone do something to you?" I said. "Did someone hurt you?"

I'd wondered about it before, many times. I'd known her only a few months and Diane was so quiet, so private, not like any of the rest of us. Private in all the body ways, taking her gym shirt off only behind her locker door. And in how she dressed, like a virgin princess.

Or maybe I assumed that of everyone. It seemed like everyone had sad stories if you scratched deep enough.

"No one did anything to me. I'm talking about something I did," she said, eyes lowered. "I'm talking about myself."

"What did you do?" I couldn't imagine Diane doing anything that wasn't careful and correct.

"I can't say it out loud. I've never said it."

With anyone else I knew, I could think of a million possibilities. Stole a sweater from the mall, cheated on a test, rolled on molly all through the school day, too much Baileys and three furtive blow jobs before the party was over. But not Diane.

"Did you crash your granddad's truck?"

"No."

A sinking feeling began. A feeling of circling something dark.

"Are you pregnant?" I asked, even though it seemed impossible.

"No," she said. And I heard something *click-click* in her throat, or mine.

She looked up at me, those golden lashes batting fiercely, but her voice even and calm: "It's so much worse."

Smart never mattered much until you, Diane.

I'd always gotten good grades, maybe good enough to get a scholarship at City Tech. But I wasn't thinking even that far ahead, much less as far as you.

You had a plan for yourself, for what you wanted to be, and you weren't taking any chances. You were relentless. Everything had to be perfect, fingernails precise little half-moons; those goldenrod mechanical pencils you used, the erasers always untouched. Your answers were always right. Every time. Teachers used your tests for the answer keys.

What I didn't know then was that all that perfection, held so tightly, can be a shield, either to keep something out or to keep something in. To hide it.

And your ambition was itself a gift—to us both—but also some dark evidence.

"Mom," I said, "she's so serious. She works all the time. She gets up at five to run and then do an hour's homework before school."

"Good for her."

"She's learning German on her headphones while she runs. She says she's going to be a scientist and work for the government."

These were things I didn't think real people did.

"We used to call them grinds," my mom said, smiling. "But good for her."

"Mom, I just…" A yearning inside me I couldn't explain, to know things, to be bigger, to care more. I'd never felt it before Diane, but now it was there, humming inside. And my mom seemed to sense it, eyes resting on me as I twisted my hands together, trying to explain.

"Well," she said, "you're the smartest person I know."

Diane, after you told me your secret, I'd lie awake at night, staring at the light on my phone.

I'd think about you. Picture you closing your books at last, scattering eraser rubbings (you had to erase sometimes, didn't you?) into the trash. Scrubbing your face. Brushing your hair until it gleamed moonlight.

I wondered if you thought about what you'd done all the time, like I now did.

Did you rest when you finally shut your eyes?

Or was that the worst moment? The time when you thought of what you'd done, and how, maybe worse still, you'd gotten away with it. When you get away with something it's yours only, forever. Heavy and irremediable.

*   *   *

Sometimes I wondered: Why did you pick me? Attach yourself to me on your first day at our school? Was I the nicest, the friendliest? The easiest, the smartest, second-smartest to you?

Or was it mere chance, the two of us landing side by side at cross-country, legs bent, at the gate? The two of us in chem lab, elbows on the slab, working the math of it all?

Or was it me who picked you?

NOW

The halls are quiet, soothing.

I always try to get there at least an hour before the others, if I can. Sometimes, I skip the elevator, slow and halting. Take the stairs two at a time, coffee splashing up my wrist and arm, trying to beat the clock, beat the relentless ambition of the other postdocs and near-postdocs.

Dr. Severin probably won't be in for hours, her schedule mysterious and unpredictable, but we swipe security key cards to get in, so she'll know I'm here. Somehow, I think she'd know anyway. *The hardest worker I've ever seen*—that's how all my past advisers always described me. I want her to know too, and the card is proof.

In the fourteen months I've been working at the Severin Lab, I've been the first to arrive every day but two, once after being sideswiped by a pickup truck en route and once when I was stuck in the elevator and the lab tech with the sequoia-thick arms had to pry the doors open.

But today, it's more important than ever to be first.

*   *   *

In the custodian's wheeled trash can, I spot the plastic cups from the day before, champagne foam dried to fine powder.

I smile a little just thinking about it. A nervous smile.

We'd been summoned to the conference room at five o'clock for the announcement we'd all been waiting for. It was delivered by Dr. Severin in her usual dispassionate tone.

"We've received news," she said, back of her hand smoothing the skunk swoop in her black mane. "Our NIH grant application was successful. Planning will begin immediately."

As if by magic, Dr. Severin's assistant arrived with a jumbo bottle of California's finest and a sleeve of plastic flutes.

We all tried to match Dr. Severin's cool, but it was a losing battle. Me with my dumb grin. Zell's face Swedish-fish red. Juwon, unable to stop rocking back on his heels. Even Maxim, reserved and watchful and the most senior of us all, looked like he might weep with joy. We'd all been waiting so long. I can't pretend my heart didn't lift like a fist in my chest.

There were toasts, tongue-tied. *Here's to snagging that last fleck of fat on the federal budget!*

After one twitchy-mouthed sip of Barefoot Bubbly, Dr. Severin made her excuses and we all drifted back to work, keeping our excitement to ourselves.

I imagined Dr. Severin going home, popping open a bottle of real French champagne with her lover, whoever that was, sliding off her expensive shoes, and tasting sweet victory from one of those special glasses shaped like Marie Antoinette's breast.

For us, it had been different, all of us heading home to our various postgrad shoeboxes, eating microwaved burritos, hovering over our laptops. All night, we'd engaged in a group-text crop-dust, the announcement like a starter's pistol firing. The news was the best we could hope for. But now came the big decision: Who among us would be chosen for the research team?

The rumor is there will be only three of us on the grant. Someone saw the staff line on the proposed budget. It's a collaboration with Neuropsych, which will eat up most of the funds, leaving room for only three postdocs out of a pool of nine. Inside, we were all surely thinking the same thing: *It should be me.* All of us toiling years in the lab, our necks permanently crooked over microscopes, our faces cadaverous from never seeing the sun. We all felt we'd put our time in, and we all shared one thought: *This chance should be mine.* All of us, the rest of the day, watching one another over our slide trays, through our Erlenmeyers, our clamped columns of ether. *This is mine.* I thought it, a lot.

Eh, Alex, the newest among us, teased, *who really wants to spend two years delving into the dark heart of PMDD?*

We all do, I said. *And you know it.*

Premenstrual dysphoric disorder, that's the subject of the study. A set of symptoms with no agreed-upon cause. Some kind of catastrophic monthly dance between hormones and the feeling and thinking parts of the brain. Striking every month, it's like PMS only much, much worse. Debilitating mood swings, uncontrollable rage. Abnormal signaling among cells, that's what scientists only recently discovered. An intrinsic difference in the way these women respond to sex hormones. After decades of doubt about whether it even existed, now science has proven PMDD is not only real, it's part of the genetic makeup. The women can't help it, are slaves to it.

Behind their hands, behind their smirks, some of the postdocs call it Hatchet PMS. Medusa Menses. They're all men except me, and they can't even talk about it without twisting their mouths or ducking their heads or making *Carrie* or Lizzie Borden jokes.

But they all want in on the grant. It's the sexy one, maybe a career-maker. I've been waiting for it, working for it so long.

It's not even seven a.m. when I ride up in the elevator. With the grant news strumming through my head all night, I couldn't fall asleep and finally gave up trying.

The minute I step off the elevator, I notice the smell.

Hot, sharp, scalding, it gets stronger as I head down the long, frigid hallway, its browning ceiling tiles and peeling plaster, the mausoleum feel.

At first I think it's some unholy mix of Cheese Nips and the off-brand champagne. But the smell coming from the animal unit is too powerful, powerful enough to feel like a warning.

"Don't go in the feed room," a low voice calls out, and it's Serge, my favorite fellow early-lurker, fluttering like a skipper moth down the hallway toward the colony room.

Serge is the head lab tech: tall, Russian, with a severe jaw and black eyes. Quiet and fastidious and always a little sad. Alex calls him the Cat because he moves so silently—slow, stealthy, his feet never making any sound. Once, over tea in the break room, he told me he took ballet until he was fourteen and his father got a good look at the dance belt he was supposed to wear. *He informed me it was time to start looking like a man.*

And he smiled that sad Serge smile.

Despite his warning, I can't help but stop at the door of the feed room, propped open by a biohazard bin.

Coffee cup against my chest, hand over my mouth, I see it, the slick pile of rotting mice on the floor, tumors splitting their violet skin, loose and massing.

There must be a dozen of them.

Serge arrives behind me, the only sound the slight squeak of the lab gloves he's putting on.

"Watch your head," Serge says, pointing one long gloved finger to a browning ceiling panel. "There may be more."

I step back quickly, lifting my eyes to the ceiling tiles, swollen with age, heat, air.

"I don't think I've ever looked up before," I say. And it's true. At least, not in a long time.

We walk together, Serge carrying the mice in one of the red bio-hazard bags.

"At least it wasn't the ferrets," I say. We had a pack of them for the gonadal study. All the techs hated them, their heavy musk and screeching.

"These are not our mice," Serge says. "Ours are secure. And much more refined. These are mutts. Maybe visitors from Panda Garden across the street."

"Do they really think our feed is better than theirs?" I say, smiling, but inside I'm thinking about the bits and pieces still on the floor. Serge will have to go back with a mop.

"So I guess you heard about the big grant?" I say.

"Oh, yes," he says. "I can smell it."

"What?" I pause. "The adrenaline?"

But he merely smiles in that way he has. "Have a good day," he says, heading toward the animal-waste dock, waving the bag slightly, like a bullfighter's cape.

When I step inside G-21, Alex is already there, Styrofoam cups in hand, a pouchy-eyed wink.

Alex.

Alex always brings me a milky second coffee from the Snack Hut. Just like he always has gum in his pocket for me and will join me in my takeout order from the egg-sandwich place. And when Zell makes one of his *Mother, you be trypsin* puns, or Maxim unpacks his fastidious, girlfriend-prepared bento boxes for lunch, or that time one of Dr. Irwin's postdocs was spotted walking the old man's sheepdogs, we share knowing glances.

Alex doesn't usually come in early, but he often stays late. A few times we've found ourselves in the lab alone together close to midnight, both working under the fume hoods, our faces close. We are the only ones who don't seem to have anyone waiting at home.

"Thanks," I say now, taking the cup, "early bird."

A few gulps and I start working, checking my cell cultures under the microscope, then carefully returning every flask to the incubator.

He's watching, glancing at the newspaper, sipping.

"You are so damn precise," he says. "The way your hands move. In ascending order, I like to watch you cutting, scraping, tweezing, pipetting."

"And with my dainty girl hands," I say. "How could I possibly get them to do such complicated things?"

He leans down closer, his elbow to my elbow alongside our gray coffee. "Don't take this personally, Kit, but your hands are really big. Did you rassle steer?"

"No steer," I say. "Only small-handed men."

"I figured you for one of those 4-H champs on some Kansas prairie. Five brothers and you. Hands like wooden paddles."

"It's amazing I can even button my own shirt," I say, splaying my fingers.

"Sometimes you miss a button," he replies. "But don't worry. No one ever notices."

He's like that, the strangest kind of flirt, and I love it, used to so much worse, the shoulder-squeezing predations of the older researchers. The fumbles and porn-slicked joking of the postdocs, never sure what to do with females around. When you meet the women in their lives—Maxim's multilingual, opera-singing girlfriend, Juwon's dazzling mathematician wife—it becomes more confusing.

Moments later, when Alex has turned back to his coffee, which slaps all over his lab bench when he sets it down, I sneak a look at my hands, palms up. I can't tell if they're small or large; they're just hands, blue-gloved and functioning. But it makes me think about touching him, or him touching me, or something.

Which, I'm sure, was the idea.

In my secret thoughts, I imagine Dr. Severin will pick Alex and me for two of the three slots on the PMDD grant. Together, we'll devote ourselves to the potentially groundbreaking work that she and her colleagues over in Neuropsych will produce. Together, we'll toil, head to head, for two years or more. It will fill our days and evenings and inspire and frustrate and impel us. It will be a thing we share. And it is, as Maxim once admitted, the kind of study that can *make your career. Make your name.*

I think about it a lot because the nights are long and lonely and I've always been partial to men like Alex. The ones whose eyes dance when I appear, who so clearly like me but also never bother me about it. Never demand too much from women, least of all from a woman who works sixty hours a week and has the lab hands—rough, scrubbed raw-red—to prove it.

If I didn't know better, had I never heard the Ivy League ease in his voice—the voice of someone who'd always been listened to, whatever he said, his whole life—I'd think Alex was nearer to one of the boys from back home, the Golden Fry, the speedway, a million years ago. Because he's easy. Carefree. Or is it careless?

He's the only one in the lab without a coal-miner cast to his skin, all of us sealed up in there, seldom seeing high noon, our bodies like the skin under an old Band-Aid, puckered and tender.

But not Alex, with his golden skin, a look of striking health.

Give him time, Zell insisted when Alex first started a few months ago. *He's still got blood in his veins.*

I always know I like a man if I can't remember what he looks like when he's not around. When Alex isn't here, all I can picture is how tall he is, and how he's always smiling at me.

There's the sound of swooping wings in the air just before ten a.m.

It's Dr. Severin arriving, her coat open, billowing behind her.

"I heard Irwin's postdocs conspiring in the men's room," Juwon says. "They're angling hard for the PMDD slots. When do we find out?"

"It might be today," Maxim says, feigning nonchalance. "But it might be next week."

"It better be soon," Juwon says, shaking his head. "I've been at labs where the longer the wait, the more people start to go crazy."

"Crazy?" I ask.

Juwon nodded. Maxim did too. I didn't like the looks in their eyes. I'd heard their tales from other labs, postdocs contaminating each other's reagents, mislabeling bottles, swapping lids on cell cultures. *Labotage.*

"There will be blood," Zell says, grinning widely, nearly swirling his tongue, never tiring of menstruation jokes as long as Dr. Severin isn't around. But the excessive delicacy and squirminess of the other men, except Alex, is even worse.

The truth is, we all know PMDD's hot stuff. Rumor is Dr. Severin is closing in on *something,* maybe even approaching something that approaches a cure. A cure, that is, other than having your uterus and ovaries yanked out. A cure for a condition only marginally treatable, if it even exists at all, which not everyone believes it does. Dr. Severin believes it does. I do.

At its worst, it's led women to self-destructive acts. Or destructive ones. In the lab, we've all heard the horror stories: Women in its grip hitting their boyfriends over the head with frying pans, rear-ending their children's teachers' cars in the school parking lot. Road rage, baby shaking, worse.

What woman can't imagine it? Dr. Severin asked me once, one of the few conversations I ever had with her alone.

Imagine what? I asked. We were standing at the dented tampon machine in the ladies' room, no less.

That, one month, the usual cramps and moodiness might suddenly spiral up into something larger, something you can't control.

I thought about it while trying to fall asleep that night, minnowing my way through the murk of all the women I'd known who'd made wrong choices or suffered diabolically or made others suffer, even me. Don't we all feel we have something banked down deep inside just waiting for its moment, the slow gathering of hot blood?

We take our seats around the battered conference table, waiting.

"'PMDD is a disorder that affects three to eight percent of women,'" reads Zell from the research précis, adding, with a faint jeer, "and I know them all."

"Dr. Severin thinks it might be closer to ten percent," says Maxim. "That it's underdiagnosed among the women better at controlling it. Or hiding it."

They all look at me, as they do whenever anything related to the female body comes up.

"Well"—Alex jumps in, thankfully—"if men could get PMDD, we'd have all these answers already."

I can't help but smile even as Zell rolls his eyes and makes a jacking-off gesture with his hand.

In front of me is a packet of the case studies that have been circulating. I can't stop reading them, like the old *Police Blotter* magazines my grandfather used to keep in the basement. The British woman who stabbed a fellow barmaid to death. Another who fatally pinned her boyfriend to a telephone pole with her car. The teen who set fire to homes all around her drowsy suburb. The woman in Texas who attacked her sleeping mother, beating her with a hammer until she was dead. All of these laid at the feet of PMDD by canny lawyers, enthralling the tabloids, titillating the public.

Those are the extreme cases, but they're the ones we discuss in the lab. They're easier to talk about than the average PMDD patient suffering her slow burn of monthly anguish, crying jags, bad thoughts whirring, boomeranging all day, the crushing thunk of insomnia, lying in bed, sweat-soaked, waiting for the blood to come.

So, Owens, Zell once asked me, reading from one of the studies, *have you ever sobbed for six hours straight because your cat looked at you funny?*

Do you find yourself consuming entire pound cakes before that time of the month?

Have you destroyed all your relationships because you can't manage your emotions?

What relationships? I wanted to say with a laugh. My head down over my work for the past decade (a doctorate by age thirty doesn't happen any other way, I told my mom), I haven't had any time. And I've never even suffered from cramps, but since I'm the only woman other than Dr. Severin (and we never talk about it in front of her), I'm supposed to know more, know differently, know something about the purple marrow of female rage. The fear all men have that there's something inside us that shifts, and turns. A living thing, once dormant, stirring now, and filled with rage.

"Yes, yes," she is saying into her slender blue phone as she strides into the room.

Dr. Severin doesn't waste time on anything, including greetings, pleasantries. When she does, they are delivered with mild contempt.

"Can you see what her folder says?" whispers Zell, but I won't look at him, at the moisture blistering on his pimpled prodigy forehead. "Is it the grant budget?"

But none of us want to be caught looking and instead we ponder the long conference table, its old wood clouded with coffee rings.

Occasionally, I sneak a glance at Dr. Severin. That face so long and severe, her mouth always brightly colored—today's lipstick I would call placenta red—and teeth white as a shark's. She moves with the brisk efficiency of a general and no one has ever seen her eat, drink a cup of coffee, or hold an umbrella.

Sometimes, as I squeeze coffee from my shirt cuff or chew through a full pack of gum in a single hour or dig into the burn gouge on the toe of my low-top from that time Zell spilled sulfuric acid, I wonder how it is that I'm here at all.

But it was no accident. Dr. Severin plucked me from the masses of pedigreed doctoral students, the only one who's ever come from her undergrad scholarship pool, the only one with a bachelor's from a state school at all. The only one with a laptop that wheezes like a wind through an accordion when you turn it on. The only one with a second job (cater waiter), much less a third (tutoring), until she got me more fellowship money.

At the original interview, Severin claimed she remembered me from that scholarship ceremony years ago when she handed me the check in a cloud of perfume, the click of her heels on the spit-shined stage.

You were the only one with a serious face, she said.

Once, I spotted an age-browned photo on her desk, a girl with slack black pigtails who might have been a young Dr. Severin, cowboy hat and cutoffs and hooded eyes, biting into a piece of fried rattlesnake.

Somehow it fits with her python boots, her zebra-streaked hair.

She rarely speaks to me but occasionally winks in a way that might be a facial tic, but I'll take it for something else.

I've been around strong women my whole life, and I know their ways.

"Yes. Got it," she says.

We all watch as Dr. Severin finishes her call (no *Good-bye*, no *We'll talk later*), slides the phone into the smooth leather fo-lio. Sitting down, she trains her eyes on us, settling in her chair, neck gliding back like a satisfied snake, its gullet thick with warm mice.

"I have some more news," she says, then her eyes drift to a paper in her hand, and we all wait again.

Finally, I blurt out, "What is it?"

Everyone looks at me, and Severin does that twitch that just might be a smile.

"We're going to have a new addition to the lab starting tomor-row," Severin says.

All our eyes blink in unison. *What does this mean about the slots—*

"Don't overthink it," she tells us. But in that instant, we already have.

No one says anything. We know we'll confer in hushed asides under the fume hoods later, over honey buns at the rust-pocked vending machine.

"And she's a catch," Severin adds, setting her paper down, looking over, I swear, at me, her eyes with those strange vertical-slit pupils, like a cat's.

A she, I think. *Worse still. It's a she.*

I swear, this is true: The second before Severin says her name, I feel it. I feel it under my fingernails, feel it buzzing in my ears.

How can I know? I can't. I haven't heard or uttered the name since high school. But I know.

"Her name is Diane Fleming. Harvard. I poached her, snatched her right out of Walter Freudlinger's wrinkly old hands."

THEN

Later, too late, I would understand how important my first encounter with Diane Fleming was. How everything was right there,
if I chose to look.

It was more than a dozen years ago, at cross-country camp, the
summer after my sophomore year. She was running next to me,
and you don't forget a gait like hers. Legs that went on for miles;
she seemed to float. No matter the temperature, she never had
more than a fine arc of beads at her hairline, like a halo.

I sweat all the time, wildly, like a sorrel mare in heat. The first
day, I sweat so much I ended up tearing off my T-shirt and tucking it through the racer back of my bra and got detention, which
I didn't even think you could get in camp.

She was fast, but I soon figured out she was not as fast as the
promise of those long legs. Sometimes I'd think if she let herself
sweat, she'd be unstoppable. Her jaw so tight, her brow furrowed
like our bull mastiff's. I wanted to try that hard.

"You're a sprinter at heart," Coach Holmby had told me. "Fast-
twitch all the way."

Fast-twitch. I looked it up after and found a picture of a cut-up chicken, just like we served up at the Golden Fry. The dark meat is where the slow-twitch muscles are, the legs. The white meat was fast-twitch, for flying. When, I wondered, would a chicken have to fly? I guess when it needed to the most.

I know I wanted to beat her. In part because she didn't seem to be competing with any of us. She never even looked at other runners, only the shimmery aerosol haze on the horizon.

But neither Diane nor I was ranked top tier. I always had to duck out for my afternoon shift and if I left early, I could get a ride with Malcolm, the good-looking fry cook. And Diane spent most of her time off studying under the awning by the Y's snack shop or talking on her phone, her hand over her mouth. She was one of the overnight campers even though she lived over in the Foothills, only twenty miles away. Mornings, I'd see her walking, head down, from the bunkhouse showers with her little toiletries bucket, rubber flip-flops inexplicably silent on the concrete. Someone told me she had trouble at home.

I kept my eyes on her. She was always reading, and sometimes I'd write down the book titles and get them at the library. One was about Marie Curie, and though Marie wasn't nearly as pretty, something in her photo on the cover reminded me of Diane, that same determined expression she wore while facing down the camp's dust-cracked trails. I never knew anyone before her who read books no one had ever heard of. It seemed like she might have some kind of secret knowledge.

"Is that good?" I asked her once, pointing to the Curie book.

"Listen to this," she said. *"My head is so full of plans that it seems aflame."*

I paused, turning the words over in my head. "Marie said that?"

"Yes," Diane replied, looking down into her book again.

27

My head is so full of plans that it seems aflame.

"Jesus, it's great," I said, even though I didn't know what it meant, yet.

The last week of camp, Diane's mom visited for the first time. She'd missed all our meets, but now I spotted her huddled with Diane at one of the picnic tables, sharing a tin of mini cupcakes and whispering conspiratorially, their gazelle legs twisted under the wooden benches. She was as lithe and long as her daughter, both of them model-tall, and she kept playing with Diane's hair, pushing it into up-dos and side knots.

I liked my mom, but the only time we ever cuddled that cozy together was the night we ate a whole box of stale Russell Stover one of her bad dates had given her two weeks after Valentine's Day. One of her crowns came out in the molasses chew and it cost twelve hundred dollars to fix and two years to pay off.

Later, I saw them saying good-bye, Mrs. Fleming stepping into her car, which was large, sleek, and so white it hurt your eyes, like looking into the sun.

Even though we hadn't met, she waved at me too, like a pageant queen making a grand exit, greeting all her admirers.

I walked over to get a better look at the car. Inside was white too, like the smooth curves of a giant molar. And the gold trimmings like molar crowns.

"Mom," Diane said, untangling her hair, "this is Kit."

"Kit," she said. "Pleased to know you."

"That's some car," I said.

Her smile, which reached up to the bottom rims of her gold sunglasses, was so warm it made me sweat a little.

"Honey, this isn't a car. Do you know what this is?" she said, sliding into that white leather front seat.

"What?"

"A promise."

It sounded like something my dad would say, and that made me feel sorry for Diane.

"My boyfriend is trying to entice me to move in with him," Mrs. Fleming said, tilting the sun visor down with a flash of her hand, showing a big, fireworks-size sparkler on her ring finger. "To entice us both. Don't you think Didi would love celebrating her sweet sixteen on the beach?"

"Sure," I said, looking over at Diane, who, with her ramrod posture and gold post earrings, her immaculate sneakers (scrubbed, no doubt, with a toothbrush and bleach each night), looked like no Didi ever in history.

"Didi," she said, "think about what we discussed, okay?"

Then, with one more flash of her hand, that asteroid-size ring, she turned the wheel and drove away.

Diane and I both waved until our arms ached, like this was the last time Miss Suncoast Peaches might visit our town.

Then, the last full day of camp, on the overnight trip to distant Rialto for a track meet, I had the talk with Diane that would knock around in my brain ever after.

We were bundled four to a room at Wheels Inn, which was what they called a family hotel, with an enormous foggy aquatic atrium at the center, like a hothouse for dying grandparents and abandoned children. Two waterslides and a bumper-boat pool and the sharp echo of kids screaming all night, their throats gurgling, as though about to meet their watery graves.

I shared a room with Diane and two girls from Valley East, Shauna and Sarina, and we swapped secrets all night, which is what you do on overnight trips, especially when you might never see these girls again, different schools, different worlds.

You felt like you could say anything. Be anyone.

Shauna confessed she'd stuck a fork in her brother's ear when he was a baby and now he had only 80 percent hearing and no one but her knew why.

Sarina confided her boyfriend sometimes choked her until she passed out, which made me feel bad for her and for all the girls like her. Except girls like her made things harder for the rest of us.

Diane, however, wouldn't share anything. She said nothing had ever happened to her.

"Not even at Sacred Heart?" Shauna asked. It was a private girls' school so it seemed exotic. There were always rumors about it, about death cults and sex games and anything else we public-school kids could conjure, all of us piled on top of one another in windowless basement classrooms, no disposable income and no mystery at all.

"No," Diane said. "We work really hard. There isn't really time for anything else."

"Are you religious?" Shauna asked. "Maybe that's why nothing's happened to you."

"No."

"Did your dad make you go there so you wouldn't get pregnant?" Sarina asked. "Because it's always Catholic-school bitches who get pregnant."

"My mom liked the idea," Diane said. "She went to an all-girls school too."

"But you live over by the Foothills. Big bucks. What's it like there?" Sarina demanded, a look on her face I didn't like, but what could you expect from a girl named Sarina?

I thought I saw a throb of panic at Diane's temple, and it was my turn anyway, so I told them the story I wish I'd never told. About how I used to dog-sit a pair of liver-coated baying bloodhounds in the Foothills for a man my mom knew from the rescue clinic. We called him Stevie Shoes because he was a sales rep for some sports-wear company and always had a trunkful of sneakers. One night, he came back early from a business trip and offered to drive me home, which saved me a half hour and a bus transfer. On the drive, we got to talking about music and the way certain songs seemed written just for us and before I knew it I'd let him put his hands down my jeans, and it was all thumbs and fingers, hip bone pressing. The radio was playing old songs I didn't like, the Eagles even, but somehow they sounded soulful at the time and he'd been telling me how hard his divorce had been on his kid and all these grown-up things and soon enough hands were in all places, both of ours, and my chin was buried in his shoulder, breathing so hard from all of it.

The whole time, I kept my eyes on the mini dream catcher hanging from his rearview mirror, its purple feathers tickling my chin whenever we pushed forward.

"We didn't do everything," I said, and I could smell the car freshener and feel the funniness of his business suit, his grown-up belt, its buckle pressing against my cheek. "But pretty close."

"I bet he was married," Sarina said. "No single guy has a dream catcher in his car."

"He was divorced," I repeated, "but he was still really old and not appropriate."

Which was what Ms. Castro, the guidance counselor, had said.

I didn't tell them how, when he dropped me off, he gave me a pair of brand-new running shoes with pink spikes from his trunk, the same ones I was wearing now.

I found myself looking down at them, touching a finger to one of the rubber studs.

As if she could hear my thoughts, Diane was looking at them too.

And then I couldn't believe it, but I started crying. Shauna and Sarina put their arms around me sloppily, patting me like a punched dog. They were crying too, for their own reasons and their own secret sorrows. We were just a quivering mess of hard shins and soft flannel, of Sour Patch–fueled girl misery.

Sitting on the opposite bed, Diane watched, immobile.

Finally, she looked at me, tucking a stray silk bit of hair behind her ear, and said she was sorry.

"It's okay, Kit," she said. "My mom always says, you don't have a self until you have a secret."

I didn't know what she meant or how she meant it.

I remember looking up, my hair and Shauna's hair tangled in my face. And Diane just kept looking back at me, those blue eyes like daubs of paint.

"Diane's right. It's fine," Sarina said. "But did you let him put it inside?"

Later that night, just as we were starting to settle in, tank tops and shorts, sharing two bottles of beer we'd stolen from a room-service tray and rubbing our feet with smelly lotions, Diane started to feel sick and bent over the trash can by the bed.

"Don't be embarrassed," I said, holding her hair back in case.

My hands kept fumbling because her hair was so soft. It felt like what I imagined Cinderella's might.

"It's probably the cheese sticks or the gummies," Shauna said to me.

"It's okay," I whispered to Diane. "Most runners do it once in a while."

"I'm not doing it on purpose," Diane said. "I swear."

"Bingeing is bad for your electrolytes," Sarina said, overhearing us. Lying back on the other bed, legs swinging over the edge.

"She didn't eat anything," I said. I'd never seen her eat anything ever. Her legs like a stork's in her running shorts.

"I'm sorry," Diane kept saying, her chest heaving. Nothing was coming out, not even a long, lean spit string like when I tried to purge up a half a bag of Chips Ahoy or a whole jar of Jif or some other poor choice before cross-country weigh-ins.

I believed her and felt bad for her, her long face and pale eyebrows and ears with no lobes and still the prettiest girl I'd seen in real life.

"Just throw it all up, then. By throwing up you acknowledge your binge was bad," Shauna said, "and you're fixing your mistakes."

Diane didn't seem to be listening, her eyelids glistening, face flushed, like how I pictured Cathy in *Wuthering Heights*, which we'd just read for school. Cathy was wicked and wonderful and I'd never known a character could be both at once. Everyone in class hated her except me.

"Lie down, Diane," I said. "Don't listen to them."

"It's just my period," she whispered. "My period must finally be coming."

I said she must be right.

At last, I settled Diane into bed and got in next to her. From the other double bed, Shauna and Sarina watched like we were putting on a show, sniping and calling me Madame Lezzifer and making kissy faces, but I didn't care. When I went to pull up the tatty hotel bedspread, Diane reached for my arm as if to hold it there, to comfort her. I'd never spooned with anyone other than my mom when I was little and she'd lock my dad out and he'd come pounding on the garage door all night till the cops came, shaking their heads, flashlights resting on their shoulders. But I spooned a little with Diane, or almost spooned, our bodies close enough that I could feel all her breaths, ragged and high. It was more like sleeping with a big doll.

For a while, it felt nice taking care of someone so timid and distressed. Until finally it felt strange, even though she never even moved. Strange because Diane was strange—wasn't she? A locked box without a key.

The next day, camp was over, and that's when I first saw Diane's dad. He stood outside the field house, a man with a trim mustache, even though no one really had just a mustache then, not even cops. He was leaning against his car, jiggling his keys, his business suit blazing under the late-afternoon sun.

"Do you know Diane Fleming?" he asked. "Is she inside?"

"Yeah," I said. I'd seen her lingering over by the showers, brushing her wet hair in long strokes. "I think she'll be out soon."

He smiled, nudging his sunglasses up the bridge of his nose. "I was worried I had the wrong place. We're driving to Johnny Hall's for dinner."

I'd never been to Johnny Hall's, but I'd heard about it because it rotated while you sat and ate oysters, and its domed ceiling twinkled with artificial stars. "Do you want me to tell her you're here?"

"She knows," he said, waving his phone as some kind of proof. "Guess no one your age is in a hurry to spend the evening with her dad."

I smiled at him without saying anything because there's no good response to that.

"Well, if you see her...," he said, and I felt a swell of feeling-sorry for him so heavy it ached.

When Diane came out of the field house, I watched. They were very formal together, her dad opening the door for her like they were on a blind date. She didn't look at him.

"I don't feel very hungry," I heard her say, "and I need to see Mom."

A few days later, I got a postcard from her. I don't know how she got my home address, and I'd never known anyone under sixty who sent postcards.

Kit, thank you for making me run faster. Remember: you don't have a self until you have a secret. Thank you for sharing yours.

I smiled, but then came a funny quiver.

"What secret?" my mom asked, holding the postcard up to the light as if it were a cipher.

"Just some running tips," I said, shrugging. "Like where I got my shoes."

And that was it. The whir of school and work, the stink of chicken fat, a junior-year boyfriend of sorts, and I mostly forgot about Diane, except for every time I pulled my Marie Curie book, now accruing a small fortune in library fines, off my shelf. The picture on its plastic dust jacket, fogged over Marie's stern face, somehow merged with the picture of Diane in my head.

But then, more than a year after cross-country camp, I saw her again. Wearing that same look of grave purpose as she walked through the water-stained halls of Lanister High.

It was the fall of our senior year, and Diane was a new student, a transfer. Amid the sea of lank ponytails, a spray of tattoos, of crop tops and low jeans, she stood apart from everyone. Her focus always seemed elsewhere, head down, lost in her own thoughts, a shadow falling between her eyes like a warning.

I was seventeen and there were so many things I didn't know yet, but I knew about hiding.

"I know her," I said. "I know that girl."

"Who?" asked Alicia, poking her head around my locker. "Church Barbie?"

With those bluebell eyes and uptilted nose, she was even prettier than she'd been at fifteen. But if she had Barbie's molded breasts, they were well covered by her shirt, the ruffled white blouse of a Sunday organist, and if she had Barbie's long, rubbery, toe-point legs, they were cloaked by a pleated circle skirt hanging past her knees.

"Didn't you hear?" chimed in Ashley Moon. "She's the one with the dead dad."

"What?" I said. "I met him." As if that somehow meant it couldn't be true.

"Yep," Alicia said. "It's going to be like Tyrus Turner." After Tyrus's mom died suddenly from meningitis, no one talked to him for months. It was like something black and poisonous was coming off him. He was invisible, but worse.

"Do you know what happened to him?" I asked. "Her dad?"

"A heart attack, I think. So, what's she like?" Alicia asked, her hand on her hip, the wariness of teenagers everywhere, watching Diane make her brisk way down the long hall.

"She's very serious," I said. "And she's . . ."

I didn't know how to finish the sentence, so I just let it drift.

Next period, in gym class, we were side by side again, right at the start line.

Her eyes were on my running shoes. Everyone's always were, the pink spikes glaring like bloodied teeth.

"Hey, Marie Curie," I said.

She turned and smiled, just a little. Which is the most she ever smiled except that time with her mom. It was like she was afraid to or her face didn't work that way or something.

"I think we're in AP Chem together," she said. "Fifth period, Ms. Steen."

"Yep," I said. And I found myself swallowing twice. "See you there."

We ran together that day, never more than a stride apart. I didn't have her long legs and grace, but I made up for it with sheer pumping power. She made me work harder, and I made her work harder too.

By the end of practice, I knew it was time to replace my running shoes, the spikes whittled too flat now, and I'd have to go back to the outlet-mall ones I'd worn before.

She turned to me, those little beads of sweat like a delicate tiara around her golden-brown brow, and said, "You've gotten so much faster."

"You too," I said, because we'd finished on the very same foot stroke.

"We're both so much better," she said, eyes on me. "No one can touch us."

NOW

Diane Fleming. The name, Dr. Severin's scarlet-rind mouth saying it, hovers over me.

We all watch her leave the conference room, her phone hissing, the *shush* of her crepe trousers. Behind, the tart smell of her perfume.

"You'll have to tell me what this means," whispers Alex as we shuffle out, a gloomy pack of lightless grad students and postdocs, our pockets stuffed with energy bars.

"What this means," I say under my breath, "is there's one less spot on the PMDD study for us. And you didn't need me to tell you that."

"I guess not," he says, holding the door for me, "but it sounds nicer coming from you."

For once, he doesn't smile.

"Well, condolences, all, but she's hot stuff," Maxim says. "Fleming's the rising star on Freudlinger's team."

His expression is the gravest among ours. Maxim has worked for Severin for six years, longer than anybody, nearly a perma-doc.

He even provided the only sliver of personal information we've ever heard about Severin: that she once had a lover named Diego who dove off oil rigs for a living and took off his shirt at the alumni banquet to show off a chest scar from an encounter with a moray eel. *He was a peacock,* Maxim told us with a look of distaste.

With his dark hair and his hooded eyes and his Italian shoes, Maxim even looks like Severin. He's a long shot for the PMDD team, though. There's a feeling that she barely notices him anymore and that he should have moved on long ago to another lab, a faculty job.

"I just texted my friend at MIT," Juwon tells us, looking at his phone. "He says she was the most talented undergrad they ever had. She was working with Cooper her sophomore year."

"I saw her once at ACS," Zell says, his face unusually grim. "In the elevator. Man. She was..."

His eyes unfocus mysteriously, like they do when he talks about huffing propofol at his old job.

"She was what?" Alex asks.

"You'll see," he says, shrugging. Subdued for the first time ever, even in his SCIENTISTS DO IT ON THE TABLE PERIODICALLY T-shirt.

"Severin poached her," Maxim says. "That's what counts. That's one spot down."

We all look at one another. Nine junior researchers—five of us and four from Irwin's gonad team—competing for three spots. Now only two. This is how it is in our tiny, thankless world. Always looking over your shoulder, always someone gaining on you. You must rely on your fellow postdocs, but you never trust them. *There is no* team *in* I, Maxim always says.

"We'll just have to see what she has in mind," I say, poker-faced, bending over my lab bench, busying myself.

*   *   *

The PMDD study was the star shot; we all knew it. But even more than that, we'd all come to the lab because of the celebrated Dr. Severin. We all wanted to work on the research that mattered most to her. I did. I'd wanted it for as long as I'd wanted anything. Maybe since I first heard Dr. Severin speak, the summer before my senior year of high school.

"You shouldn't worry," Alex says as we walk to our lockers to retrieve my stash of Mexican candy from the dollar store.

"I'm not," I say, handing him a Pulparindo. "But you better."

He laughs, but it's all bluster. I didn't go to Caltech on an IBM fellowship like Juwon, and I don't come from a Big Pharma fortune like Zell. I didn't, unlike Alex, grow up with a stepdad who worked at NASA and a mother who taught experimental particle physics at MIT. I didn't grow up feeling smart and special, the world my oyster, born with a silver shucker in my hand. *No one works harder than you*, that's the way Zell and Juwon like to put it. Everything I have is because I was the dutiful worker bee or because I have no other things to distract me, like girlfriends or wives, like mewling kids or family dogs or a love of weekend brunches and fantasy football or a single, sad hobby, like solitaire or the Sunday jumble. I have this.

It took me until I was seventeen to imagine my own brain as something with all kinds of hidden channels and crevices and drop chutes leading into glittering chambers of even greater possibility. It took me, in some ways, until Diane Fleming.

And now, at a mere twenty-nine, having bolted through undergrad in three years and propelled myself through grad school at a ceaseless pace, who knows what else might lie in those watery neuro corridors? Who knows but that I might be somebody no-body ever guessed?

Except now there is another woman in the mix, stripping me of any advantage I had. And that woman also happens to be brilliant Diane.

Brilliant and strange and extraordinary, as she is in my dreams still, standing next to me at the long slab table in our high-school chem lab, her pin-neat notebooks and her keen gaze.

In the always-empty ladies' room, with its ancient globes of soap that leave pink soot on your hands, I hold my phone high to get a signal and try to look her up.

The first listing I see is a bio on the Freudlinger Lab site (. . . *receiving her BS with honors and the distinction-in-major award before pursuing her PhD in biochemistry and molecular biology . . .*); I read just enough to know she finished her degrees even faster than me, one step ahead to the end. I skip her citations, all the publications, invited seminars, poster presentations at the finest universities on the opposite coast.

I've never looked her up before. I've always been superstitious, just like my lamentable old dad. *Don't count the cars in a funeral procession. Never move a cat. Drop a dishrag and it means someone dirtier than you is coming.*

In some animal part of my brain, I guess I thought looking her up might somehow summon her. So I never did. And she came anyway.

Tell a bad dream before breakfast and it comes true.

In the lab that evening, they all drift away, one by one. Juwon to his pure-mathematician wife and split-level; Maxim to Sophie, his long-legged opera-singer girlfriend who proofreads all his articles for him and pours him brandy and kneads his weary neck; Zell to his home computer, his gaming chamber, the dark web, who knows. Even Serge is gone from the vivarium that is nearly his home, off to wherever he lives, with his classical music and his two-year-old Persian and his ten-year-old Russian blue.

"Do you ever call it a night?" Alex asked me once. "How come you're always the last one?"

The answer is: Jenny Hsai. Jenny was the only other woman in the lab when I joined. Jenny, who had two babies at home, fat-cheeked beauties I spotted once at the lab picnic, their weary house-husband dad wearing them both in a kangaroo carrier slung across his bloated stomach.

The whole afternoon, Jenny never looked at those kids or her husband once. She didn't want Dr. Severin to catch her in an act of divided attention, she said. (It was unlikely Dr. Severin would have noticed. Sometimes she looks at us as if we were as indistinct as the glum little inbred mice lined up in cages in the vivarium.)

Six months ago, Jenny's husband revolted and accepted a position in the state capital, and Jenny went with him, taking an industry job. Her last day, her notebooks and Koosh Balls and pipettes and Kimwipes piled high in her dimpled new-mom arms, she had a look of impending and permanent loss on her damp face. Sometimes she e-mails me (*Is it still like it was? Is it still that intense? Pharma is not intense*). Once she said, *Kit, run it as hard as you can while you can.*

Kit, I'm so bored here.

Kit, it feels like my heart stopped.

"We're a nest of vipers," Alex says when it's just the two of us left. "We've got PhDs in protein chemistry, bacteriology, molecular biology, even psychology. And we're all used to winning."

"It's just nature," I point out, wiping my lab bench, the sweet smell of the ethanol solvent. "Put animals in a small, closed space, and the one with the sharpest nails, the pointiest teeth wins."

He grins. "Or maybe it's just like musical chairs?"

It's a luxury to view it so lightly. But I nod. It's best never to let them see your teeth.

"I bet," he adds, "you have a mean elbow hook."

I don't say anything, racking the clean pipettes, but he keeps going.

"You won't need it, though."

"So you keep saying," I say, wetting a Kimwipe, rubbing the bottoms of the beakers and tip boxes. "Is it the elegance of my ovaries that'll push me over the edge?"

"I don't doubt their elegance," he says. "But no. It's because she took your Bunsen."

I try to hide my smile. It's the moment to which I cling. A month ago, Severin came into the lab late after an awards dinner, her color unusually high, her Russian-red lipstick slightly stained with a dark wine, a slight give in her step. She found a handful of us in the lab and we didn't know why she was there, but in her mouth was an unlit cigarette, hand clasped over a Pall Malls pack like the one forever drooping in my grandma's shirt pocket.

"None of you smoke," she said, sounding like Marlene Dietrich in some frond-draped nightclub between the wars. "This is what's wrong with your whole generation."

I don't know what came over me, but I thrust forward my Bunsen burner. Gallant, aggressive.

She paused barely a second before leaning toward it, toward me. Smelling strongly of expensive things, she murmured under her breath, "Clever girl."

Oh, how many times I've replayed it in my head, her smoky

tones, the faint growl in her voice. I didn't mind her calling me a girl. I loved it.

"C'mon. Who's your competition?" Alex says now. "Zell, who's more likely to steal ammonia tanks for a rolling meth lab than to get this gig? Or Juwon, who's probably going to ditch us all for the CDC by spring?"

"How about you?" I say, taking one last swipe at the bench, resin gleaming like black stone.

He laughs. "Maybe if I had your brain, your jumbo hands, and that cute gap between your teeth."

"The better to pick clean the carcass of competition like you."

He looks at me, grinning still, and tells me I have the funniest way of flirting. Then adds, quickly, "You were flirting, weren't you?"

I just smile, zipping my backpack shut.

That night, I sit on my balcony, a mere three feet by six feet but the first I've ever had, hanging out like a stubbed toe over the parking lot. But beyond, if you squint, you can see a streetlight-studded expanse that absorbs me every night. A long snaking strip of Quik Lubes and box stores, rippled by brume and the bus exhaust, that extends all the way into the hot brutalist maze of campus, four miles away, nestled deep in the sinking lemon groves.

I've always lived in sprawl, so it feels like home. There's something crazily beautiful about it, the banks of stacked illuminated signs—Sauna Hut, Sheer Elegance, Waterbeds USA, Chiropractic Here, Benihana, Ideal Uniform—gorse rolling from curbed island to curbed island, across the endless parking lots like suburban tumbleweed. Last week, I watched one roll over a lit cigarette, flaring brightly. If there'd been anything natural in its path, it might have started a fire.

The main thing is this: I can't see the lab itself from here, not with the smog. Even squinting, I can't see the building, a sealed box, grim and featureless. Windows like mean slits, vertical fins on either side offering narrow places to smoke, scream. Inside, it's far cozier, the grunting comfort of work, routine, concentration. But each night, stepping from its great concrete maw at eight, nine, ten o'clock and walking the two miles home, the neon springing from the horizon, I always feel lifted the minute I taste real air. The minute I see the sun-scorched signs, the swaying traffic-lights. The lab is gone.

But not tonight, it seems. Tonight all I can think of is Diane Fleming rolling into town, starting fires.

One beer later, I'm on my hands and knees, digging through my closet to find the old milk crates and sunken file boxes from home.

I don't have anything of hers. Nothing to document our friendship, if that's what it was. There are a few senior-year mementos—a tasseled leather bookmark Ms. Castro gave me that sits forever in my copy of *The Origin of Species*, a beanbag bunny in a State U. sweatshirt, a graduation gift from the Ashleys—but none are from Diane. I didn't ask her to sign my yearbook, which I find in the very back of a crate, wedged between my childhood teddy bear, flat as a gingerbread man, and my diploma. We were no longer friends by graduation.

The only piece of Diane I have—the one I've kept through countless cinder-block dorm rooms, sweaty, crusty-carpeted college co-ops, through university apartments with broke-back sectionals and the smell, always, of industrial glue—is the piece I'll always have.

By which I mean the neural snag she left in my head, the mad drone of her toneless seventeen-year-old voice that long-ago night, the burned-into-my-brain image of her cross-legged on my twin-bed-in-a-bag comforter, purple paisley, as she told me her secret. And showed me what darkness was, and is, and how it works, and how it never goes away or ends.

Because the bad things you do become part of you, literally. This is no metaphor. They become part of you on a cellular level, in the blood.

That night, lying in bed, waiting for my nightly antihistamines to fan out across my brain, I read. Papers on PMDD. Dry scientific articles about progesterone and $GABA_A$ receptors, genetic vulner-abilities.

Indeed, many in the field continue to express concern that raising the profile of PMDD will further stigmatize women as emotionally and physically unstable, providing additional mechanisms by which men can claim women are not equipped for positions of power, sensitive positions, etc. —

Other articles. Case studies from Severin's past research going back years.

I tell my friends, "I'm not myself right now," Elizabeth H. stated. *"I'll call you back when I'm Elizabeth again."*

And another:

At age twelve, Nina's mother, who Nina believes also suffered from undiagnosed PMDD, gave her a rabbit's-foot key chain. Nina notes that when "the feelings came, I'd stroke it and stroke it, hoping they would go away."

But all I can think of is Diane. And that old Diane feeling, like walking in deep water, the weight against my legs, the unstoppable drag.

It's late, very late, when the buzzer in the living room shrieks. I bolt straight up, wait a moment, then rise and creep into the living room, my eyes on the white buzzer box, glowing in the dark, the living room lit by the strip-mall signs outside: MEATS HERE. GUNZ AND GOLD, BOUGHT AND SOLD.

"Hello," I whisper into the vibrating box. "Who's there?"

But there is no one there. My fingers to the intercom, I think I can hear something, though. I think I can. Someone pulling hard on the heavy door downstairs. Someone breathing. Or the wind.

"Diane," I whisper, crazily. "Diane, is that you?"

Later, I wonder if I dreamed it. I wake up and I'm sitting on the edge of the bed, my body upright, my hand on my chest.

All my papers, once stacked neatly on the bedside table, are scattered across the floor, binder clips like little bats, nesting.

THEN

AP Chem brought us together. We went shoulder to shoulder amid all that fire and smoke and mystery.

It was fate, Diane would later say.

Two days before she arrived at Lanister High, Benjy Dunphy, my lab partner, got suspended for throwing a fist-size chunk of potassium into a sink full of water, shattering the sink and setting a girl's hair on fire. I never liked Benjy, who had a hundred jokes about stopcocks and a hundred ideas of how to use science to rip girls' dresses off or maybe make their bras fall open.

"Kit," Ms. Steen said, "meet your new comrade in arms."

Diane took her place beside me at the lab bench in her Peter Pan collar and smooth headband and an expression I remembered well from camp: focus, intensity, a wriggling vein at the temple. The tidiness of her notebooks, the bright and crisply cornered textbook cover of *Chemistry in Action and Reaction!*, it all spoke to me of seriousness and purpose.

Up front, Ms. Steen was giving titration instructions.

"I don't know how I ended up in AP," I said, trying to find a piece of paper in my notebook, stained with my mom's coffee from the jolting drive to school. "I should have taken the rocks class. But Ms. Steen made me." I rolled my eyes. "She believes in me."

Diane looked at me but said nothing.

Then she pulled two pages from her spiral notebook and handed them to me, their edges neatly shorn. "Use this."

Side by side, we moved through the titration lab, using the juice from two fat cabbages that Benjy surely would have held in front of his chest like big purple tits and I probably would have laughed.

Hair pulled back into a glossy barrette, Diane began labeling everything meticulously: Dr Pepper, Rockstar Energy Drink, tap water, Febreze, hand sanitizer, milk. I poured the cabbage juice into a watch glass and then into our sample cups and I was careful too.

Leaning in close for each reaction, I called out the colors: "Coke, orange—acid! Febreze, clear—base!" Diane recorded them with her little mechanical pencil.

When it was over, she wrote out the report on the spot in her even, exact handwriting, her pencil swirling and equations appearing.

"You can take that home and do it," I said. "I mean, we can. It's homework."

"That's okay," she said. "I've done this lab before."

"At Sacred Heart?"

"No, before that," she said. Later, she admitted she'd mastered it for her fifth-grade science fair. I wondered how it felt being here with all of us. With me.

When the bell rang, she was still washing a burette with a long brush.

"That's fine, Diane," I said. "That's plenty good enough."

"I want to do everything right," she said, shaking the burette dry. "I don't want to make mistakes."

By the end of the first week, Ms. Steen took us aside after class to compliment us on our lab reports and our A+ quiz scores.

"You're going to be good for each other," she said, smiling. My face went warm. *A+*.

"Maybe we should study together sometime," I said to Diane as we walked out.

"Maybe. Sometime," she said. If your dad dies, I thought, maybe even studying with a classmate takes you out of mourning or something. But even before, even at cross-country camp, I'd never known anyone so private. It felt like you could hurt her just by looking at her, or you could never hurt her at all.

Later that day, I spotted her leaving the school library, backpack heavy with books. I found myself following her.

You always wonder, when someone is trying so hard, what it's really about. Whenever my dad started calling more or took me out for a surprise dinner at Benihana or sent me leopard-pom booties for Christmas as if I were twelve (or a stripper), it was always because he'd lost his job because his boss was jealous of him or he'd gotten married again to a woman he'd met at the OTB and, anyway, there would be no monthly support checks forthcoming, and *Maybe you could even talk to your mom about floating me a nickel? How 'bout a hundo?*

Maybe, for Diane, working really hard was a way of crouching low in her grief, of staying under the radar. Of hiding.

But in other ways she was impossible to miss. In class, her hand was up all the time. It was something to see, the way her mind wrapped around things. The way she'd always ask questions

("I'm just wondering why the chapter doesn't mention stem-cell research even once?"). Sometimes, she even disagreed with something in the textbook or something Ms. Steen or Ms. Cameron, the English teacher, had said. I'd never see anyone do that before.

I wondered what it was like to care so much about ideas from books and to think about things like why we dream and if female brains are different from male ones. But maybe I cared too, because sometimes I found myself wondering about those things. I just didn't show it. It was high school; you didn't show things.

I followed her down the hall, only stopping when she did, drawn by a glossy flyer on the bulletin board by the counseling office.

Later, I'd remember the way she summoned me over, like she'd known I'd been following her all along.

"Kit," she said, her fingertips light on my arm, "look."

The flyer, stern-looking with a vaguely Germanic font, announced the application deadline for the DR. LENA SEVERIN STEM SCHOLARSHIP FOR WOMEN IN SCIENCES.

"The winner gets a full ride to State," she said. "Tuition plus room and board. A stipend too."

"Severin," I said. "I saw a Dr. Severin at STEM camp over the summer."

"It's the same Lena Severin." She said the name as though she liked how it felt in her mouth, and there was something about the way she pressed her fingers against the poster, like it was a piece of fine-spun silk. "I saw her talk once at the science museum. It meant a lot to me."

"Me too," I said, only realizing it now, after Diane said it. There had been something so exhilarating about it, the first woman scientist I'd ever seen and still the smartest.

It was just a few months ago, at the summer science program Ms. Steen had talked me into, even though it was embarrassing having to show my mom's paycheck stubs to get in free. Six weeks of me racing between the Golden Fry and the lab at City Tech, injecting samples into the gas chromatograph while smelling hotly of chicken grease.

Most of the time, we were just doing grunt work—counting, washing and spinning cells, injecting those samples—but sometimes we had lectures from visiting big-time researchers who explained how they were going to change the world through polymers or a nanotech moisturizer that would speed the healing of diabetic skin wounds.

One was a biochemist, an MD/PhD who wore the highest heels I'd ever seen in real life, shaped like black cones. Her name was Dr. Severin, and with a name like that, you could never be a soft wisp of a girl. No, you were destined to be *this*.

At first, all I could do was stare at the pictures projected behind her, which were brain scans but looked like something you might see in astronomy or your most deeply felt, late-into-the-night dreams. But then Dr. Severin started talking about the female brain before, during, and after menstruation, which made at least one boy burst into nervous laughter.

I was the only girl in our school's group of seven STEM scholars, and the boys seemed glad the room was so dark because Dr. Severin's talk, as scientific as *luteal phase* and *increased amygdala response* sounded, seemed to speak to them of all the blood-horrors of being female. I don't know how many of them had ventured into girl bodies or how deeply, but they had the look of small boys expecting to find teeth between every woman's legs.

"And isn't it interesting—significant, even," Dr. Severin said, looking at the squirmiest guy, the red-faced, white-lipped one down front, "that menstruation is a source of so much horror in our culture?"

The boy nodded grimly, as if conceding something.

"After all," she added, "to quote Deuteronomy, *The blood is the life.*"

Which is a line I remembered from Dracula movies.

I loved hearing her, not just because she was a woman scientist and young with a skunk streak in her dark hair and earrings that were little silver scythes, but because she talked with such fervor about her mission: to unravel the enigma—"and plague, really"— of PMS and something called PMDD, which was even worse. In the old days, if you had it bad, they used to just cut out your ovaries to "cure" you. "Snip-snip-snip," she said, making a little scissoring motion with her hand.

"But how far are we, really, from that?" she asked. "There are still those who deny that these conditions exist. Medical students are rarely trained in diagnosing or treating them. When women come for help, they're frequently dismissed with a roll of the eyes. Worst of all, research is scant and, frankly, sad. I aim to change that, to stake a claim for the health of women caught in these unbearable snares, prisoners of their own bodies."

Up on the screen, the last scan hovered, ghostlike. The brain of a woman with severe PMDD. I couldn't stop staring at its shape, like a strange mushroom you'd find in the woods. All its shadows and hollows—you could almost see a face in it, eyes like caves and a mouth open like a scream.

"So think about that when you decide your own path in the sciences. Think about where you want to go, what dark terrain you want to uncover. The mind, the body, the complicated junction between the two—it's dangerous stuff. It's thrilling stuff. What you do will matter."

When she finished, slapping her laptop shut, a cluster of Severinites, graduate students in versions of her oversize glasses and dustless black attire, followed her from the lecture hall, their dark bodies moving like a snake's winding tail.

For days after, I imagined myself as one of those chic Severinites, trailing her, joining in her grand mission. By the end of the summer, I'd decided to change my senior-year schedule like Ms. Castro had wanted me to, enrolling in AP Chem instead of accounting, physics instead of communications.

"She was my favorite," I said to Diane now. "Her whole lecture was about periods."

"Yes," Diane said, then, lowering her voice, she said with a sneaky look, "All that blood talk."

"The blood is the life," I said, grinning. *"The blood is the life."*

Diane smiled widely, the first time I'd ever seen it. A dazzling, even-toothed smile with something wicked in it.

"The boys all looked like they were going to throw up," she said, covering her mouth, hiding that smile.

From the counseling desk, Mrs. Kreuzer shot us a snippy look, but Diane didn't see it, her eyes back on the flyer.

"It's for girls. Just for girls," she said, palm flat on the glossy paper. "I'm going to apply. You should apply too."

"But you have to be in the top two percent of your class in science," I said.

"Yes," she said. "That's right."

I can't pretend I didn't feel a rush of something come upon me then. Could I? I thought. Because if Diane Fleming thought I could . . .

"Maybe I'll apply," I said, surprising myself.

Diane nodded, as if to say of course I would, and turned back to the flyer, her lips faintly moving as she read the requirements again, committing them to memory.

*   *   *

That night, I ran the numbers on my GPA. I'd have to get perfect grades in my three science courses the first and second quarters. It didn't seem possible. Except maybe it was.

Before Diane, I mostly just focused on the math of it. I was always good at that, balancing my mom's checkbook and working the register at the Golden Fry. I guessed I'd be a CPA, maybe, or work at a bank. But lately I'd started to feel like there was more there, hovering. Maybe it was the Severin application. It gave everything we were doing a center, a unifying force. It wasn't about the grades, but what the grades could get you. Where they could get you. Places no one in Lanister, or at least my corner of it, had ever been.

I asked Ms. Castro at the counseling office about it.

"This is smart, Kit. I've been telling you, you can't apply only to City Tech," Ms. Castro said, reading glasses low on her sloping nose. "You have to apply to State. Your grades are competitive. Your test scores are strong."

But in my quieter moments, standing over the Henny Penny fryer at work, my skin feeling tight and crisp as the staggered chickens', roiling, all I could think of was the students I'd seen at STEM camp. The way they spoke about DNA nanotechnology and super-resolution microscopy, the paper-thin laptops and tablets they carried, and the group of Severinites trailing their chic idol through the sleek auditorium.

"You should really do it, Kit," Diane whispered to me in AP Chem the next day. "Who in here's smarter than you?"

You mean other than you? I thought. But there was a stirring in me, a flutter of sparrows in my chest.

NOW

The next morning, I leave my apartment so early, the parking-lot lights are still on.

My heart bucking and bounding in my chest, I tell myself it's just nerves about the PMDD slots, but I know it's about Diane Fleming.

Twelve years later, and the thought of her still feels like a living thing in my head. Something humped, pointy-eared, its claws out. Like the thing I used to dream about when I was a kid. *That's your shadow*, my mom told me once. *You need it more than you think.*

The walk helps me shake it off. The wind-whisked highway has a kind of somber beauty at that hour, the concrete streaked with oddities, forlorn trash, a forty of Olde English, the plastic bags wrapped tight around light posts or soaring like doves. On Sundays, there is always at least one woman's shoe, a stiletto like a vinyl boomerang or a sad kitten heel, crushed flat.

At the lab, I feel better. I always do.

I label bottles. Clean my pH meter. The simplest of tasks, just to get my brain firing, to give me peace. I move as much as I can before drifting to the cell-culture room, where I will soon be hunkered down for hours at the fume hood, my back curled to a clamshell.

There is something beautiful in it. Like when I was little, when my parents were still raising our roof semiregularly, and I'd sit in my room and alphabetize all my books or align my pencils by length in their case. The Beanie Babies my mom always bought me from Rite Aid, their soft necks arched. The pair of bunnies, all ears at the same height, pink nubbins pointing straight.

If everything is ordered, maybe something momentous will happen. Like the relationship, however mysterious to others, between the molecular formula you'd write on the page—$C_{17}H_{19}ClF_3NO$, abstract, so much hieroglyphics—and the wild thing happening in front of your eyes, between your hands.

Nothing else could promise both things, could it? To be so ordered and so out of control.

An hour later, the parade begins. First, Juwon, with his Stanley thermos and shrieking headphones, or Zell, with his pair of tightly wrapped frozen burritos and his TV recaps, or one of the techs, coffee in one hand and slinging on his gray lab coat with the other, his cell phone tucked under his chin. And the fluorescents inevitably sizzle to life (along with them, the usual jokes come: "Why don't you ever turn on all the overheads, Kit? Were you napping? Developing film? Self-pleasuring?"). The fume hoods hum loud, the storage cabinets bang open and shut. Then comes the vague buzzing of nervous coughs, jaw clicks, mild curses, and the tight jarring energy of personality and bravado starts.

By nine, the place is alive with nerves. Will we find out the PMDD slots today? Will we meet the new lab team member today?

The second question is answered swiftly.

"She's here," comes Zell's whisper. Men can hiss at least as well as women. "Diane Fleming. She's down by Severin's office."

I don't say anything, which is easy in the lab. Often, we don't reply to questions, don't even nod hello.

"She's just like I remembered," Zell adds, as if his elevator-riding experience with her were deeply significant. There's something in his expression. That slack, stubbled, colorless lab-rat face looks newly—maybe for the first time ever—filled with feeling, heat.

"I look forward to meeting her," I say, "after hearing so much."

I'm not sure why I don't say I know Diane. It's a conversation I'm afraid to start because something in me isn't sure I'd know how to stop.

She told me, once, the worst thing anyone's ever told me.

If you knew what she did, you would go running for the door.

Other than my mom, I've never talked to anyone about Diane. And I couldn't tell my mom everything, not even at the end.

I walk down the hall toward Severin's office, all the flyers and posters and leaflets ruffling as the air conditioner shudders on once more.

The dropped ceilings, the colored signs (BROWN-BAG LUNCH FRI AT 1!), the gust of ammonia, latex. The half-muffled laughter of awkward young men at their lockers.

In an instant, I know time, its passage, is meaningless, and when I turn the corner, I'll be back in high school, another fluorescent-banded labyrinth, or back in my tiny Lanister bedroom with its shag carpet and the low-tide sink of my twin bed, and it'll be Diane across from me, her great sweep of hair, the pearls of her teeth, and when she opens her mouth—

"So, just take these and fill them out when you can," someone is saying, probably Ilene, the lab administrator. "Happy to have you here."

I'm so close. I'm twenty feet away.

"Diane," I say.

It's like those moments when you catch yourself in a store window or a pair of smeary elevator doors without knowing it's you. Or you see a picture of yourself you don't recognize, an angle you'd never catch in life.

You know something's wrong, but you can't name it, place it. When I was a kid, my mom told me that Mr. Mott, the retired cop who lived down the street, died after slipping in the shower. A year later, I served Mr. Mott at the Golden Fry. It turned out it was Mr. Mertz, the retired insurance agent, who'd died. But I stood there and handed Mr. Mott his chicken on a stick and it felt like I was talking to a dead man, or else a man who could never die.

When she turns, it's like that. It's like seeing a ghost, or worse.

But if she's a ghost, she's changed. Her body is so thin, a whittled twig, collarbones poking through her pale blouse.

But it's the hair that confuses me. Gone are those fairy-princess locks I knew so well. Shorn nearly to her scalp, her pale-gold hair is not half an inch long. It's Mia Farrow–in–*Rosemary's Baby* hair, except it gives her not a pixie look but something more striking and grand. Under the hard fluorescents, she's like a saint mortified. And that blue look we all have—from vampiric lab life—is even bluer, conjuring a tubercular beauty. A sunken glamour.

The severe hair makes all her features jut and tremble. Cheekbones and jaw both knife sharp, and you can see her skull; you can see everything, maybe even her wormy black brain.

Eyes like bruises now, as she turns fully, looking straight at me.

*   *   *

"It's you," she says. "Oh, Kit."

As she walks toward me, all the Lanister High tall-girl awk-wardness, the darting eyes and earnestness—earnestness that made you want to cry for her—that's all gone.

There are diamonds in her ears. Her shoes are finely made, un-creased. No wriggly vein at her temple asserts itself. The pen in her hand is silver, expensive, impossibly thin. Like a tiny, precise wand.

She is the golden girl she was always destined to be.

Except this: I can look in her face and know her for who she is, what she is. A devil, a goblin damn'd.

"It's you," she says again, but her eyes show no surprise, which means she's seen me already or prepared herself to. And practiced her response. Adjusted her face.

"Diane," I said. "After all this time."

"I always knew you'd be a success," she says, her voice jagging ever so slightly. "The smartest person I ever knew."

She is so close, so close, it's unbearable.

"Took the words out of my mouth," I say.

There's a swinging of doors and the swirl of Dr. Severin's per-fume—mossy and sweet today—and, after a flurry of introduc-tions, Severin pivoting her new hire from postdoc to postdoc: Zell, Maxim, Dr. Irwin's stubbled disciples, all their boy faces rubbery and grinning, Diane is gone again.

We're short on lab coats so Diane is wearing hers from Freud-linger's, logo-embroidered, flame-resistant, expensive. It's wine-colored, and excessive.

We're watching her as she stands at the end of the hall speaking to Dr. Severin, the two of them so tall, such high shoes and narrow legs. They're like gazelles, I think. It reminds me of something, but I can't hold on to it.

"That coat, Jesus," Zell says, transfixed.

"Freudlinger's a showboat," notes Juwon, chin resting on his thermos as he watches her. "He's not just doing research, he's staging *Sweeney Todd*."

Alex walks up beside us. I try to catch his eye, but he's looking at Diane.

"The blonde in blood red," he says approvingly.

I look away, trying not to flinch.

"She's in the culture room now," Maxim whispers to me. "She didn't say a word about our shoddy incubators. I can't imagine how it looks compared to Freudlinger's operation. He's got a three-D suspension array system. Real-time PCR detection systems."

"So why did she leave?" I say, my whisper more like a hiss. "Tantalized by our low stipends and battered spectrometers?"

"She wants to work with Severin," he says, turning away a shade too quickly. "That's why we're all here, right?"

Of course he's right. It's what Diane and I always wanted, back in high school, and now.

Within the hour, I'm back at work in G-21, and next to me is Diane.

We stand a half a dozen feet apart at our respective fume hoods for hours, the exhaust pumping noisily, churning. We stand and we work. We concentrate.

At first, I can't help feeling like we are being observed, as if our history, our shared secrets, hover between us visibly, like

a series of stretching strings. But it's really Diane they're looking at. That scarlet coat, the fume-hood illuminator making her
glow.

Across the room, Zell, with his beady intensity, grips his flask
and stares. Juwon occasionally peeks, head tilted in analytical wonder: *What makes her so special and how does it affect me?* And Maxim,
the slickest of the lot, or at least the most accustomed to new hires,
offers to "orient" her, but she says she doesn't *need any orienting,
but thank you.* Zell brings her coffee, but she doesn't drink coffee.
Maxim carries over a cup of tea, but she doesn't drink that either.
Nor the Red Bull that Zell offers next, nor even the water from
the glugging watercooler.

"Do you drink anything at all?" Juwon asks, head tilted the
other way now.

"Are you a vampire, is what he means," says the just-arriving
Alex, skating effortlessly over the all-thumbs fumbling of these sad
little boys. There's a wince inside me as I watch him eyeing her. *Et
tu, Alex?*

But Diane doesn't respond. I don't think she even smiles. She
gives them nothing. Which, for these boys, is everything they want
most.

Most of them—except Zell, who's only twenty-seven, a
prodigy, and Alex—are attached, some married young and already
with a kid or two. You would never know it, though, were it not
for the occasional vein of dried spit-up on Juwon's backpack or the
intense drinking some of them do on their rare nights out.

It isn't until that moment that I wonder: Could Diane be
married? God, could she have a baby? The thought makes my
teeth ache, and I steal a glance at her hands, narrow delicate fingers
like harp strings. No ring, but most of the others don't wear rings,
all of us changing gloves five or ten times a day.

*   *   *

Diane disappears before lunch.

"I saw them leave together," Maxim says, rubbing his artful stubble.

"Who?" I ask. For a crazy moment, I picture Alex taking Diane to the Snack Hut instead of me, making sure they give her extra hot sauce like he does with me.

"Dr. Severin and Diane. I bet she takes her to the French place."

My relief is fleeting. Dr. Severin has never invited any of us to lunch, not even Maxim.

None of us go out for lunch anyway, snarling over cling-wrapped sandwiches in the lounge, microwaved Banquet chicken fingers, pizza rolls, the hot stench drifting from the greasy sack sitting by Zell's bench while he finishes centrifuging.

Later, we hear Diane is on a tour of the rest of the lab, the colony room, the cage-wash room. Maybe she's even touring the neuro lab in the east wing, meeting the brain jocks.

I don't see her again that day, even though I stay late.

I won't let her think she's thrown me.

It's after eight and Alex and I are the only ones left. Wry, winking Alex and me. We share cold noodles from Panda Garden, huddle by the vending machine, gossiping over stained coffee cups.

Today I'm more glad for it than ever.

"Too fast, too fast," I say. "You're gonna have too much air."

He's running a flash column, forcing the solvent down a glass tube to separate its components, to make it pure.

"Always rushing things," I say. "Did your ex-girlfriends tell you that?"

"Never with such charm," he admits.

There's one like Alex in every lab. Sloppy, a little slapdash. It upsets Serge, annoys the other lab techs. Equipment perpetually crusted, stain-slicked, his fume hood dusted with silica, his lab coat, which he seldom wears, frayed and graying at the cuffs, sprayed with pinhead holes from the sulfuric acid. Once I found a crushed box of horchata wedged between his bench and the floor.

We both watch for a moment, the mixture separating itself in the foot-high glass tube, first like an orange push-up, now a tequila sunrise. His moves are deft but careless. Soon enough, the tube makes the tiniest pop.

"You cracked it," I say, pointing to the little star in the glass. "Better start over with a new one. It could shatter." I've seen it happen, especially with undergrads, who are always putting too much air in and sending glass into their too-cool-for-safety-goggles eyes.

But Alex just shakes his head and says, "Been lucky all my life."

Then, he goes back to his story, about the time he fell in love with a girl in his orgo class his freshman year of college. A girl with a killer dimple, Sally Woods. *Beautiful,* he says, *and she could titrate like a motherfucker.*

"I was determined," he says. "I just had to get a game on."

"So how'd you pull it off?"

"Easy. The flame test."

"C'mon. That's for kids."

"Not," he says, voice husky and sly, "if you're doing it right."

I pause, but only for a second. "So show me how you did it," I say. "Show me."

"Are you sure?" he says, slanting his head. "Because it's been known to overwhelm women."

"I'll try to control myself."

All it really is, the flame test, is taking a wire loop, dipping it in one element or another, and holding it in a Bunsen flame. Each yields a different color, a luminous one.

But what Alex knew then, and still knows, is how intimate the experience can be, lights dimmed, bodies so close, soft explosions of color.

Because here we are, the lab a blue cave, standing over the lit Bunsen burner together, leaning close against the cool ledge of the lab slab. Everything is fire and magic. The soft hiss of the Bunsen, Alex's wrist flicking, the loop's platinum flashing, yielding all the sumptuous jets of color.

He dips the loop into each sample, one by one, then into the fire. First unfurls the acid green of boron. Then the filmy lavender of potassium. The scandalous violet of rubidium. Lithium's searing fuchsia.

"So this worked with Sally," I say, swinging my hip against his, sister-like but also not.

"Of course it worked," he says, maneuvering that loop so smoothly. "On me."

He explains how Sally Woods took him back to her dorm room—the smell of microwave popcorn and hairspray, hot-pink string lights draped in a heart over the bed—and made sweet, sweet love to him all night.

"A happy ending," I say, feeling a vaguely jealous twinge.

"Three weeks later, she dropped out of school to follow a guy in a band. His name was Skippy, the unkindest cut of all. Anyway, I never saw that dimple again."

He lowers the loop once more—"Let's see if you can guess this one"—and the flame streaks apple green high as my chin.

And there it is.

I look at it, his hand behind the flame, its color like sour taffy, a goblin, the green eyes of a green-eyed monster.

"Barium," I say, my voice sounding funny, small.

Green like the bottle flies that feast on garbage, roadkill, dead things. Green like the ooze from a body bloated then gently rotting.

So fast it happens, my knees soft as pea tendrils, my fingers clamping onto the lab station's resin edge, then reaching fast for the sink's gooseneck faucet.

A flash in my head of cut-pile carpet, a pair of twitching loafers.

"Hey," Alex says, a look of concern that hums inside me like a chord, "you okay?"

He must see something, something barefaced and awful, because he says, hand on my shoulder, "Listen, how about we ditch this joint? Maybe get some beers?"

Is it the third Long Island Iced Tea that makes it happen?

I suggested the Irish place, the grad student hangout, but Alex shook his head.

"We're going someplace where no one's heard of a reagent or spectrometers or peer reviews."

So here we are at Zipperz, a year-round-Christmas-lights bar near my apartment. I've been inside only once before, to play video poker and drink Jack and Cokes with my cousin Scott who'd come to visit after losing his shipping-and-receiving job for selling buttermouth perch out of his trunk in the parking lot. (*I only ever did it after I'd clocked out,* he said. *You know me. I'm highly regimentalized, like all the Owenses.*)

We're drinking the Thursday-night special, two-for-one Long Island Iced Teas, which Alex can't believe I've never had before even though he hasn't either. They come in tall glasses, lemon peel spiraled like curling ribbon, and taste both nasty and perfect, teeth-stinging, sour-smack.

Alex has all the bar gallantries—*You need a fresh coaster? Here's the hook for your handbag . . . you don't call it a handbag? Let me show you the cool, old-timey cigarette machine, c'mon, don't you wanna pull the crank?* And somehow I've forgotten about the lab and Diane and the green lash of barium, and we're talking and talking and laughing, and his right knee keeps jostling my left.

"I don't get it," he says, spinning my coaster. A fiddler, a fondler; at work he's always nudging upward the sleeve on my coffee cup rather than his own, and here he is now, peeling with faintly callused fingers the LADIES DRINK FREE paper bracelet from my wrist. "Why are you so worried? You're in. You're a sure shot. You're the only one I'd put money on for Severin's team."

I fight off the perpetual instinct to offer *Thanks, but no, there's so many qualified . . .*

Instead, with the blaze of rum–vodka–triple sec–tequila–gin, a five-gun fusillade, charging through me, I say, "She *should* pick me."

"No one'll work harder," he adds.

I look at him. That phrase. *No one works harder than you.*

But then there's a *sizzle-pop-pop* from the PA system and a stir of frayed shorts and greasy ball caps by the small stage, and, God help us, live music is coming.

"Maybe I had a chance before," I say, leaning closer, talking louder, my thoughts blurry and my shoulders sinking. "But not after today."

"What do you mean? Little Red Riding Hood? Eh, she——" He waves his hand dismissively. "I suppose a world-class CV means something to *some* people."

The picture comes to me, the way Diane looked today, sauntering down the hall with Dr. Severin like invited royalty, lab coat like an imperial cape.

"She came up just like me," I say. "Me plus money."

"Then you'll be fast friends in no time," he says, watching me more closely now. "You have so much in common."

"We don't," I insist, louder than I mean to. "And we won't. And we're nothing alike."

"Got it," he says, lifting his hands in surrender. "Don't let Zell hear you. He'll start making those catfight sounds."

He's kidding but somehow it's unbearable. He's light and laughing because he doesn't know. If he knew, if anyone knew— and suddenly that's what I'm saying.

"You don't know about her," I insist, my words coming in hard bursts. "I know about her."

"Know what?" Alex asks, leaning forward too, one hand on my shoulder now.

No, no, no. I start counting in my head, counting to clear my head. Behind Alex, the band is taking the stage, stepping over cords, the sizzle of the amps, the *whoop-whoop* of a few rowdy women, swiveling jean hips. I remember a long-ago night, the only time I ever went dancing with Diane, the complicated pleasure in her eyes, how she started twirling with the song, her hair curtaining, hiding her face, all her bad thoughts.

"Nothing," I say to Alex, my voice nearly drowned out by the bray of tuneless guitars, the screech of feedback. "Nothing."

And the music swallows everything.

Saved by the noise, we have another round.

They're terrible, Alex mouths, pointing to the band, but in that moment I love them.

The music is mostly just noise and bombast, but like most bar music, it has the sneaky power to insist, and when the set kicks up, it's suddenly as if, although I'm not even watching the stage, the fuzzing guitars start cycloning inside us, our faces LED lit, bar stools vibrating, the thrum and vroom from the blasted-out speakers on sticks, and we're facing each other, knees grazing, fingers touching forearms, leaning in to hear, and I've been alone a long time, so many nights, and now here I am, here I am...

And then there's the sweet musk of the second Long Island Iced Tea.

"Twenty-two percent alcohol?" Alex guesses, our heads close so we can hear each other.

"And seventy-eight percent heaven," I add. My drunken tell always the same: my tongue searching for a teenage piercing long healed.

"You swear you never had them before?" he asks again and it's starting to feel like it means something.

"You swear you haven't?" I ask. "But how have you had anything other than single-malt scotch and fine champagne?"

"Oh," he says, laughing, "and, what, just Mickey's Big Mouth and Ripple for you?"

Before I can pause on that, on whatever idea he has about me, he's leaning forward, strong hands on my knees, and whispering in my ear.

"What's a guy gotta do to get a dance from you?"

So maybe it's not even the third Long Island Iced Tea so much as what follows: the frenzied whirl around the floor he gives me after the next song starts, his grip stronger than I've felt in so long, maybe ever. The song is that creaky old warhorse about friends in low places that I haven't heard in a dozen years or more, since my dad's second wedding, the one to Debra, the real estate agent with the cigarette-crimped mouth and a talent for short sales. He made the band play it, then he took the mike and sang—he bellowed it, oh, did he, slipping in his too-tight rented shoes, landing on the laminate, and nearly bringing Debra down with him. And my mom, who'd been trying not to cry through the couple's first dance, burst into laughter instead and shouted, hands cupped around her mouth, from the back of the sticky-walled catering hall, *He's yours now, Debra baby! The prize is yours!*

Hearing the song now, as Alex's arms relax for a spin, loose like a marionette (*I want him to pull me close again, just to feel the hard tug*), I can almost hear my mom laughing even though she died two years ago, untethering me from all the things that kept me whole and real, and Alex keeps smiling at everything I do or say, some private pleasure over my littlest gesture, my sad little boot scoot, my even–better–than–Sally Woods's dimple, the way I keep spilling my drink on myself, on him, on everyone because I just will not set it down.

"I always knew you'd be like this," he says, mouth sweet with rum, triple sec, sticky things.

"Like what?"

"I don't know," he says, gigolo-dipping me. And he says something else I don't even hear.

When he pulls me up again, a dizzying smack of leftover solvents from the lab hits me, sharp and eye-stinging, but I don't care about anything but the softness of his shirt and the crooking of his fingers in the small of my back.

And the music slows and we do too, one long, lingering dance to a song I don't know and will never remember except that it's big and sorrowful and the middle-aged singer with the frayed shorts and crab-red face suddenly seems like Johnny Cash brought back to desperate, broke-voiced life.

"This is so much fun I could die," I say. And I mean it, my chest aching from the smoky air-conditioning and the experience of actual air whenever the back doors open. *It's been so long*, I think. *So long since any of this. There's never time for any of this.*

My head is swimming, that's what they always say in old novels, the sensation of everything around you and in you all at once, and the firm fingertips of a lanky, adoring-me man and the way, when we sit back down, he pounds the bar jauntily for more drinks, *More for the beautiful lady! She shall not go undrunk!*

Pound, pound, and then a wink for the stone-faced bartender:

"A kingdom of Long Island Iced Teas for the queen," he says.

I take three long sips, the last one lost to the bar floor, some big-armed passerby in a searing neon-green T-shirt that actually reads BITCH! on the back, his meaty elbow to my rib. *Wait*, I think, *I know*—

But a warm hand on my forearm. Alex.

"You," he says, "are as fun as you are smart, and you're the smartest motherfucker I ever met."

"You have no idea," I say. No idea at all.

"So stop worrying about Diane Fleming, okay?" he asks. Then, putting one hand on either side of my bar stool, his face so close: "And don't listen to the other guys. Just because she's a woman doesn't mean Severin won't pick you."

My face runs hot in an instant and I can't guess why he's decided to spoil things.

"I know," I say. "I know. This isn't about that. This is something much, much bigger." The words come from my mouth without my actually choosing or forming them.

"Bigger how?" he says, leaning forward, the heat of him on the heat of me, and whose heat is greater? But it's the stage of drunk when you're not even sure if you're saying things or just thinking them until suddenly you're shouting them.

It comes so fast. A push of feelings in my chest and I can't stop myself.

"I know Diane Fleming. From before. Diane. I know her. And I'm nothing like her."

His eyebrows lift.

This time, there's no stopping me.

"I know Diane," I say, and my mouth is humming, "and she's a really bad person."

We're on the back patio now. The boom-boom-*boom* of the juke-box hurls itself into an old song I know, from when I was ten years old, headphones pressed tight, rolling around in my bed and dreaming of places other than Lanister, my dander-thick house, the great muddy sweep of the ugly old town.

"Hey, what did you mean earlier?" Alex asks, and somehow it's come to this, his hand dancing along the lace edge of my bra, plucking at the tiny pink bow (if I'd anticipated this, I wouldn't have worn my milk-fed, tenderfoot, junior-miss white).

"Let's not talk," I say, my back arching, body wriggling to get more room, the two of us entwined on one of the Zipperz settees, the rain just starting and no one but us back there. "I'm tired of talking."

This is what you do, my mom told me once, wondering about the men, few and briefly, who'd flickered through my life, *to avoid everything else.*

What did you mean, Mom? I want to ask, but she's a sack of ashes now, the saddest and sweetest, and she never was any kind of expert on men, the woman who tangled with my dad for a dozen years, though she saved me from much worse than this.

(When your mom is gone, the thing no one ever tells you is that the little compass needle inside keeps spinning around and around, never finding north.)

"When you were talking about Diane Fleming," Alex says, a long finger under my bra clasp. "A bad person how?"

"She was my friend in high school," I say, and his leg is shaking beneath me and my thoughts are coming in fits and starts. "Or I was hers. And she told me something once."

I can feel his grin, his teeth against my neck. "You, my girl, are a charming and mysterious drunk," he says, and *pop*, his bare hand under my unloosed bra, my skin both hot and cold under his palm.

And I stop talking.

THEN

Those first few weeks Diane and I were lab partners, I never asked her anything about her dad or her family. Then one Sunday I was out walking the dogs and I spotted Diane and an older man in a suit and string tie at the cemetery over on Fall Road. They were carefully placing a big spray of white flowers on a headstone. The man, who must have been her granddad, hair white as frosting and face tanned and serious, was sobbing, while Diane stood rigidly, arms at her side.

Tugging at his leash, Grimm let out a yowl.

Diane didn't move, but I kept going. Walked faster, head down.

That night, I looked it up online. The death notice.

Bruce Allan Fleming was born on August 14, 1964, and passed away unexpectedly on Wednesday evening, November 23, 2005. He is survived by his father, Warren Fleming, and his loving daughter, Diane Marie. Services will be held Sunday, November 27, at 2:30 p.m. at St. Bonaventure Chapel in Lanister with Rev. Rob West officiating.

Interment will follow in St. Bonaventure Cemetery in the Fleming family plot.

There was really nothing there to see except for the blurry photo of a stiff-backed, mustached man trying very hard to smile. And those words *passed away unexpectedly*, which I guess they always say when you die so young.

By then, Diane and I were studying together almost every night.

I was working harder than I ever had, my calculations telling me I had to get a ninety-seven on my AP Chem midterm to qualify for the Severin scholarship.

No senioritis on you, my mom kept saying, somewhere between wariness and pride.

There was a satisfying, soothing rhythm to it all. Diane with her mechanical pencils and me with my green-capped Hickory Hill Animal Rescue Bics, the two of us exchanging our formulas, checking each other. Diane, pencil tapping on lip, reading over my combustion analysis, and me trying so hard to find errors in hers, any error. The one or two times I did, I could barely bring myself to tell her, not wanting to see that nervous crumpling over her eye, the twist of her mouth.

Sometimes we ran together too. Diane wanted to get her Lanister letter in cross-country to match the one from Sacred Heart. It was funny to think of how much it had mattered when I got mine last year, when I'd never even heard of the Severin scholarship and wasn't sure I'd take AP Chem because would City Tech really care?

One morning before school, we ran clear to the interstate, where I spotted Tanner and Stacey opening things up at the Golden Fry, its fuzzy neon lights coming on and the smell of chicken fat making my mouth water.

"Looking good, Kitty Kat," Tanner shouted, big smile gleaming.

"You have so many friends," Diane said, after.

"Work friends," I said. "Sometimes we drink out at the old speedway after closing."

We were breathing hard and I felt the sweat everywhere. We'd run for so long. Sometimes it was like Diane forgot we were still running, her body just moving, always, forward.

"My mom says that's important," Diane said. "Friends, dances, parties."

It was hard to picture Diane hanging out with girls like Ashley G. and Rachael Schreiber, who spent their free time dyeing their hair pink and going drag-racing under the viaduct with Emmet Diaz or Jeff from the taco place or Matt Stollak, who came from Texas and could do backward free throws on one bounce from the far end of the court into the basket.

Walking down the halls, she always seemed a girl apart. All around her, kids might be buzzing and swooping and swinging their bags and waving their phones like bright flags, but she never seemed to belong to any of it.

"But it's just not that important to me," Diane said. "Not like the Severin."

She smiled a little and I smiled too.

I'd have traded Alicia and Rachael and both Ashleys for Diane's brain. All the friends in the world weren't going to get me out of Lanister.

Then Diane said the funniest thing.

"Except sometimes I see you walking your dogs," she said. "You've got your earbuds in and the dogs all tangled in your legs, and the way you're walking, like...like there's nothing in the world to worry about it. And I think, *That's what I want.*"

"But that can be you," I said. I was thinking of our bull mastiff, Grimm, and Fudge, our German shepherd, and Old Sam, the dog they were meant to replace. When my dad ran over Sam with his Mustang, I cried for three days. I thought I'd never stop crying, my face swollen and pink like an Easter Peep. "Anybody can do that," I told her.

It felt like she was seeing something in me that she wanted to, something I had that she didn't. But it wasn't really a thing I had, or a thing I was. It was just part of being in the world, of living. You cared about things. People, animals. That was what you did.

"I'm going to try," she said. "I'm going to try to do that."

"Kit," Ms. Castro said, waving me into her counseling office one day, "I'm really glad you and Diane have become such fast friends."

"You mean you hope she'll rub off on me," I said, smiling. Ms. Castro never really liked my hanging out with the Ashleys or Alicia or, worse still, wild Michelle Turlock, now transferred to St. Martha's, with whom I used to duck out of last period to play pinball and smoke cigarettes with my cousin Scott.

But Ms. Castro's lips became a line, like they did when she had bad news (*Your father didn't send the check for the cross-country uniform or your letter jacket, Kit*).

"No, I meant you're helping her," she said. "She's had a hard time. Shuffled around from Mom to Mom-and-boyfriend to Dad. Then he passes away and she's packed off to her granddad..." She shook her head.

Until that moment, I hadn't realized Diane had been living with her dad when he died, and suddenly everything seemed so much worse.

"I just want to make sure you understand," Ms. Castro continued. "A parent dying—it changes a person."

"Yeah, I know," I said. "Everything changes you."

Ms. Castro paused like there was something she wanted to say but wasn't sure how. Finally, she nodded, pushing her glasses back up the bridge of her nose.

"It can do things to a person," she said, turning from me. "And sometimes it takes a long time to figure out just what it's done."

That night, she came to my house to study, appearing in our driveway behind the wheel of a big truck like the kind wealthy ranchers drove on TV. Seeing her descend from its high haunches in her cream sweater and long braided ponytail was always memorable, like seeing a pale angel alighting from the clouds.

"Whose is that?" I asked, remembering Mrs. Fleming's speckless white sedan, grille like a tombstone.

"My grandfather's," she said. "He lets me take it whenever I want."

"Do you ever get lonely out there?" I asked. Her grandfather's house was all the way over in Frontenac, seventeen miles away, on a fifteen-acre place nearly in the mountains.

"No," she said, curling her fingers around a bunny-paw key chain, so girlish for Diane, and I wondered if her mom gave it to her. "My mom and I talk on the phone every night."

"My room's pretty small," I warned, escorting her through our pocket-size house quickly, the smell of carpet deodorizer and my mom's Corn Huskers moisturizer, her arms always red to raw from the chemicals at the clinic.

The room seemed even tinier when we both stepped inside, barely space for us both to stand with our backpacks, my narrow bed, plywood desk stacked high with books, a thin strip of carpet between the two.

But Diane didn't seem to notice, looking around at my goofy

dog poster, my running shoes flung over the desk chair. My books wedged tight in milk crates.

"I have this," Diane said, her fingers touching the crinkling plastic library-book cover of *Marie Curie: A Life*.

"Do you?" I said, smiling.

Before we started, my mom appeared with a tray of sodas and chips, the thick-ridged kind, and Diane acted like it was caviar and champagne.

"Your mom's really nice," she said when we were alone again. She was holding a chip in her hand like it was a baby chick you'd better not squeeze too hard.

"She's pretty okay," I said. "You must miss yours. How come she's not here?"

"She moved to Florida with her boyfriend," she said, setting the chip down, uneaten. "I decided to stay here to finish school."

"You guys seemed tight," I said. "Maybe she'll come back. She's gotta come for graduation."

"Maybe," she said, turning away, reaching for her bookbag. "I don't know. She's always loved the beach."

It seemed like a funny kind of answer. Then she opened her wallet and flapped it at me: a snapshot of Diane and her mom, two blond beauties with legs a mile long in matching white one-pieces at some pool, that big sparkler I'd seen at camp flashing on her mother's finger.

"That's from last summer," Diane said. "When I visited."

My mom was only thirty-four and we even liked to swap jeans sometimes, even though it meant her lying back on her mattress and wriggling like a dog tick to zip them up. But I couldn't imagine the two of us hanging out in bathing suits and getting our picture taken.

There was something in the snapshot—edges curling, a thumb smudge on one corner from so much touching—that made me sad. I wondered if Diane's mom looked at it half as much.

"Do you wish you were living with her?" I said.

"No," Diane said, not meeting my eyes.

"Who wants to live in Florida?" I said gently. "Alligators and serial killers."

"So you've met her boyfriend," she said. And I laughed. *Diane had made a joke!*

"Parents' love lives are the worst," I tried. And I explained how, one night, soon after my mom had kicked my dad out for good, he'd shown up and plowed across the lawn in his blistered Firebird (*Cash-poor, hood-rich SOB*, my mom would say with a sigh), then went careering into the backyard, uprooting our old swing set by its haunches, like in a video game.

"My dad always hated that swing set," I said.

"Why?" she asked.

"Broke his leg jumping off the top of it on the Fourth of July," I said. Then added, "I may have dared him."

Diane let a sneaky smile appear, the rarest of things.

"You should've tried it with your mom's boyfriend," I said.

"They have nine lives, those men," she said, more softly now. "Don't they?"

I nodded. Nothing ever felt so true.

She turned away from me and began removing her books from her bag one by one in the slowest, most methodical way.

"We better start," Diane said, pointing to my bookbag. "There's not much time."

It wasn't until hours later, both of us jittery on Diet Coke ("My grandfather won't have any soda in the house," Diane told me, slurping greedily. "Grandma died of diabetes"), when we'd nailed the last of the net ionic equations, eraser dust flying, that I got up the courage.

"Hey, I saw you on Sunday," I said. "At St. Bonaventure's."

"I saw you too," she said, surprising me again. I'd never seen her turn her head.

"Whose grave was that?" I asked.

She looked up. "My dad died last year. I thought everyone knew."

"I wasn't sure," I said, my face burning. "People say stuff."

There was a pause so long I thought maybe she'd never say another word.

"I remember him from when he picked you up at camp," I said, finally. "He seemed really nice."

She still didn't say anything, so I tried to touch her hand, like my mom always did when people's pets died. But she was cold to the touch, cold as the door to the walk-in freezer at the Golden Fry, and I could tell she didn't like it.

"I'm sorry," I said, pulling my hand back. "I mean, about your dad."

"Thanks," she said. "We weren't close." She paused a second, looking at me. "It's sad, though."

There was something so odd about her face, how it didn't change. The skin smooth as sweet cream and lashes like a doll's hairbrush.

"A heart attack, right?" I said, scrounging for things to say. "It's . . ."

"It's strange," she said, nodding thoughtfully. "It's just strange sometimes that he's really gone. We didn't know each other that well."

"That doesn't seem strange," I said.

"He didn't really know much about being a dad," she said. "My mom used to say he was a haircut in search of a personality."

I looked up, surprised. Seeing my surprise, Diane suddenly looked surprised too.

"She didn't mean it like that. She's just always wanted me to want to be with her."

I nodded, but as I did I felt the same faint chill I'd felt watching her at St. Bonaventure. Something in the way her face rested, in the way her hand lay, palm open, on her lap.

"My grandfather put this framed picture of him in my room," she said. "And every night, I stick it in the bedside drawer. Every morning, I take it out again so he won't know."

It was the most she'd ever said about anything other than titrations and scholarship-application deadlines, but she said it in almost the same way, just slightly flatter, the words so matter-of-fact.

"I get it," I said. "When my grandma died, I used to dream about her standing at the foot of my bed yelling at me. Asking why we put all that dirt in her mouth."

She looked at me, and for a second, it felt like something was lifting from her as we sat, as if her squared shoulders rose higher and her eyes tugged back from some darker place.

"I just wanted her to go away," I added, unable to stop now. "But every night, there she'd be at the foot of my bed."

Both our gazes turned to the edge of the bed, its cramped foot. The dark space behind it, the sharp surprise, though we both knew it was there, of the stick-on mirror on my closet door.

"Yeah," Diane said, turning away quickly, looking down. "I have those kinds of dreams."

When she glanced up again, her face looked so tired, like an old woman's.

*   *   *

"Be careful with that one," my mom said later, smearing her face with lotion in the bathroom.

I stopped in the hallway, wondering if she'd heard something. "What do you mean?"

"Remember that Birman we had for a while?"

The cat with paws like snowy mitts. I was nine or ten, and one day she darted out from under the sofa and chomped me on the wrist. I suffered through a rabies shot and cat scratch fever that made my underarm bulge like Popeye's. It turned out she'd fractured her ulna and it had made her scared and mean.

"We didn't know until we did the X-ray," my mom said. "You had to look really close to see it, but there was the tiniest hairline fracture. Watch for the crack in the prettiest bone."

"What about the whipworm I got from the schnauzer you brought home so they wouldn't croak him? Or the second rabies shot I had to get from that old bat?"

"That bat was not my fault," she said, snapping a tissue from the box, wiping at her hands. "He was hiding in the tire swing."

"Uh-huh."

"Listen, Kit, there are some people who are trouble. They can't help it," she said, watching me in the mirror. "But let them in, and they'll swallow you whole."

I didn't say anything for a moment, but the hallway felt hot and I wanted to leave.

"Mom," I said. "I know about those people."

Besides, there was no time to worry about Diane, especially not when she was helping me. Just being around her made it seem like studying all the time wasn't a burden but a plan. A way out.

Even now, I'm not sure what drew us closer: these few confidences, a dark sharing, or the Severin. That's what we called it now. Just "the Severin."

By December, my AP Chem grade was up to ninety-five, and I had a ninety-six in physics.

"You should be really proud," Ms. Castro told me. "You're going to make eligibility, I know it."

"Don't jinx me," I said, crossing myself.

"Just keep going," Ms. Castro said. "You've got this."

So I kept going. I studied all through Christmas Eve stocking-hanging and my mom's eggnog-and-tree-trimming holiday-movie sob-a-thon. I even skipped the secret, after-close New Year's party at the Golden Fry.

In the last few frigid January weeks before midterms, I'd come in the door at eight, and if Mom was home, she'd send me to the shower immediately to wash off the stink of the Golden Fry, especially those nights after I'd bricked the grill and came home slicked in oil and feeling mean. But by half past eight, I'd be elbow-deep in the books.

"Kit, don't you wanna take a break?" my mom asked me one evening, her night off. "How about we go to Pinky Toes? My nails are trashed from all the Bru-Clean. Oh, honey, I had to hold this rabbit during surgery today. His legs were like a teacup handle."

But I didn't want the gel mani. Or to walk the dogs to the rail trails or eat peanut butter and banana sandwiches while watching the tanned women on reality TV.

I didn't even care when Keith Brandt said I had a banging stride at cross-country that day and maybe we could get together. My stride *was* banging. Concentrating so much more on everything made me run better, faster. I was thinking all the time.

I was thinking so much, so fast, so hard, that sometimes I

dreamed about ionic compounds. Ms. Steen told us a famous chemist named August Kekulé once fell asleep while working on a problem and he dreamed of atoms dancing into the shape of a snake, which then turned around and bit its own tail. When Kekulé woke up, he realized that benzene molecules were made up of rings of carbon atoms, and that opened up an entire new field of chemistry and gave everyone a new understanding of chemical bonding.

What if, I wondered in bed every night, someday I dreamed of something like that?

But other times, it all felt so far away. And seeing all the one hundreds on Diane's grade sheets, and that thing Ms. Steen said about maybe she should just hand over the class to Diane—sometimes it seemed impossible. The Severin and everything else.

"Maybe it's not for me. Maybe I don't care enough," I told Diane after a rough lab full of screwups and my forgetting to preweigh the flask, throwing off our results. "Not like you do."

Watching her in class, the way she knew the answer to every question, and the complication to every answer.

"Kit, let me show you something," she said, opening her laptop.

The screen lit up brilliantly. It was a series of short films shot with high-definition cameras—simple chemical reactions, but magnified, intensified, until they became magical explosions.

"This is my favorite," she said, showing them adding zinc metal to a lead nitrate solution. In seconds, a silver-tipped winter forest from a fairy tale emerged.

"They put it in a soft gel," she said, "to preserve it."

The gel's bubbles looked like giant globes.

We watched again and again as the glinting and intricate forest seemed to paint itself before our eyes, the simplest of chemical reactions.

If you've never seen it, you should.

"Dr. Severin has these cameras in her lab," Diane said. "These are from her lab. The Severin Lab."

By this point, her name had become like an incantation.

"You can do it," Diane said. "Science is facts and results. It's not messy. It's precise." She placed her palm on the cover of her AP Chem book. "Everything makes sense here. It's the safest place."

I looked at her. "For people like you."

"But you are like me, Kit. You're just like me."

NOW

We're running across the parking lot, Alex grabbing for my hand, me tugging my bra back up under my shirt.

Then we're inside his car, and Alex insists he can drive—he was at least one Long Island Iced Tea behind me, and did he even finish his second?—and I say I can walk home ("Like the beginning of every true-crime show ever. They'll find one of my shoes and a barrette gleaming in the dirt"), but he seems to be driving anyway.

We're only a mile from my apartment, after all.

"You did the right thing," he's saying, and I'm nodding and nodding because I think he means letting him drive me home.

But in that moment, his head turning slowly—*like slow motion, like a movie*—I have a full and complete vision of something else, something I'd been missing. It's gone before I can hold on to it.

In the soundlessness of his car—the quietest I've ever been in except the time I drove the provost's tipsy wife home in her Town Car after the Breaking the Magnifying Glass Ceiling women alumni reception—I sit back, watching all the lights of the city scatter across me, and everything is slow, voluptuous, beautiful.

My stomach lifts at the sight of Alex's ragged linen cuff over the gear shift. The heedlessness with which people like Alex wear such fine clothes; ink jab, acid spray, what does it matter?

Alex glances over once, twice, his long and graceful hand reaching for my leg, fingertips grazing the inside of my thigh with such ease, the ease of a single man in a hand-harvested linen shirt driving a car that pipes cool air the minute the ignition strikes and makes no sound even when coasting above all the pots and pits of Route 310 as we near my apartment, all the Quik Lubes and Sun-less Tan-o-Rama and Family Doctor Here and Party Dawgs that beat a golden path to my home.

What if it were always like this? I wonder. A whole life like this, with cars that always run and never make a sound, a life with savings accounts and heavy glass bottles of Italian water and organic milk in the glass-doored fridge, a life where there are fam-ily homes with spare rooms and tablecloths on long rollers, and Christmases in family cabins and always-new computers and the latest quantitative software and an aunt who knows the head of the PharmaTherapeutics Research unit at Pfizer and a college friend who edits the *Journal of Biological Chemistry* . . .

. . . and waking up mornings with a smile pressed into a pillow-case, spiderweb-soft, because he's there and his ceiling has never leaked once and the *Journal of Biological Chemistry* would be happy to accept the article and meanwhile, a French-press plunger gently plunges in the kitchen and then he's right there, palm to mattress, grinning and saying, *By the way, while you were sleeping, Dr. Severin called and she would love to take you to La Belle Vie for pâté and rosé and to talk about your future.*

But then the moment passes, and we pull into my pockmarked parking lot, and experience tells me, even through the golden haze of Long Island Iced Teas, that none of those things will happen, and the only guarantee is that, in seven to ten minutes, I'll have this grinning man in my bed and maybe it'll pull me, for seven to ten minutes, from the leachy hold of the lab and PMDD team selection and the long, unlovely corridors of the Severin Lab, the click-clicking of the HEPA filter, the ventilation blowers, and most of all, maybe it'll pull me from the hold, more than a decade old, of the seventeen-year-old girl standing in that far corner of my head, the one glaring at me, needy, full of thunder and consequence.

We stumble up the steps, Alex's foot catching on the downstairs neighbor's ashtray forever resting on step three to the right. The tin clinks and ashes scatter. His arm around me, his hand tickling my torso, finding any bare space of skin.

My keys are nowhere in the all-purpose dump of my purse, flash drives and hand sanitizer, tampons and gum sleeves, Tylenol blister packs and a rubbed-out emery board, laundry sticks and a Kit Kat wrapper.

And it's Alex who dips a pair of fingers inside and lifts the jangling tentacles of my keys.

It's Alex who unlocks my door.

It's Alex who hoists me in the air, and my right shoe catches in the door and tumbles to the ground as he carries me inside. *Across the threshold, triple sec streaked up one arm (the bartender promising he'd made that last Long Island Iced Tea "extra-long"), and what could be more romantic, blooming bruises on my shins from rassling on the Zipperz patio and—*

(In the morning, I'll find the shoe—one of my favorite low-tops—in the hallway, its canvas tongue torn loose.)

*   *   *

When it starts, all the laughing stops and everything feels rushed and mysterious. He's so much graver in the act itself, all the smiles gone.

If I look at you, he says, head down, *it'll be over too fast.*

I remember that, remember him saying it, when my eyes slap open, 3:00 a.m. blinking on the digital clock and a pair of dark eyes in front of me, shutting themselves.

I remember.

Sorry, I said after—I remember this now too. *Sorry,* I whispered, his hand on my pounding-pounding chest, my lungs, a hook of worry over his brow, *I couldn't catch my breath.*

No, he says, *that was me.*

My hand to his beating chest, *th-thump, th-thump*; he's right.

In the dream, I'm in G–21, that narrow L-shaped room where we spend more than half our lives, a long black-topped bench snaking along the wall. The place where all my evening hours, my Friday nights, my vacations and holidays vanish like smoke. The safest place in all the world.

But then Diane appears in the doorway, in a lab coat the color of a spleen, its sleeves so long they cover her hands.

She's heading toward me, walking stiffly, her arms in front of her, her legs as stiff as those broomstick arms.

Diane, I say. *You're not supposed to be here.*

But she keeps walking, right up to me, leaning close as if to whisper something in my ear.

When she opens her mouth, a puff of vapor slips from her lips. Apple green, sickly green, and filling our nostrils, our mouths. Its smell so sweet it hurts.

*   *   *

"You were crying," Alex murmurs from the far side of the bed, his faced turned away from me in the dark. "In your sleep."

"I wasn't," I say. I say it twice.

The morning comes before it should, the vinyl bedroom blinds in a tightly knotted bundle against the wall because, I remember now, at some point before the bed captured us both, I'd decided I needed to get an eyeful of the great big Lanister sky.

Of course, I haven't lived in Lanister since I was seventeen, even though its smells and languor sink inside me like an industrial sludge every time I catch a whiff of benzene in the lab. Or, more recently, when Mother's Day cards fill the drugstore racks. The last time I saw its blush-red, aerosol-thick skies, I was there for less than twenty-four hours, just enough time to fill three dumpsters with family heirlooms (those magnetic photo albums from the eighties that ate away at the pictures; my toddler handprint in plaster) and drive two Lab mutts and a sad-faced boxer to animal rescue. The tickle in my throat from the sulfur, the orange flares—will it ever leave me?

"Alex," I say, his name fumbling in my throat, but he's gone save for the blinking text on my phone: *Morning, you. See you at the lab xo.*

The walk is bracing, the chilly expanse of parking lot after parking lot, four strip malls in a row before the far north end of campus.

It didn't happen, it didn't happen, it didn't.

The memories come in pieces. Little bits of grit too small to pick up even with a wetted finger, too small even to hold in my gaze.

Except this: At some point in the triple-sec-stuck night, before the bed and what we did in it, my hand on Alex's collarbone, my voice urgent, desperate, came forth.

Diane Fleming. My words hot and daring. *Diane Fleming. Listen to me. You have to listen. She's a killer.*

A secret I held tight so long, lodged deep in some vapor-tight box in some shut closet in my head. But then you came back, Diane. You came back.

It's the latest I've ever arrived at the lab, nearly eight thirty.

At the end of the west hallway, I see her long before I'm ready, coffee churning high in my throat. The wine-colored coat. I'm not prepared, not even close.

But there she is. Half enveloped by four pale lab coats: Zell, Dr. Irwin wiggling his mischievous gray eyebrows, two grad students hovering around him. All the men but Zell are taller, but still she looms larger, head dipped low, listening to them or pretending to, as they press forward, jabbering advice, offering guidance. Their hunger to impress her is heavy, embarrassing.

Seeing her, though, I can feel my face burning, like a criminal's.

I didn't say anything, I tell myself, *that wasn't true.*

"Did you hear?" Maxim asks me the minute I step into the lounge.

I stare dumbly at him, hoping he can't see the hangover slick on me, regret so thick it's like a film on my skin and impossible to hide.

"So how bad do you think it is?" he asks, close to me.

"I'm sorry," I say. "How bad is what?"

That's when Juwon appears, sleep-creased, rubbing the scruff on his new-dad neck.

"It's starting," he says. "We better go."

"Severin called a meeting," Maxim tells me impatiently. Then he adds with surprise, "You don't know anything. You know less than me."

"There's a rumor," Juwon tells me, "that they're redoing the budget for the PMDD team. And that's never good."

That's when Alex appears down the hall.

My wrist throbbing from the jug of water in my hand, the biggest the Quik-E-Mart had, I find myself backing away. My bleary head and the slight ache between my hips and the feeling my mouth has been sucked dry from booze gives it all a harrowing quality, like one of those old movies where the hero blacks out and wakes up with a gun in his hand and his wife dead on the floor.

"Conference room," Juwon says, pointing.

Alex looks at me. "Well," he says, hair still faintly shower-wet, the loose, buoyant face of the sexually triumphant, "timing is everything."

They're all looking at me. Alex keeps trying to catch my eye, and then there's Diane, whom I can feel approaching from thirty feet away, the swirl of scarlet.

Moving quickly, I fiddle with my bag, its shredding plastic handles, the heft of the water jug, ignoring Alex, who looms closer.

"It was hot a half hour ago, I swear," he's saying, his hand outstretched with a stained paper cup of cooling coffee. "First time I ever beat you to the lab."

I shake my head, try for a careless smile, the smile of a distracted colleague.

"Hey," he whispers, leaning close, smelling like my soap, "can we talk later?"

"Sure," I say, my head lifting in what feels like slow motion. "Sure we can."

*   *   *

As we wait at the conference table, I bow my head, doodling with aggressive concentration, my pen pressing into my notebook. Not looking at Alex once.

When I was a kid, I checked out *Call of the Wild* from the library and inside, on one of the chapter pages, someone had drawn, with sharply pointed pencil, the most meticulously detailed sketch of a swollen penis and an enveloping vagina. It vaguely terrified me and the words beneath it (*Just one squeeze and . . .*) even more so and for a few years, until I crossed the great divide myself, I couldn't shake the idea of sex as being this contorted, ugly thing, a gaudy cartoon.

The big surprise came later when I learned the scariest part about sex wasn't the swell and heave of body parts, its comic grotesquerie, but the shattering intimacy of all of it.

How it made you feel, in your shuttered-up heart.

"Just a quick meeting to update you all on the PMDD grant," Dr. Severin says, glasses lowered on her nose as she looks at the piece of paper in her hand, one flimsy sheet. "I've been working with Finance on the figures. My good friends in Neuropsych, as usual, are being greedy."

My pen point rests on my paper, a blotch spreading.

"I have my techs lined up. I'll need a neuro postdoc for this, and maybe a neuro grad student. So it appears, looking at the numbers, that leaves me space for two of you."

She looked around at us, a faint twitch over her left eye. No one can say anything. *Two. Only two. Is that what she said?*

"I know some of you have been speculating that I'd bring on three of you, but that didn't come from me. We need a line for Serge. Serge is very necessary."

We should have seen it coming. Serge has worked for Dr. Severin forever, longer even than Maxim. I'd never seen an animal unit run with more rigor and precision, a closer adherence to rules and protocol. Sometimes you would see Dr. Severin and Serge walking together or conferring in the vivarium, dark head bent to dark head, and you had the feeling they barely needed to exchange a word. They both have a very clear sense of how things should be done. They are both relentless workers.

"Don't worry. I'm not kicking anyone to the curb. There's plenty of work on Dr. Irwin's hypogonadism grant and other, smaller projects," she continues. "But two of you are all I need, if they're the right two. I'll let you know on Monday."

She taps the paper, a flick of the wrist. All our fates imperiled in an instant.

"Dr. Severin," I say, and I can't guess what's come over me, except the sticky syrup, last night's renewable gift from Zipperz, sluicing up my windpipe, "do you already know who the two will be?"

She looks at me; everyone does. Is it just me or does the pressure in the air feel like we're all in a submarine, barreling through deep waters? "Because if so, why not just tell us now?"

Alex clears his throat three times, and I think that's his leg under the table brushing against mine.

Dr. Severin continues to look at me, a pause that feels like a wink. "Bright girl," she says.

But she doesn't answer and instead asks Juwon to update her on the CCK results.

"Some balls," Zell says to me under his breath as we walk out. "Did you really think she'd give it up like that? She likes to keep us fingers-on-the-ledge."

I don't say anything. I'm watching as Maxim hands Diane a new lab coat to replace the scarlet one. She slides it over her water-colored dress, the color of an expensive oyster, like a lick of mercury. So different from the prairie skirts and cowl necks she wore in high school. Her "apostolic wear" was what my mom called it, my mom most comfortable in cutoffs and scrub tops. My mom who told me never to be ashamed of my figure, which unfortunately never gave me much cause for shame.

I watch her walk down the hallway, her head slightly slanted as though thinking. Diane is always thinking.

And then I see Dr. Severin catching up to her in tight, tidy steps.

I've never seen Severin try to catch up with anyone. Maybe the FedEx guy.

"And then there was one," Zell says, watching them too. "Sorry, Owens."

"What does that mean?" I say. But I know what he means. If they wanted a woman on the grant, now they had one. Why would they have two?

"Goddamn," Zell says, not answering me. "I'm gonna be buried in Irwin's gonads forever."

I don't say anything, turn to walk the other way.

I stay under the fume hood most of the morning and no one bothers me.

Two spots, and one will be Diane. If there was a "woman" spot, there no longer is.

It's the worst kind of news to come with a hangover, the hangover already scraping the bottom of my bad thoughts, lifting them for inspection. At one point, I have to walk swiftly to the ladies' room to try to throw up. In high school, among the cross-country runners, and in college, when I lived in that ramshackle co-op with sixteen other women, I used to see them do it all the time, but it's harder than you think, even with all the water.

A memory flash comes of me hanging off the bed at two a.m., my head dizzy with drinks and desire, and Alex laughing in the dark.

All of it seemed like such a great idea twelve hours ago. Sometimes your genes rise up. My dad never thought ten minutes ahead. He once figured out he could set up phony orders at the electronics distributor he worked for, and he didn't stop until he was caught starting an eBay store (LettheLightinHere) to handle the good business. Twenty-four months at Wasco for his trouble.

So not only do I open my legs at the first chance for my sweet-breathed, fine-limbed lab crush, I tell him all my secrets too.

Well, one. The only one that counts.

I know it's coming—that moment, Diane and me alone together for the first time.

Why not, I think, *make it now?*

She's alone in G-21. Four lab benches away, toiling quietly, setting up slides, acquainting herself with the work of the lab.

Things are stirring in my head. There's a two-pound sack of flour on my neck and I haven't eaten since the cone of free popcorn at Zipperz. Something makes me start talking. I want to be the one who starts.

"Diane," I say. "I just wanted to congratulate you. On all your successes."

I see her mouth open slightly even though her gaze remains on the slide tray before her.

"Thank you," she says softly. "You've had quite a bit yourself. I'm not surprised."

"So how's your family?" I keep going. "Your mom?"

Diane's eyes lift from the slide tray fleetingly before sweeping down again.

"She's fine," she says, her fingertip moving across the slides as if counting.

"Diane," I start, but I have nowhere to go, a sudden flapping in my chest.

"Is there something," she says, turning to face me now, "you want to talk about?"

Once she's called me on it, I can't think what to say. She parts her lips and I remember my dream. Diane, the green gust from her mouth.

"There *is* so much to talk about," she continues, lowering her tinted goggles to her neck, looking at me. Her voice is stronger than I anticipated, and forthright. "Seeing you here, I keep thinking about fate."

"What?" I say, thinking I've misheard. "What did you say—"

"There's so much between us," she says, softening her voice to a whisper. "The things we shared." She places her hand on my forearm. "My best friend."

At that moment, the door clicks open and Alex stands there, his key card in hand.

I step back from Diane quickly, nearly stumbling. Looking at me, face pale, Alex somehow decides on a smile.

"Hey, you two," he says, his voice a little too calm. Then, turning to me: "Can I borrow you for something?"

I look at him and back at Diane, her goggles nudged up and flashing like an insect's jeweled eyes.

THEN

"Kit, there you are, there you are!" Diane said, pointing, rocking in her cap-toe flats.

January 29, midterm grades in, I'd met the GPA requirement for the Severin scholarship. It was right there in black and white on the big bulletin board outside of Ms. Castro's office.

Diane and me. Me and Diane. The only ones from Lanister High.

Ms. Castro emerged from her office and hugged me. When she saw Diane, she tried to hug her too, though Diane's body stiffened like it always did if you stood too close, and Ms. Castro stepped back, uncomfortable.

"Now you're my toughest competition," Diane said to me.

We both smiled, but it was true.

"But you don't have to go to State. You can go anywhere," I said, unable to stop myself. This was the sneaky truth of it. Diane had her pick of schools, schools far better than State, and it seemed like she could afford them, with the money from her father's will and from her grandfather, who was rich enough to own all that land in the Foothills.

She looked at me, something crackling between us.

"But I want to go where she works," she said. "Dr. Severin."

"The blood is the life," I said, looking back up at the list, our names side by side. "You're that into PMS?"

"No," she said. "But you know what? My mom's periods last a whole week, sometimes longer. She goes through twelve tampons a day. She keeps an index card taped to the inside of the vanity door filled with little hash marks."

It was such an odd detail I was almost sure I'd misheard it. The bell rang, and all I could think of was Mrs. Fleming bleeding in her white, white car.

"It started after her miscarriages. She had three before she had me. And one stillbirth. She said she went a little crazy and thought for sure the baby was coming back. She kept buying presents for her for weeks after. They were all girls, all named Diane. She says they were all trying to become me. Until I became me."

All the way home I kept thinking about those dead Diane babies.

"I used to dream about them," Diane had said before the second bell rang. "All in bed with her, nestled like baby mice."

Maybe everyone has strangenesses tucked deep inside. When I was little, I used to eat burned match heads and chalk. My dad kept a list of all the women he'd ever kissed. At least that's what he told me it was when I found it in his wallet, soft as a puppy ear, so soft it might fall apart in my hands.

"When you were first born," my mom confided once, "I used to have nightmares that I'd done something horrible to you. Like I'd dream I opened up a KFC tub and it was full of my babies all covered in honey. I plucked one loose and it smiled at me so I ate it like a chicken leg."

And she laughed and laughed, and I did too. My mom never even liked chicken, and only my dad ate from the tub.

The next night, when Diane came over, I didn't feel like studying for the first time in a long while. I told her we should celebrate instead. Celebrate getting this far toward the Severin without thinking too hard about how now we were each other's primary competition.

"Come on," I said. "Just one night. I gave up a senior-year boyfriend just for you."

Which was true, in a way. I hadn't had time to do any of the things that lead to having a boyfriend, like driving with the Ashleys to Cresper's Peak with a cooler of Mickey's, those green bottles like grenades, until we found the spot where all the college guys dragged along the viaducts, or taking up Marcus Bell on his offer of a midnight tour of the fun park where he worked. He said we could dive Coyote Canyon to loot out the day's trash and that I could meet all the feral cats who took over the place from one a.m. till sunrise.

And I'd missed all the parties that fall. I never cared much, not when I saw the pictures everyone posted, the vomit shots, a nipple hanging out for all to see. Sometimes the girls' drunken faces looked so old, like liquor-blossomed, beer-bloated visions of their future selves. Selves that would take up jobs at the hospital, Mather Electronics, or the water-treatment plant, marry in five years, and start pushing out whey-faced runts and sweet muffins and never, ever leave Lanister.

I didn't need the parties. But I wanted to celebrate with Diane.

*   *   *

I called up my cousin Scott, and four hours later I had two driver's licenses in my hot palm. A pair of blondes pushing twenty-five, hard-faced and aqua-smeared.

"I need these back," he'd warned me. "They're on loan. And the owners don't know they're on loan."

I looked at them. Would I be sullen Amber or defiant Bailey? Both had at least three inches on me and neither had green eyes. I wasn't sure how Scott had gotten them, but he was on my dad's side of the gene lagoon, so I knew better than to ask.

"Kit, I don't know," Diane kept saying as I hovered the mascara over her lashes. It seemed wrong, like layering kitchen sludge on angel wings, but it made her look four years older in an instant. Just hours before, we'd gone to the mall because she didn't own any jeans. She'd stood in the mirrored dressing room looking like an Amish girl gone to Vegas.

"My mom doesn't like jeans," she'd said. "She says they're un-refined."

"Well, your mom's not here now," I'd replied, thinking of Mrs. Fleming posing with her daughter in matching bathing suits. "And you look great."

We ended up at an old place called Barrelz and Bootz because it was as far out of town as we could get and still make it home before my mom's late shift was over. Oh, to see it shimmering on the horizon, the two of us so hopped up on diet soda and our own febrile energies: a massive tin building made to look like a barn, with a neon barrel pouring neon hay over and over again onto the roof. The parking lot was jammed with parking-lot drinkers, and just over the door where a big bouncer loomed, a sign assured us: SORRY—WE'RE OPEN! In back was a deck lit with a campfire and chili-pepper lights where a quick-draw tequila contest was under way.

"This is perfect," Diane said, and I'd never seen her face glow like that.

We drank three foamy beers apiece and danced with at least twice as many men, two of whom wore pinch-front Stetsons and one who had a flaming-pistol tattoo on his hairy forearm. He made me dizzy inside and my high heels tangled with each other, and he caught me just before I hit the ground, my forehead grazing the floor's simulated sawdust, the crunching peanut shells.

And Diane—you should have seen her. Those long legs strutting, and breasts bobbing up the top of her tank as she two-stepped and hip-swung and boot-scooted; who could take his eyes off her?

And these were men, not boys, and because they had never seen Diane perform a fetal-pig dissection with the fluency of a star surgeon or seen her balance ionic equations, they did not shrink back in awe or intimidation.

There was no one to tell them that she was too brilliant for them, or anyone.

All they saw was her hair swinging like in a shampoo commercial, her skin rose-tinted under the dance-floor lights, and a smile—a smile I'd never seen on Diane before, a smile that was open and wide and pure, one that said, *Untouched, please touch, never been touched, dying to be touched, come show me the big, wide world.*

So they all wanted to dance with Diane and wind their arms around her wasp waist. They wanted to dance with both of us, and everyone was loving us, but most of all we were loving this. And I loved you, Diane. That night, I thought, *I'm doing this for you, Diane. Because I never would have even tried for the Severin without you. Because I never dreamed far beyond Lanister until you.* And because that night all I could think was *Diane, you changed my life. You made my life.*

*   *   *

Nearly one, and well past any curfew, I couldn't find Diane. Not in Dart Alley or the pool room, not out on the raucous, sticky-planked deck. A girl with a beauty mark drinking beer from a big, kingly goblet said she'd seen her kissing the singer in the alleyway and I panicked.

But no, it turned out Diane was crouched behind the batwing doors of one of the Cowgirls' stalls, like she was hiding.

"What's wrong, Diane? What's wrong?"

"I forgot where I was," she said loudly over the music. "I forgot who I was."

"What?" I said, laughing a little. "You're drunk."

So she made the motions of laughing too, though it didn't seem like a laugh but something trickier.

I told her we had to leave, but when I reached out for her, she backed herself farther into the corner of the stall, one hand on either side.

"Kit," she said, "you're my friend, right? You're my friend forever."

I took one of her arms hard in mine, but I didn't reply. I never replied to *forevers*. Life was long, and full of surprises.

Later that night, after my mom yelled at us halfheartedly for our coming-on-two-in-the-morning arrival, we settled in (Diane zipped tight in my old Ninja Turtles sleeping bag on the floor) and, our guts rumbling with bar nachos and corn-dog niblets and maybe even sawdust, recounted deliriously all our dances, especially those last slow dances, the way the men crushed so hard against us.

"That's when you feel how different they are," Diane whispered, her teeth glowing in the moonlight. "Men. They can't hide it. They can't hide anything."

Because we both looked down and saw the imprints on our stomachs from the big belt buckles pressed there.

*   *   *

Sometime in the night, I felt Diane's hand on my wrist. My mouth cottony, my head sleep-heavy, I shook her off twice, but she was insistent.

"Kit," she said from the floor. "Are you really sorry you don't have a boyfriend?"

"No," I whispered. "It takes up a lot of time." It seemed to, all the talking and making out and birth control and being scared of getting pregnant or worrying about doing something wrong in bed or having something wrong done to you.

"My mom's always asking about it," she said. "Every time she calls. But I'm not interested. I want so many things."

I lay back and nodded because it was all I could do. Because it felt so real and true. I'd had full-on sex with two guys. The first was Patrick, my junior-year boyfriend whom I loved like my old teddy bear, and the second was just a few months ago, on the French club's train trip to Montreal. After too many cans of sparkling Canadian wine with a college guy, I woke in the upper berth without my underpants. I was too nervous to get out of his bed and pee so I got an infection too. *It'll be different after high school*, my mom had said after she took me to her gynecologist for antibiotics. (I told her I must've gotten the UTI when dirt flew up my shorts at cross-country and she just laughed, a little sadly.) *It'll be different once you're out of Lanister.*

I was pretty sure she was right, but no one in my family had ever left our town, and none had finished a four-year college.

Suddenly, I felt Diane's hand on my wrist again, hotter now, night-sweated.

"Remember back at cross-country camp?" she said. "You told that story about you and that older man, the shoe salesman."

My eyes shuddered open, suddenly. "Yeah."

A whispered confidence, elbows pressed to nappy bedspreads at the Wheels Inn two summers ago, three girls I'd thought I'd likely never see again. I'd shared the whole sordid story of Stevie Shoes, the clutching encounter in his car. The way men touch you is so different from how boys do. Like they know all the handles and levers. Which felt so unfair, really.

Now, a year and a half later, it felt like a kid's mistake, but one that made me feel naked all of a sudden. Or one that had left a big target in the center of my chest. But I never thought it would be Diane who would raise the bow, draw back the string.

"It just sounded so awful," she said, eyes glowing in the dark below. "The two of you, and his car. It made me never want to do anything like that, ever."

"What?" My face stung as if she'd slapped me. "What does that mean?"

"I'm sorry," she said, that disembodied voice down there on my flattened-pile carpet. "Forget it. I'm sorry."

"It's not scary," I lied. "Sex isn't scary."

"It's just...how do you know how it'll make you feel? You start something and you don't know what it'll do to you," she said. "How far you'll go with it."

"I don't—"

"Sometimes I get scared of myself."

In the dark, all I could see were those big eyes of hers. And somehow I knew we weren't talking about boys anymore, and maybe not even about sex.

"Sometimes, Kit," she whispered, "I don't know what I'll do."

NOW

Alex and I are the only ones in the lab lounge. No one wants to take the chance of being seen lounging today. Not with those PMDD slots waiting to be filled on Monday and Diane Fleming emerging as an early favorite. The final day to show Severin what we are made of, but I'm shiny and twitchy-eyed, last night's excesses seeping from me, scooting off to face last night's shame. Trying not to think about Diane, her hand on my arm (*My best friend*) . . .

"Hey," he says. "I guess this is a little weird."

It's the first time I've looked directly at him since whatever whispered dirtiness we passed between pillows at my apartment. His rumpled oxford seems no more or less rumpled than yesterday. His shrugging, gangling pose I'd long thought of as that of an aw-shucks cowboy from a TV Western feels different now. Lurching, grasping, looming.

He is the same, I realize, but I've ruined him for myself.

Not with the intimacies, not by encouraging his roving hand on the Zipperz patio, finding places for him to rest his hard fingers, my knees, my shins—I remember now—on the wall-to-wall.

No, I've ruined him with my secret. Which is Diane's secret. Except it's also mine. The minute she told me, it became mine too, this black-browed albatross.

"Could we..." He starts again. "What if we had dinner later? Or a drink?"

I feel my stomach pitch. "I can't."

"But," he says, and I recognize the sickly look on his face. My infection is now his too. "But you told me something really big and I..."

"I'll say anything when I'm drunk," I say, then, narrowing my eyes, low and mean, I add, "I'll do anything too."

He pauses just a moment, the faintest of flinches.

"Got it," he says, nodding, stepping back slightly. I begin walking away just as he adds, strong and clear, "But I don't believe you."

The feeling is off, tilted. It's in the air. A crackle of pressure, something. Is it possible for a person to change the barometric pressure in a space?

I start to walk back to G–21, but then swivel and turn the other way instead. I know just who I want to see.

At the end of the hall, I dip my key card into the colony room outer door, then again in the inside door. It's the only part of the aging lab with truly modern security, three swipes of the card (elevator, entry to the floor, finally colony room itself), plus PIN codes even to get inside. The safest place in all the lab. All the world, maybe.

"Ah, there she is," he says, sliding his headphones off.

Watching Serge always comforts me. The *hmm-hmm* from his headphones as he moves through the quiet space, tucking nesting material, an ear of corn's gleamy floss, in the mouse cages with long gloved fingers. The skitter and scuff of his mice.

The mice love Serge more than any of the other techs and rumor is it's because of his smell, something he wears, because usually mice don't like men. They spike their stress hormones, or so some believe. I tease the other postdocs about it sometimes, all these men in the lab, and such smart mice.

"Are you hiding?" he asks with a wink. For a second, I wonder, and not for the first time, if he likes me a little. I'm the only postdoc whom he's never written up for mouse-protocol violations.

Approaching him, I get a whiff, and the smell is nice. Organic. Mysterious. Loamy. He makes me put on a smock. The shoe covers too.

"You work so many hours," I say, not answering. "Don't you ever take a break?"

"I am not here on Monday," he says in his formal way (*Guy's allergic to contractions*, Zell always said). "I worry about them while I am away."

"Where are you going?"

"The dentist," he says. "Wisdom teeth. Ten years overdue, I am told."

"Ouch," I say. "I hope you have someone to drive you. And feed you milk shakes after."

He looks at me, puzzled.

"That's what my mom did for me," I tell him.

"Of course," he says, smiling at me in a warm, sad way.

Once, on World Cancer Day, I told Serge about my mom and he asked if that was why I worked in a lab. I told him it wasn't, that I'd always worked in labs. *But maybe it is different for you now*, he said. Later, someone told me Serge's sister had died from leukemia when she was very young, so I suppose it may be true for him.

I wonder what it feels like, giving the mice—the soft squishes of mice—the same kind of poisons that had killed his sister. Sometimes it feels like life's about understanding how much opposites meet. Kill to cure, poison to immunize, sacrifice to save.

"Do you wish for a mask?" he asks, watching me.

That's when I start to notice other smells—mouse dander and mouse food, mouse feces. It's heavier today than I remember. So heavy I feel like I'm swimming in it.

The swarm of pale brown coats in the cage out of the corner of my eye.

"There's something wrong with the air today," I say.

Serge smiles gravely and I can't tell if he agrees or is humoring me. He reaches into his pocket and offers me a face mask, but I shake my head, not wanting to seem too delicate.

"I once read something," he says, adjusting one of the food hoppers, the nuggets inside like miniature wine corks, "about Venus."

At first I think I've misheard him beneath the low whir of the ventilated racks, the click of a drop feeder again and again.

"Venus?"

"The planet, not the goddess," he says. "The atmosphere is so thick, we have never seen the surface. Even our most powerful telescope cannot penetrate the dense layer of clouds that surround it. Protecting it."

"I don't think that's true anymore," I say, though I know nothing about astronomy.

"At some point, it repaved its own surface. The lava is now on the outside, as if the planet turned itself inside out." He opens one palm and flips it in front of me. "And in so doing, it erased all evidence of any old damage. It made itself new again."

He looks at me earnestly, as if moved by the notion that one

could remake oneself. Serge often seems moved, even by the rodents slinking around his hand, waiting for their estrogen, their
fluoxetine.

"You sure know a lot about Venus," I say, my hand over my
nose now.

He smiles in that Serge way, somber and knowing. "I suppose
I am a romantic," he says. "But we all are."

I pause. "Russians?"

"No," he says. "Men."

I smile, though I'm guessing not for the same reason as Serge.

"Well," I say. "They're not all as sincere as you."

He lifts one of the mice, examining its coat. Its smell is sweeter
now, just being in Serge's hand. "You know the tall one, the messy
one—Alex—he was in here looking for you earlier."

"Oh," I say. "I saw him."

"There is a feeling about him," he says. "I am generally correct."

"He's okay," I say, but my brain is going places. "You just don't
like him since you caught him clipping tails." You weren't supposed to clip mouse tails for a DNA sample without permission,
but Alex never followed protocol. *It is barbarism,* Serge said, walking into G-21, mouse in gloved hand. Alex laughed and then
apologized. I don't think Serge will ever forget it. There's a rumor
he keeps a Log of Animal Cruelties in his office.

"He is very confident, that one," Serge says now. "I am not
sure he understands Dr. Severin. What guides her choices."

"What do you mean?"

He strokes the mouse, turning it around, looking for something: a fight wound, a patch of missing fur, a sign of the hair-
chewing that can happen with mice housed in groups.

"My sense is that he believes her a political animal. She is not."

"Hold on," I say, my hand in front of my mouth, the smell per-fumy now, whatever Serge is injecting in the mice, some ketamine cocktail for Irwin's study. "What are you talking about?"

"His uncle is on one of the boards at the National Institutes of Health."

I drop my hand. "How do you know?"

"I have heard him tell Dr. Severin, more than once. He thinks it is significant to her. To others, such a connection would be. But to her..." He shakes his head. "No."

I shift my feet a little, the shoe covers crinkling. One of the feeding tubes clacks, a mouse straining beneath it.

"He is the political animal," Serge says. "He is the one."

"He never said anything," I say, keeping my voice even. "We talk a lot. He never said anything."

Serge looks at me and holds my gaze. "Didn't he?"

What does it feel like? the young woman on the screen says, her aer-ated voice wobbling gently. *Is that really what you want to know?*

In the library, in one of the plywood carrels, smelling thickly of glue and loneliness, I watch PMDD videos for the rest of the afternoon, far away from the lab.

This interviewee has freckles, sweet curves, the small white face of Kathleens and Fionas everywhere. But something is wrong. She's rubbing, tugging the space between her eyes like a woman in an old aspirin commercial.

Yes, says the unseen interviewer, Dr. Severin herself. *What does it feel like?*

The woman smiles. *Well, first you get hungry. Then you get hor-monal. And then*—she pauses, her eyes darkening—*you want to die.*

The next woman is older, African American, with glasses she keeps taking on and off.

I couldn't stop eating. I threw up all day and drank all night. One night, I threw up so I hard I tore my esophagus and had to go to the ER. It was like red ribbons, that's what the doctor said.

The last one is tanned and bright-teethed, big enamel hoops clicking at her ears.

What does it feel like? she whispers, her lip gloss glinting, the girl at the health club, the hostess in the short dress at the low-sofa, throbbing-music restaurant. *It feels like there's a bomb inside me. It's about to explode.*

Her eyes grow large and confused.

The last time, on the last day, just one hour before the blood came, I'm cooking eggs and my boyfriend is asking me, for the hundredth time, where his phone is. I don't even remember throwing the frying pan at him. His head is, like, collapsed in the center. And his skin is, like, sizzling.

Her hand stretched before her, her bracelets clattering like cymbals.

And then, while I was sitting in the police car, the blood came. Right there on the back seat.

The knock on the door comes late, near midnight, and I'm afraid it's Alex. No one else knows where I live.

It's raining outside at last. Serge told me it would start at ten p.m. and it does.

Laptop open in bed, I'm watching the reality show about the women with the shiny legs and tight faces. All of them live in the same glamorous city filled with rooftop bars and white-lined spas and the thump-thump of rose-gold limousines, champagne from gold bottles. Everything is theirs, yet they are always drinking and fighting, and when they do, it feels the same as many of the women back in Lanister—my mom's coworkers at the rescue clinic, the assistant managers at the Golden Fry—except usually the Lanister women were softer and sad, beaten smooth by various disappointments and eager, always, to seek the corners of joy available, the Bloody Mary bar at Tomfooleries after church, the pet-photo contest at the clinic, a bridal shower in the covered smoke patio behind Mama Cuca's.

The knocking at my door goes on for some time. Finally, I rise and move from bedroom to doorway, fingers curled, across the rasping wall-to-wall, edges stiff with decades of tenants.

As I get closer, I hear rustling behind the door, and something wet.

"Why are you here?" I'm peering through the yellowed peephole in the door. The fisheye shows only her golden head, the glassy black of a wet trench.

"Kit, let me in." Through the peephole, Diane's face, broad and white as a moon.

I open the door.

"How did you find me?"

"You can find anybody," she says, standing there dripping sheets of rain from her coat, black and sleek as a crow's wing. "Do you have newspaper?"

"What? No."

But she's already inside, sliding off those expensive loafers, now rain-swollen and unhappy-looking.

"Maybe some paper towels?" she asks, holding both dripping shoes between her long fingers, her eyelids dewy with rain.

I take a breath. "Yes."

The entryway getting wetter and wetter, her whole raincoated body like a flicking butterfly, a black witch moth, I let her in.

She's so wet that it's as if her wetness is her only response. Little pools caught in the folds and furrows of her raincoat. My floor beneath her glossing.

"Diane, why are you here?" I say. "We have nothing to talk about."

She looks up, pulling off her coat. "You know that's not true," she says. "We have everything to talk about. Everything."

We settle on my sofa, the smell of rain and Scotchgard. She's slipped her hat from her head, and that hair, so short and pale and drenched, reminds me, fleetingly, of my dad after a stormy night working security at the speedway, soaking my mom's wall-to-wall like an old kitchen sponge. My mom would run a hair dryer over the spots so we wouldn't get mold again.

Except really this is nothing like that because, as always, Diane is beautiful, and not exactly real.

"You live alone?" she asks.

I nod. "Do you live with someone?"

Diane shakes her head, almost a smile at the very thought.

"I guess it's hard for us," she says.

Something bristles inside me. *For us.*

"I was engaged," I find myself saying. "After undergrad."

"Oh," she says. "What happened?"

His name was Greg and we met in biochem. After graduation, he started teaching middle-school science while I raced straight into the fast-track PhD program. He wanted to get married and have little science-nerd kids, but after missing our romantic getaway to the redwoods so I could get my professor's grant application in on time, after my hours-late arrival at his parents' twenty-fifth anniversary party and forgetting the gift in my lab locker, after falling asleep at the library too many times and not coming home . . .

"It didn't work out," I say, wishing I'd never brought it up.

The longer you're with someone, the heavier it all is, on top of the heaviness you carry inside yourself. It was too much, taking on all of someone else's feelings.

That was four years ago. At some point, without ever really knowing when, I'd stopped taking on new passengers. There didn't feel like room enough.

Diane looks at me. "You asked me about my mom," she says. "Today. In the lab. You asked how she was. That's all over. She's gone."

Something creaks inside me, a forgotten crawl space reopened.

"Oh no," I say, my voice losing sound as I talk. "Mine too. Cancer. Cervical."

She leans back against the sofa.

"Kit. I'm so sorry," she says. "When?"

"Two years." Apart from my cousin Scott, she's the first person who knew my mom that I've told. Scott had to chase down my dad at a dog track in Hialeah to let him know. That was it. I have no one else to tell.

She nods, eyes darkening, hands folded in her lap. An amnesiac tenderness momentarily hovers between us, but neither of us was ever the hugging type.

"How about your mom?" I say. It seems impossible, both our mothers so young.

"Oh." She looks newly stricken. "I'm sorry. I didn't mean my mom's dead." She pauses. "Just gone. As far as I know, she's somewhere in South Florida right now. Singing her twins back to sleep, kissing that husband of hers good night. I haven't talked to her since college."

She stops and looks at me.

"But your mother," she says. "She was so kind. That must be so hard."

I don't say anything. Somehow it all feels like a dirty trick.

For a moment, she stares down at her hands, stretching her fingers. They were always the only unpretty thing about her. The way they'd turn red, tight and veined, like an organ, a liver, or a heart.

"I've thought about you a lot," she says. "About what you did for me. I never forgot it."

What I did for you.

"Kit," she says, "you're the only one who really knows me."

I feel that old, familiar clasping, grasping inside me. The desire to lift the drawbridge, sharpen the battlement spikes, raise up the walls so high I can't even see the killing field.

"I didn't ask for it," I say, coolly. "It's a curse."

She smiles a little. "I forgot how you talk," she says. "How you say things."

But it's Diane who always talked that way. Her words so big, like the Shakespeare tomes we read together, like the Technicolor melodramas I used to watch with my mom, florid skies and desperate clinches, long-lashed and golden-skinned doomed lovers.

"By telling me, you trapped me," I say through my teeth.

"By telling you," she whispers, rain still glistening on her, "I was free."

Her face beatific, the shorn blond saint, her eyes glowing and sanctified. A kind of rapture.

THEN

"I'm not going to English today."

It was the Monday after the news about our Severin scholarship eligibility, after our Barrelz and Bootz night. (The morning after, groaning like the rattle of a spoon in a coffee can, I'd looked down and found my sleeping bag rolled tight and Diane gone.)

She looked at me now, wan and slightly greasy in a way Diane never was.

"You never miss class," I said. "Didn't you read act three?"

"Of course I did," she said. "I read the whole play."

"So come on, then," I said, putting my hand on her arm harder than I meant to—I almost never touched her; who could?—her body shuddering into the classroom, its lights so bright.

Maybe I was mad still about the things she'd said Saturday night. Maybe I was mad because Sunday morning after she left, I sat and stared at those sneakers Stevie Shoes had given me, buried in the back of my closet. Finally, I dumped them in the trash beneath coffee grounds and potato peels. No running for me until payday.

"There you are," said Ms. Cameron, smiling at us, her star pupils. "Now we can begin."

*   *   *

"Class," Ms. Cameron announced, "something is wrong in the state of Lanister High." It was just the kind of so-lame-it's-cool thing at which Ms. Cameron, with her Call of Cthulhu T-shirt and her Buddha bracelets and her thick sandals even in the winter, excelled.

"Ugh," moaned Ashley Moon, barely looking up from her phone. "Ms. Cameron, it's too late for Shakespeare. We graduate in a few months."

"That's why it's exactly the right time," Ms. Cameron said.

She loved to tell us that Hamlet was the ultimate adolescent. Childhood suddenly over, disillusioned by adults, lust-conflicted, seeking to supplant his parents. All of which made adolescence sound so dramatic, which maybe it was and maybe was why I wished it were over.

"Can we talk about when Ophelia gives Hamlet back all the stuff he gave her?" asked Melissa, chewing hungrily on her pen. "And he tells her to become a nun?"

All the girls in class loved Ophelia because in paintings and in the DVDs we watched, she was so fragile and ethereal and doomed, one after the other, pale blond nymphs with long wispy tendrils and flowers falling in slow motion, Ophelia sinking into a stream, a swimming pool, a bathtub. One glorious, glamorous scene after another of Ophelias erasing themselves.

She was not for me. My legs were thick and strong and I never spun languorous in floral dresses or let a boy call me a whore. Even my mom—once a pliant woman, or why else did she put up with my dad for all those years?—was still the type who, when not bagging dead cats and taking hacksaws to rabid dog brains, might choose to wield a hot clothes iron rather than let my dad sneak off with her car after his got impounded. We were not Ophelias, even though we had our weaknesses.

But I loved the play. There were so many parts that sang darkly in my brain. *You would seem to know my stops,* Hamlet tells his back-stabbing friends. *You would pluck out the heart of my mystery.*

Sitting in class, looking at that line, I thought of Diane. Diane and the things that had happened to her and how much I knew, yet how little. Was that what I was doing with her, circling closer, trying to pluck the heart of her mystery?

"So, let's turn to Hamlet's treacherous uncle," Ms. Cameron said. "What do we learn of Claudius in act three?"

"That he did do it," I said. "That he killed Hamlet's dad."

Diane's head was bobbing a little. She hadn't said a word since class began, her book still closed on her desk.

"That's right, Kit," Ms. Cameron said, eyes now on Diane. "And how do we know?"

Next to me, Diane pressed her fingers to her temples. Her face looked soft and waxy under the fluorescent lights. Almost like an apple gone bad.

"He talks about the whole thing," piped up Tim Streeter from the back. "I don't get why villains always do that. Like in *Batman*—"

"Is Claudius the villain here?" Ms. Cameron replied, looking first at Tim, slack-mouthed at the question itself.

"He has no conscience," I said. "That's what he says. He confesses everything."

"Yeah," Tim shouts out, nodding his head vigorously. "He's a psycho."

I sneak another glance at Diane, her face almost greenish now, and a knot in her brow.

"Well, let's look at what he says," Ms. Cameron said. "Page sixty-two."

A grunting whir of pages, spines cracking.

Ms. Cameron looked at Diane, who sat motionless, her spine curled.

"Open your book," I whispered, nudging it.

Diane turned and looked at me, eyes glassy and black.

"Diane," Ms. Cameron said, walking closer to us now, "how about you read Claudius's soliloquy for us?"

Diane's head lifted, then fell again. "I don't..."

"Come on, Diane," Ms. Cameron said, walking to Diane's desk, rapping her knuckles on the laminate top. "Let's hear the confession."

"Ms. Cameron," she whispered, "I..."

"Confess! Confess!" shouted Tim, playfully pounding his fist on his desk.

Diane's head darted around, and the black look she gave him made him nearly jump back.

"I can do it," I volunteered, a queasy feeling rising in me.

But Diane opened her book, her hands looking damp. Her familiar leather bookmark on the exact right page.

"*O, my offence is rank, it smells to heaven,*" she read, her voice high and not her own. "*It hath the primal eldest curse upon 't.*"

For a second, that voice quavering, I thought she might be about to cry. But Diane never cried. Her face white, and lips white too, like a vampire in a movie, she kept going.

"Diane," Ms. Cameron started, "are you—"

But Diane talked right over her, her voice drowning her out, pitching suddenly loud and strong and throaty. Then she rose to her feet, as we were supposed to when we read, and all of us watched, heads twisting, craning, to see.

"What if this cursèd hand were thicker than itself with brother's blood?" she read. *"Is there not rain enough in the sweet heavens to wash it white as snow?"*

She read it all. Each word like a hard blow, and everything sounding so much darker and more dire on the page.

"But, O, what form of prayer can serve my turn?" Diane read. *" 'Forgive me my foul murder'?"*

Beneath the desk, her legs trembled, an ankle turned against itself. And that hand at her side, her fingers pushing together, pressing into her leg.

By the time she reached the end— *"My words fly up, my thoughts remain below"*—she wasn't looking at the page at all and her face, tilted high, caught the light, eyes shut like a church-window angel: *"Words without thoughts never to heaven go."*

None of us knew what we were seeing and I was just as blank and dumb as all the rest.

That night was the night. Diane came over to study, *Hamlet* in hand, bookmark hanging like a dark tongue.

"I wasn't sure you'd come," I said. "You were so strange in class."

She looked at me, her winter scarf bundled around her neck as she shivered in the doorway.

It felt like she saw a hunger in me, but there was a hunger in her too. I felt it.

"Kit, do you think I could sleep over?"

I said yes without even asking my mom.

As soon as we settled in my room, she called to get permission.

"Is it okay?" I asked when she hung up. I still hadn't met her grandfather, but my mom said she'd heard from a nurse who volunteered at the rescue clinic that he was sick.

"He's glad," she said. "He worries I work too hard. He thinks we're going to, I don't know, do our nails and watch music videos."

It wasn't until then that she tugged off her gloves, unfurled her scarf, neck and hands ruddy and angry-looking. She turned to me, solemn and serious, and suggested we get started.

But she didn't really seem to want to get started. She kept fanning the pages of the Signet *Hamlet* in her hand, as if looking for something she never found.

"Diane," I finally said, "is this about what happened in class today?"

But she insisted nothing happened, except it was clear that it had, and was still happening because finally she looked at me and said, "Did you mean what you said in class today? About Claudius having no conscience?"

"Sure," I said. "He kills his own blood to get what he wants. Which means he just has no morals."

She looked down at the book, palm pressing the gloomy-faced man on the paperback cover.

I waited, and that was when it happened. A click of her jaw, like a pit bull's or cobra's unlocking, and she asked me, "Kit, do you think it could happen in real life?"

"What?" We were talking about *Hamlet,* except we weren't.

"For someone to have no conscience."

"Yes," I said, quickly. Because I did. But also because it felt like she was going to tell me something, a secret. Diane's secret at last (as if any of us had only one).

I remembered what she'd said that night after Barrelz and Bootz. All her talk about sex and scaring herself.

"Diane," I said, "what is it?" I paused. "Did someone do something to you? Did someone hurt you?"

I would regret saying this, asking this, more than anything else in my whole cramped life.

Her head turned to the side; she glanced at me, showing me only the white of her left eye, gleaming like a pearl. Her hand wrapped about the locket, chain pressing against her neck.

The first thought that came to me was her dad. That phantom with the mustache, the dad-khakis. The awkward arm around his daughter's tense shoulder. Everything that had seemed earnest and sad turned ugly. *Molesting,* or *incest,* an even uglier word. Is that why she never talked about him? Had he done something?

But she shook her head. "No one did anything to me. I'm talking about something I did. I'm talking about myself."

There's a churning in me, like there's no going back now, but why had I pushed myself here in the first place?

"What did you do?" I said.

"I can't say it out loud. I've never said it."

"Did you dent your granddad's truck?"

"No."

I paused. "Are you pregnant?"

"No." She looked at me and, voice even, said, "It's so much worse."

I didn't say anything at all.

"I killed him," she said. "I killed my dad."

NOW

"Diane," I say, "it's time for you to go."

Other than Alex, no one's ever been in this apartment before. I haven't had a single guest in two years. And these intimate encounters, it's like they're not just in my apartment but in my brain, whispering demands.

"But I came to tell you something," Diane says, straightening. "It's about the lab. I'm going to be on the PMDD team. I'm one of the two."

And there it is. I nod, hide the wince expertly. Hide everything, my face still, and still hungover.

"Well, good for you," I say. "That's goddamned wonderful for you. You always land on your feet, don't you, Diane? On floors paved with gold."

"And you," she says. "The other one is you."

She blinks twice. My, does she flash those doe eyes at me.

"That's not true," I say.

"It's you," she repeats, a hint of a smile there. As close as Diane gets. "It's both of us."

I don't say anything.

"Now do you see what I mean about fate?"

*　　*　　*

I stand in the kitchenette, waiting for the water to boil in the dented kettle. I've never made tea in my life, but the last tenant left a faded box of Red Rose in the cupboard and I need time. I need to breathe.

"So Severin told you this," I say, returning to her with clinking mugs. "She just decided to tell you before anyone else. That it's you and me."

Diane nods, taking the mug. "She told me I'd be on the team when she offered me the job in the lab."

Of course. An incentive. An enticement, to lure Diane from a very prestigious lab to ours.

"Did she say anything about the others? Maxim or Alex?"

"Alex? The slippery one with the expensive watch?" Diane sets her mug on the table. The way she holds herself, so carefully. Like someone who always sees herself at the same time as she sees everything else. Who always thinks, *Careful, careful.*

"Yes. I mean, I guess." My fingers lift to my temples. "Slippery?"

Diane shrugs. "She never mentioned him."

"Oh." And I admit, in that moment, the fast-diminishing Alex, the Alex with the secret family connection he concealed from me, diminishes even more.

"But Diane, why is . . . why are you and Dr. Severin . . ."

"What matters is this: she wants you."

I don't let that sit with me, don't let myself be flattered by it. It feels like a trick.

"What makes you think I'd ever work with you?" I ask, my mug clattering against the sofa's rattan arm, the tea spattering red on me, on her.

"If you're the Kit I know," she says, "nothing would stop you."

"What does that mean?" I say, my voice hard.

She looks at me. "It means you're strong."

We're quiet for a moment. Her gaze wanders to the fat stack of papers on the coffee table. The case studies I'd been reading.

"Do you think it's true?" Diane asks.

"What?"

She nods toward the case studies. "That PMDD made these women do those things? Drive into light poles, shake their babies, throw kitchen knives at their husbands."

"We don't know yet," I say. "But maybe. Some of it. Some of them." I pause again. "Do you?"

She looks at me and something in her face—I feel a flash of something old, a memory of an ancient nightmare, Diane under my bed, shaking it by the springs.

"No," she says, turning away from me. "I used to but not anymore.

"There's so many things," she adds, "we don't understand, even about ourselves."

"Especially ourselves," I say.

There's another long pause. A standoff of sorts.

My brain is doing dances. *What is this really about?* I wonder. Because you never know with Diane until it hits you in the face.

"This isn't how I wanted this to go," she says, rising. "I thought you'd be glad. I thought this is what we always wanted."

What we always wanted; there's a hoary, uncomfortable truth to it.

That's when a snaky, swampy thought comes to me.

"You did this," I say. "You made it happen so that I wouldn't tell. So Dr. Severin—so no one will ever know."

Her eyebrows lift.

"You won't tell." Her voice low as a man's.

"I don't owe you anything," I say.

She slides on her coat, still wet and carapace-dark.

"I had nothing to do with Dr. Severin's decision," she says, reaching for her shoes, which are sitting in a near lagoon on my carpet. "But I know you would never tell for a lot of reasons."

"I don't owe you anything," I say, louder this time. "Not a god-damned thing."

But Diane only nods, as if crossing off an item on a to-do list or recording a final measurement in her lab notebook.

"I guess you're afraid," she says.

"Afraid?" I say, moving toward her now, following her to the door. "I'm not afraid. Afraid of what?"

Buttoning her coat, she doesn't answer for a long moment, letting me wonder into those endless eyes of hers, making me remember all kinds of things. I can smell Diane's shampoo, like strawberries and dew, and I can feel her close and remember things.

I shut my eyes for a second and picture myself lying on the carpet, my mouth open, my head jerking, crying out without making a sound.

"Afraid of me," she says, finally, moving to the door. There's an unspeakably sad look on her face that I don't know what to do with.

"I'm not afraid of you," I say, my voice suddenly rough, hang-over hoarse, "but maybe you should be afraid of me. I'm the one who knows what you are. You should be afraid of me."

But she has already opened the door, crossed the threshold. I stand in the doorway, bare feet curled. I call out after that swaying black raincoat, like a snake's tail.

"What could you do?" I shout after her. "What could you possibly do?"

She turns, pauses at the stairwell door.

"Nothing," she says, a look enigmatic and impossible, just like she is. "Bye, Kit."

The rest of the night, lying uselessly on my sheet-stripped bed, the smell of strawberry everywhere now, I can do nothing but think.

In the lab, everything is separable. Extraction, distillation, centrifugation, crystallization, decantation. Leaching. A funnel, filter paper, a flask, the vacuum outlet under the hood. Feeling for the suction at the end of the tube. The solvent passing through the paper. Whatever is left behind is what counts. Let's pretend it's gold. It couldn't be gold—gold doesn't work like that—but let's say it is. In this moment, for me, the PMDD slot is the gold. I want to feel it in my hand. I don't want to think about that dirty slurry of sand, salt, chalk left on the bottom. I only want to think about that gold—flake, nugget, or flour, raw and heavy.

I want that gold.

I've been waiting so long. I'm not like my old man with his lottery tickets and his Herbalife franchise, the Diabetes Solution Kit bought from the man on the TV. I've worked for it, neck forever crooked now, eyestrain, fingers numb from pipetting, wrist ache.

I've been working for this forever, for a decade anyway, and finally it's happening: I'm on the PMDD team. Me. I'm one of the two. She picked me. She picked me, as she picked me a dozen years ago, choosing me from a thousand applicants. Dr. Lena Severin, mouth like a razor, brain like a god's, an ion pump where her heart should be. She picked me.

Does it matter if Diane helped make it happen? Does it matter if I'd have to work side by side with her, shoulders nudged close? Elbow-deep in the purple marrow of the PMDD study?

I try to imagine Diane and Dr. Severin and me in a sturdy dinghy amid the hormonal sea of PMDD, hurling lifesavers, raising breakwaters. Waving from jetties, promising rescue.

So long working, toiling, living monkishly in strip-mall apartments, eating old salad from Styrofoam boxes, English muffin pizzas in the toaster oven, my dad's famous mayonnaise sandwiches—all to get a chance to be a part of the Thing.

If I'm honest, who deserves it more?

Not Alex, who all his life has had anything he ever wanted and a hundred things he never thought to want.

I want that gold.

So give it to me.

But, Alex said, that familiar sickly look on his face, the one I once wore, maybe still wore. *But you told me something really big and I . . .*

Alex, looming and lurching and knowing.

He could ruin everything, couldn't he? But would he?

I think about what Serge said. And Diane: *Alex, the slippery one.*

But what could happen even if he did tell? That just opens up another slot. She wouldn't unpick me because of Diane, would she? Guilt by association?

Scandal is bad for science, Kit. We have enough controversy. This study is controversial enough.

Or: *Kit, you are faithless. A lab depends on loyalty. We have no space for a Benedict Arnold.*

Or: *Kit, you are a coward. I do not want cowards working for me.*

Let's be honest: there are many, many reasons she would no longer want me.

*　　*　　*

At one a.m., the texts come:

Listen, the text from Alex reads. Then two more:

I've been thinking a lot about it and I have to tell Dr. Severin.

ASAP.

They come like that, in three sharp thrusts.

Tell her what? I type, fingers tight. *You don't know anything.*

I'll be clear that it's secondhand. Don't worry, I won't name you.

You CANNOT *do this,* saying the words as I type them. *I was drunk. You've got it wrong.*

He doesn't reply. After ten minutes, I call him directly, but it goes straight to voice mail.

"Alex, I was lying," I say into his voice mail.

"I was drunk and I made it up. I was jealous of her. I always have been."

My voice shaking now. It seems so funny to say those words.

"Alex, listen, you can't do this, okay? Call me."

But he doesn't call me at all.

THEN

This is what she told me.

She'd been living with him a month, less even.

It was all because her mom had asked her to move out, *just for a little while, I swear, honey.* There'd been that trouble with her mother's boyfriend, now fiancé. He was a businessman her mother had met at a trade show. She never told him she was older than he was—only five years—because men didn't like that. He'd been married once, but his ex and their son lived up in the Northwest somewhere so he didn't see them much. And the minute he saw Diane's mother, his heart went *gazzom.* She was so beautiful and surely a fashion model, an actress (and there was no way she had a *teenage* daughter).

Things started off with a bang, a weekend trip to the beach, tequila sunrises and soul confessions. Three months in, he invited her—and, of course, Diane too—to move into his new condo in Canyon Crest. It had three bedrooms, a Jacuzzi, marina views. Soon, he hoped, they'd all move together to Florida, which was where he really wanted to be.

But the arrangement didn't work out. He was not a good person. Diane knew it right away. He had exactly one picture of his son in the whole condo, and what kind of person saw his child only once a year?

Then she found out some things about him and told her mother. Things that showed the kind of man he was.

The atmosphere in the condo was tense. He accused her of trying to poison her mother against him. *The truth can't be poison*, she told her mother, who definitely did not agree.

For two nights, the boyfriend slept on his office couch while Diane's mother locked herself in their bedroom, which overlooked the deep water slip where his boat—the *Big Love*—bobbed. Every time Diane came to the door, her mother started crying. She told Diane she had an ocular migraine, or maybe it was Lyme disease, or maybe a tumor, or MS.

Finally, the boyfriend called Diane's father. Together, they made arrangements for Diane to move in with him.

Diane, honey, her father told her over the phone, that formal voice he always used with her, the same one he'd used her whole life, *I'm happy to have you.*

Diane's mother claimed she wasn't involved in the decision, but wasn't it the best thing anyway? Wouldn't it be wonderful for Diane to develop more of a relationship with her dad?

Diane hadn't lived with her father since her parents divorced when she was seven years old. First, he'd relocated to Nevada, then to other places. Now he lived twenty miles away, but she saw him only once a month at most, a restaurant dinner, stiff napkins and Diane watching the waiter fill and refill her glass of Diet Coke. They never had anything to say.

But Mom needs me, she wanted to tell him. When there was trouble with a man or with work, or if they were facing one of her mom's "big blues," she needed Diane to do the shopping, the laundry, talk to the electric company about the overdue bill, to chat for hours in their pajamas about what went wrong. After a breakup, she sometimes took Diane out of school so they could drive to the mountains together, or out to Anchor Lake, and think about things. They'd sleep in the same bed, her mom talking all night in that singsong voice she got after too much Chablis and those big horse pills she took for cramps. Talking about all the ways her life needed to change.

You're the only one I trust, her mom whispered. *The only one who hasn't let me down.*

Once, the two of them walking together on Anchor Lake, her mother linking elbows with her, bending her head on Diane's shoulder, a man asked if they were lovers. It was embarrassing, but people didn't understand. Her mother had just always needed her. And now more than ever.

But it had been settled.

You'll see, baby, her mother said. *I just need some time with him, to bring it across, you know? It'll go so fast and then we'll bring you back and be one happy family.*

The day came and her mother drove her to the bus station, wailing the whole way about how the two people she loved most were tearing her apart.

As the bus drove away, Diane received a text from her mother: *One last thing! Promise me, honey, you'll never love your dad half as much.*

After three stops, Diane got off the bus and hitched a ride with a nice, round-faced lady in a minivan to Sacred Heart Academy. For four days, she managed it. After school, she'd go to the library. After the library closed, she'd sneak into the utility room until morning. Her dad called twice that first night, leaving messages wondering where she was, but no one called after that.

One morning, the custodian with the Bambi tattoo on his neck found her. He felt sorry for her. They talked about families and how complicated they could be. He told her a long story about how his father kicked him out of the house when he was seventeen for disrespecting the Lord, *and yet, Diane, I tell you he never went a day without banging fifty-four milligrams of Dilaudid and what does the Lord have to do with that?*

But he still turned her in. The principal called both her parents. It didn't start things off on the right foot with her dad.

I thought you wanted this, he said, picking her up at school, distracted in the middle of his workday, coffee stain on his shiny tie. *Your mother said you wanted this.*

When she arrived at his apartment, in the big complex with the SINGLES WELCOME! rental sign, she was surprised to see a paper banner drooping across the archway to greet her: HOME, SWEET HOME! He was trying, she knew.

It was a bachelor's apartment. That's what her mom would have called it. And it was only a one-bedroom so she slept on a groaning old rollaway. He promised her he was on the waiting list for a two-bedroom and it probably wouldn't be long.

In the meantime, he said, *we'll make the best of it, okay?*

In the kitchen drawers, there was a can opener, plastic takeout spoons, a pair of old steak knives. In the refrigerator, protein powder and a bag of sliced bread. He had only two towels. He'd never taken care of anyone before.

Her mom still called her every night. Diane hid in the laundry room to talk to her, to hear all about her grand romance, the trinkets the boyfriend was buying for her, the trips planned.

Diane tried to explain how uncomfortable she felt with her father, with whom she hadn't spent more than a few hours in years. Her mother sighed and said she'd learned long ago not to expect too much from him and maybe Diane should learn that too.

When, Diane asked every night, *do you think I can move back?*

But her mom kept saying she hadn't given it a chance. And that they hadn't forgotten the trouble Diane had caused. Besides, she and her boyfriend were still getting to know each other, and that was easier without stress and complications.

The beginning of a relationship is always fragile, she'd told Diane. *Just give me some time.*

Diane didn't know what to do with her thoughts. She was used to thinking about her mother all the time. Listening to her problems with her "beaus," with her bosses, with the way she was treated by the cashier at Kroger's. She'd never spent so much time alone before, getting tied up in her own thoughts. She wondered constantly about things she'd never considered before, like what she would do when her period came. The idea that her dad would see tampon wrappers, smell it somehow, see her bloated body, horrified her. She willed it not to come, and it didn't.

Her dad worked a lot. He didn't get home until nine o'clock some nights. He had sort of a girlfriend named Joann who lived on the fourth floor. Sometimes she made crockpot stews. From what Diane could tell, he mostly lived on Steak-umms and soggy takeout tacos, watching old TV shows on the bad cable. Weekend dinners were the hardest. He said he wasn't used to talking at home. They sat across from each other at the plastic tulip table, forks scraping into tinned potpies. She tried to ask him questions about his job, which had something to do with travel insurance.

Your mom always wished I was better at this, he told her, though he didn't say what exactly "this" was.

After a week, she began to feel as though she weren't real. Moving through the halls of Sacred Heart, where everyone knew she'd been found sleeping in the basement, she came to believe she might be invisible.

They didn't have all the science classes her old school offered and, despite her protests, they'd stuck her in the same chemistry course she'd taken the year before. She tried studying advanced chem and microbiology on her own.

Coming home each night, arms aching from all her library books (there was no room for her own books in the apartment so they had to keep them in her father's storage unit in the basement, a big metal cage), she felt like a ghost. By ten thirty or eleven, her father disappearing into his bedroom or to his girlfriend's, Diane started to wonder if this was all a bad dream with no end.

Sleeping on the rollaway, the floor-to-ceiling window over-looking the SINGLES WELCOME! pool, the laughter rising in the night, squeals and splashes and cooing and great squalls of laughter, she began to get ideas. One night, at nearly two o'clock, she heard a scream so piercing she was sure someone had been murdered. She waited several seconds, sheets pulled under her chin, the pool immediately silent. Finally, she crept across the room and peered through the tinkling vertical blinds, but she saw only an orange-bikinied woman, tanned as a roasting hot dog, being heaved into the pool by two men.

Don't, she cried out, *you're killing me!*

The scream came again as she hit the water. She looked so happy she could die.

Sweetie, just hold tight, her mom kept saying on the phone. *Before you know it, things'll settle here. And you can come back and show him you're really sorry. I know you two are going to love each other, like each of you love me.*

By the second week, a C+ on her first exam because she couldn't bring herself to answer all the questions, a strange rash on her neck from her father's bath towels, everything started to get crazy in her head. Some days, if her mom didn't call, Diane didn't talk to anyone. No one talked to her.

She had nightmares: her mother and the boyfriend had relocated to Tokyo without telling her; her father came out of his bedroom one night and folded up the rollaway while she was still in it (*I forgot you were here, are you sure you're here?*). There was no getting out, no breathing at all.

She wondered how long she could take it. She began to have crazy thoughts about what she might do, and slowly the thoughts seemed less crazy.

Didi, her mother whispered on the phone one night. *You should see the freshwater pearls he bought me. We're going to Bimini for the holiday weekend. That's in the Bahamas. I'll bring you back water from the Fountain of Youth. If they let it on the plane.*

The next day, while distilling acetates in class, she realized what she was meant to do. It was so obvious. Following the directions with care, she poured the dried barium acetate into one test tube, and the lead into the other.

As she worked, Mr. Keyes, a mordant, stone-faced man, talked to them about barium acetate being so soluble, how it decomposed on heating, how it had no odor.

Mr. K., the jock with the overbite shouted out, fingers in the white powder, *can we snort it?*

Bro, another added, *don't get high on your own supply.*

That was when Mr. Keyes told the class that if you inhaled barium acetate, you would get very sick, and if you ingested it, you would likely die.

That was when she knew what she would do. After all, in so many ways, she was already gone.

* * *

Later, she wouldn't even remember scraping the powder into the same envelope that held her report card, all As, not that anyone had asked to see it, and putting it in her backpack. None of it was real, anyway.

She kept it in her backpack for a week.

But what was it about the night that it happened, right before the long Thanksgiving weekend? Joann came over to invite them both to Thursday's singles' potluck turkey dinner in the apartment complex's common room. She planned to make stuffing with chestnuts. Her dad declined. He wanted to take Diane out to dinner. He was sorry he and his daughter hadn't spent much time with each other, and wasn't Thanksgiving supposed to be for family? *After all,* he said, *we're in this together, Diane.* Then, more quietly, *At least until your mother burns through this fella too.*

That night, he'd brought home takeout spaghetti from DaVinci's. She watched him eat it, bent over the coffee table (they no longer bothered to eat at the squeaky tulip table), noodles slapping against his chin. She couldn't even bear to open the lid on her own container, the smell so strong. The Pop-Tart yesterday morning was the last time she'd eaten.

The TV was playing that air-disasters show (*Aloha 243, we are unpressurized!*). Diane knew what she had to do. Her glass of Diet Rite fizzed on the coffee table. The fizz was so loud, louder than anything she'd ever heard. *I won't even taste it,* she thought. *I won't feel anything.*

She reached under the sofa for her backpack and unzipped it. He didn't even notice that she removed an envelope. Or that her hands were shaking.

When he went into the kitchen to pour his Dr Pepper, she knew it was time. Hand on the envelope, she leaned over her glass. A cabinet door slammed in the kitchen. *Hurry, hurry,* she thought.

She could never explain it later. Her arm darted the wrong way; the powder disappeared into her father's noodle-heaped plate, the red wormed mound at the center.

Did I really do that? she thought. *Is that what I did? Is this happening?*

But before she knew it, he'd returned, cold beverage in hand, and taken his seat. Unbuttoned his collar. Dug back into that wormy mound.

She felt her mouth open, then close again.

Because suddenly it seemed exactly right. Suddenly, it seemed that he was the one responsible for all this. For her banishment, her expulsion, her imprisonment. He was the author of all her misfortune.

Wasn't he?

Something turned inside and her head jerked up. Had she really done that? Did that really happen?

She watched him hold his stomach and walk to the bathroom. He was in there a long time. For a few minutes, listening to the high, singing swoop of the cascading Aloha airlines flight on the TV, she thought he might never return.

When he did, his face purpled and a slick of vomit on his collar, she thought, *Oh no.*

Oh no, I'm going to have to get more.

But he looked at her woozily, his hands on his knees. He said his legs were stiff. He said it was like his whole body had turned wooden.

A few minutes later, he started to make a funny noise.

Where's my phone? he said, his neck so red now, red as a firecracker. But Diane didn't know.

Can you get Joann? A wheeze like a squeeze toy. *Something's not right. Can you get her for me?*

She rose, nodding. She climbed the two flights to Joann's floor and it was so strange. It was like none of it was real except the sound of her sneakers on the concrete, louder than the loudest noise in the world.

She stopped on the stairwell and stared up at the sizzling fluorescent light above.

Is this happening? she wondered. She had no idea. *Did I do that?*

Joann followed her down, asking a hundred questions and carrying a big bottle of Pepto-Bismol. When they walked inside the apartment, her dad was lying on the carpet, the TV tray on the floor, spaghetti stringing garishly across his ankles.

Oh God, Joann kept saying. *Oh God.*

There was this gurgling sound, and foam in a little curlicue in front of his mouth.

This was when she could no longer think, or speak. Because none of it was real.

Joann was already calling 911. *Did he take anything?* She kept repeating the operator's questions. *Is he on anything?* Everyone had so many questions.

When the EMT people came, they couldn't get the tube down his throat. It was completely closed.

She stood in the doorway and watched. Everyone moving around her, but she couldn't move at all. Maybe she was made of wood too. A wooden girl.

Was it real? she asked herself. *Did I do that?*

He lay on the rug, dead, his eyes open. He was staring right at her. A big, empty stare, like, *Who are you?*

Which was how he always looked at her anyway, how both of her parents did. *Who are you and what are you doing here?*

This is what Diane told me.

And when she'd finished, she looked at me, her face changed, her features dark and soft. She looked at me and waited.

NOW

Saturday, just after seven a.m., I start thinking about calling Diane.

The PMDD literature sits on the coffee table, articles spread like a cardsharp's fan. I graze my hand over it.

It's you, Diane said last night. *It's both of us.*

I think about the power she once had, a strange, drowsy, dark cloud around her that always drew me to her. That made me want to draw things out of her, to uncover her secrets. And how I fled from her the moment she offered them to me. *Watch what you wish for,* that's what my dad always said. Every time he eloped or lost a bar bet.

Checking my voice mail again, I see Alex hasn't called me back. But there's a text from Diane, who must've gotten my number from the lab directory.

Call me if you want to talk, it says. *And think about what I said.*

A peculiar feeling flits through me. An old loyalty, something.

I fight off the impulse to type back, to warn her: *I told Alex. Alex knows.*

She's here two days and, just like that, we're back in it, together.

Except this time maybe I'm the one who's laid the dark bundle at her feet.

Hey, sorry about yesterday, I text Alex, fingers white. *Can we talk?*
    The wait, phone in hand like a live thing.
    Finally, six minutes later, having felt five phantom buzzes, his reply:
No worries. I'm at the lab now, though. Tonight?

Five minutes later, I'm walking across the stretch of strip malls, making my way to campus, the brisk bright Saturday morning hours before anything's moving other than blowing trash, parking-lot tumbleweed.
    As I walk, I try to remember precisely what I said to Alex, the words I used.
    But mostly what comes are whispers, the green light of the bedroom, ATOMIC LIQUOR winking from the top of the neon-sign stack at my window.
    You were crying in your sleep, he'd said from the far side of the bed, shaking me awake.
    I guess I was. I guess I didn't know it would be like that. I didn't know it would feel so much.
    But you can undo this, I tell myself. *You can fix this.*

The campus is empty and hungover, the gray ghost of Friday-night beer and mayhem still hovering. It's not until I reach the building's front doors that I see an actual person, a shadow behind me some-where, gone before I can turn, before I can swipe my key card and step inside.
    In the elevator, the access card's edges cutting into my cupped hand, I think about what I'll say to Alex. But the truth is, you can rarely undo things. This is what you realize after one of your parents dies.

I look down at the access card: Severin Lab, my name, my institutional photo, snapped by the HR woman my very first day. I couldn't believe I'd finally made it. The Severin Lab, at last. Working with—well, *for,* but maybe eventually *with*—the woman herself. So the moment the HR woman clicked her digital camera, my face broke into an impossible grin.

Looking at it now, that smile so big and unrestrained I don't even recognize it, feels important. *Eyes on the prize,* Ms. Castro always used to say.

The lab itself is quiet, just the beep of an autoclave echoing through the halls. Weekend mornings, the place always feels haunted. Serge might be there, but he seldom leaves the animal unit unless he has to. Or Juwon by late morning, same with Maxim, who brings his own Chemex on weekends (*You have to saturate the grounds. I like to let it bloom precisely thirty-seven seconds, no more, no less*) and settles in for four or five hours of work before his girlfriend, Sophie, starts texting, and texting. Once, when she didn't hear back from him fast enough, she showed up. After a half hour of trying to find an entrance she could get into without a key card, she finally appeared, a crunchy leaf in her hair from the bushes by the back exit, the one often propped ajar by grad students without weekend-access privileges. She seemed surprised to find Maxim there, just where he'd said he would be, even disappointed in some furtive way.

You're always here, she cried out, tugging a twig from her shoe, *what was I supposed to think?*

But Maxim had said something about Sophie dragging him to a wedding this weekend. And Juwon—well, one kid with a sore throat and he might not show.

First, I look in the lounge, but it's empty. Maybe everybody's superstitious about the decision. Or maybe they're sending out CVs to avoid being stuck on Irwin's hypogonadism study. There was something so sad about the tired, hairless men shuffling in, waiting for their testosterone injections.

The closed-circuit TV screen shows the building entrance, and my eye catches the flutter of a person moving past. I wonder if it's Diane. Something in the movement, both graceful and stealthy. In the way of bogeymen in your childhood nightmares, I imagine she knows I'm here, knows I told Alex.

I shake the thoughts loose, rising.

The moment after I walk into G-21, stopping at the turn in its L shape, I spot Alex, standing under the fume hood, his headphones large and buglike.

He still looks handsome, the elegant crook of those long fingers. The delicate swivel in his sneakers as he moves from hood to bench.

This is the first Saturday I've ever seen him here. (*This weekend? A college buddy made me go out on his boat*, he'd say with rolling eyes. Or *I had to fly home for my sister's gallery opening* or *Went to Vail for my cousin's wedding*.)

"Hey," I blurt. "Figured you might put some work in today?"

The slow turn is his tell. He knew I'd been watching. Heard the click of the door unlocking before I walked inside. Thinks he holds all the cards.

He does, maybe.

THEN

"Diane," I said. "Diane. Why did you tell me? Why did you..."

I felt something in my stomach, reached out for the trash can, like I might throw up.

But I didn't. I covered my mouth, turning and looking at her.

Sitting with her spine so straight, her hands folded in her lap, just watching me.

"Haven't you ever done something in the blink of an eye and then realized it was wrong? That it was all wrong?"

"No. Not like that. No."

"And you can't believe it later. You can't believe you were that person."

"No," I said, shaking my head harder. "Never."

"I guess," she said quietly. "I guess I was wrong."

NOW

It turns so quickly. A flash, a spark, and everything changes, forever.

"I'm sorry about before," I say, walking toward him. "Yesterday."

"Hey," Alex says, looking up, a generic smile. "Okay. Sure."

He's setting up another flash column, plugging cotton wool to fill the stopcock. All you're really doing is using gas to push a solvent down a tube, but it's a delicate thing. Every time I watch Alex, I wince a little. Too much air, clamps too tight, a chip or scratch in the glass tube. Working too fast, too roughly.

"I said a lot of things the other night. Some things about Diane, but that's drunk talk. Like that time Zell downed those Old Crow shots at Flanigan's and told us how he used to wrestle girls in junior high."

Fixing the foot-high glass tube to the clamp, Alex smiles again, smiles easily, maybe even a little smugly. "That's not exactly the same thing, though, is it?"

"It is," I say, my voice lifting high in a way I hate. "Petty high-school stuff. I knew Diane when we were seniors. She was always the smartest, always beating me. It just all came back."

"We're not talking about stolen lab notes or some dry-ice

prank," he says, adding the solvent now, the bright, pungent smell of the chloroform filling the air.

"She was the best at everything. I could never beat her." I keep going, feeling a dampness at my forehead. "She was perfect, and I wanted her brain. I wanted her drive. She never stopped. I never knew anyone like that before."

But Alex merely nods as he pours the silica slurry into the tube with one tilt of the arm, doesn't even bother to stir.

"Alex, stop what you're doing a second, okay?" I say.

But he keeps going, tapping the sides of the tube. "Who did she kill, Kit?"

"What?" I say, my voice shaking.

"Who did Diane Fleming kill?" he says, looking up at me at last. "You said, *That girl, she looks so innocent, but don't believe it. She is a killer. She killed in cold blood.*"

As he says the words, I can feel them like the hard old knots in the back of my neck. I know I said those words to him because I've said them before. To myself, to someone else once. The biggest words you can ever say and still be real and not be a person in a play, Ophelia among the buttercups and nettles, the long orchids and browning daisies.

"What else?" I say, my voice like those clamps, scraping glass. "What else did I say?"

"You said you had nightmares for months, every night, that she came running after you in the woods like a crazy killer in a mask."

"No."

"You said that you stopped sleeping after, that you'd have to sneak out into your mom's car at night and blast opera or death metal to get her out of your head."

As he says it, I start remembering, those words like marbles in my liquored mouth.

"You said you nearly lost your mind," he adds. "But in the end you saved yourself."

I don't know what to say because there is nothing to say.

It was all true, but it wasn't everything. It never could be. There were so many parts that were hard to articulate, that required me to heave my heart into my mouth. And there were other parts I'm sure I left out for reasons of my own. The sneaking knowledge: Had I told him everything, he might have seen some of the ugliness in me. Not half as dark as Diane, but still full of blood.

"And then you said, *But now she's back, Alex. And look what she's capable of.*"

"I don't really know if she did anything," I say, and in some technical way this is true. "It's all secondhand, thirdhand. It's all ancient, Alex. I need you to forget it."

He looks at me, tapping the glass tube with his finger, that callused finger. The gas surging.

"None of us should be working with someone like that, Kit."

I don't pause on this. I can't. In my pocket, I clutch at my access card.

"I don't know why I told you," I say, "but—"

"I think you do know."

"What does that mean?" Maybe it's that brief huff of chloroform, sickly and strong, from the tube. *He should be under the fume hood,* I think, distracting myself so I don't have to ponder what Alex is saying. *What is he saying?*

"It means," he says, "you were right to tell me. And don't you think, deep down, you probably wanted me to take care of it?"

"Take care of it?" I repeat, which is all I seem able to do, my eyes fixed now on this easy, knowing look on his face. It's enraging, recalling a dozen, a hundred, a thousand times in my life a man telling me to *relax, be a team player, stop worrying so much, take it easy and roll with the punches. We're all on the same team.*

"You wanted me to do what you couldn't do."

"No," I say. "No. No. I was drunk. You with your *one more round for the lady.* Plying me with drinks." His eyes widen. "I'll say anything when I'm that drunk. I'll do anything when I'm that drunk. That doesn't make it real."

The slurry separating like a lava lamp, he steps forward. The usual looseness in his face, the comfort and ease, is gone for the first time since I've known him.

"Are you suggesting I was trying to get you drunk?" he says. "Because who hopped on whose lap out on that patio? You with the sneaky hands and the dirty talk—"

"Stop," I say. "Shut your goddamned Dartmouth mouth." I don't know where the Dartmouth came from, or any of it, my face hot, hotter.

"Or," he says, louder now, "are you suggesting I got you drunk not to get in your pants but to get in your head?"

I don't know what I'm suggesting, but there's victory in throwing him off his game, in watching his eyes darting, his sneakers squeaking on the floor.

"Because," he says, fiddling impatiently with the tube, turning to adjust the adaptor, adding more pressure to make it all go faster, "I don't need to load anyone up with cheap drinks for a lab spot. My work speaks for itself."

"So does mine," I say. "So does mine."

It's just a beat, a slow blink, but something lies in there, I can feel it. Something he's thinking but not quite saying, until he does.

"Being a hard worker, a good little worker bee, is great," he says. "But it gets you only so far."

The raw, ugly, mottled things you fear about yourself in your most private moments—what happens when someone says them aloud to you? The feeling like your skin slipped from your body, showing everything, red and veined.

"You don't even know what I can do," I say, and in the background somewhere I'm hearing something, some distant whistling sound. My eyes snag on the glass tube, the pressure cranked too high. The gas driving the solvent too hard.

"That's not what I meant, Kit," he says, shaking his head, his face softening.

"How would you even know? How smart I am. What I can do—"

"Kit, listen." Like every *Kit, listen* I've heard my whole life at schools, in financial aid offices, at job interviews and HR offices, *Kit, listen, community college is a good thing. Kit, listen, be grateful for what you have, don't be greedy.* "It's under control. I got this."

"Wait, wait," I say, my head throbbing, that chloroform lifting from the tube, my own bad thoughts. "What do you mean?"

He looks at me, and there's something in his eyes, the way his mouth opens as if to say something but then stops.

"Did you already do something?" I say. "Did you already talk to Dr. Severin?"

"No. It's not—" he starts, but then his head jerks, and he backs away from the lab bench, squinting down the other side of the L-shaped room. "Is someone here?" he asks me.

"Alex," I say. "Alex, please."

It must be something in my voice because finally Alex stops and looks at me, a long look.

But that's when the whistling sound gets louder. Like that time long ago, my mom put my favorite Snoopy mug in the microwave. The whistling sound and then—

I look over at the glass tube behind him.

"You've got too much pressure on it," I say, stepping forward. "Can't you hear that?"

It is both a second and an eternity, but I can see how it's going to happen. That same glass tube from the other day, its star-shaped crack now like a web spreading, the pressure inside too high.

Watch it, I try to say, thrusting my arm forward, pointing to the tube. Except I can't hear the words come out, and Alex is still talking. *The crack in the glass, Alex. I told you—*

"In the end you'll thank me," he is saying. And I can see it happening, but I can't move to stop it. I can't even get my mouth to say it.

Alex, behind you—

I can't seem to make any words come.

His mouth is still moving, voice pushing forth (*Kit, listen—*), as it happens, as the *pop!* comes, smaller than a firecracker, like the bang-snaps my cousin Scott used to twist into teardrops and throw on the driveway.

The same second, or the one after—a singing sound in between, something flying, glass flying.

Nothing can stop it now.

Pop! and in the same second, or the one after, his throat bright red, the glass shining there. A sheet of red dropping from his neck like a curtain descending.

"Alex." My voice crumples, my hand flapping in front of me like a frightened bird.

His face, his chin, as if a scarlet veil hung there, his hands grabbing for his throat, the fountain.

"You killed me," he says, which doesn't make any sense. I haven't moved. I'm not even moving. But that awful glub-glub sound.

*   *   *

The blood jet is real, obscene.

He reels back, head bobbing, one hand clutching his throat. Turning around once, grasping for the lab bench, he reaches out just as his long, narrow body slides to the floor.

There he goes, slipping to the floor and falling back in a long, red forever.

I'm on my knees, leaning over him, clasping my hands over the fountain. Pushing down. The beat of his heart beneath my forearm as I press hard against the gushing thing, his open neck, a femme fatale's wet sneer, a cleft lurid and obscene.

Inside, his slashed vein is finger-thick, a bright shoelace resting between my fingers. Taking a breath, I press hard against it. I won't let go.

Lips bluing. Those lips.

My face wet, dripping with something hot.

The cloying chloroform everywhere now.

I watch his eyes, dark and blissful, and I can see it happen. It happens right there.

One hand pressing against his splayed throat, the other landing hard on his chest.

On his heart now. On his heart.

My feet clapping on the sidewalk. They leave black marks, the chloroform melting the rubber on my sneakers.

I'm walking my dogs in the blush-red chemical haze of Lanister, leash-tugging Grimm and Fudge, both gone for years now, gone before my mom, who's running up behind me, wind in her hair, those creasy eyes and sad smile.

She's shouting something to me, her voice caught in the wind.

What, Mom, what?

She's shouting and waving and the dogs are pulling at their leashes, straining my arms, and my mom is screaming, her hands around her neck now like the people on the Heimlich poster, but her voice makes no sound.

And before I can do anything, the dogs are bolting, my arms feel like they'll be torn from me, the leashes slipping from my grasp.

Hey, hey.

Grimm stops and turns his head, looks at me, eyes gone white. Then bolts again.

They aren't dogs at all anymore but two black things small and far away.

My wrists hurt, oh God, they hurt.

Looking up, the fluorescents screaming above, I see Saint Joan from the old movie, her shorn hair, her blazing cheek. Has anyone ever been so beautiful?

And she's dragging me, my legs heavy and stiff, through a rain puddle.

"You have to get up, Kit," she says. "The chloroform is making you sick."

Diane is leaning over me, her hands gripping my forearms. And it's not a rain puddle I'm in, and there's something holding me in place, a heavy thing in my lap.

I look down and see Alex, his head slipping off my legs as Diane pulls me, my sneakers skidding, leaving black marks.

There's glass everywhere, and more blood than ever in all the world, pooling in my jeans, my shoes.

And Alex, his throat torn to red ribbons like poor old Grimm after a coyote got him and his eyes seal gray and empty and staring at me.

Everything comes back, scissoring through the sweet brume of the chloroform.

"Did you hear the glass break?" I say. "Is that why you came?"

"No," she says. "I heard someone crying. I heard you crying."

II.

We lived in a preoccupation as complete as that of a dream.

—Marie Curie

NOW

"What did he do? What did he do?"

Everything is wet.

The chloroform is gone from the air now but seems instead to all be inside me, like droopy flowers going to rot in my mouth, my head.

"What did he do?" I hear my voice saying over and over. "What did he do?"

But it isn't my voice. It's Diane's. And suddenly, Diane is there, kneeling beside me, her face a pale smudge. She's waiting for me to say something.

It all comes drifting back, like a briny tide. *I said a lot of things the other night. Some things about Diane . . . That girl, she looks so innocent, but don't believe it. She is a killer. She killed in cold blood.*

"I didn't mean," I say, words coming in dreamy pieces, " . . . to do it.

"I tried . . . to stop it."

"I know," she says, her face coming into focus now. Her eyes saucer-wide, like a picture of a girl. "You had to. You had to do it."

"Yes, yes," I say, voice dragging. "I didn't think you'd understand."

She looks at me. "I'm going to help you," she says very formally, her chin shaking slightly.

"Help me," I say, but it's really a question. That's when my head turns to one side, all the pieces inside it seeming to slide in one direction.

That's when I see him. Alex. Three, four feet from me, sprawled on the floor.

Everything comes back, the lush fountain from Alex's throat, the sharp smell, the glub-glub like the bubbler on my fish tank when I was a kid, the way he turned on his heel before he fell, like a vaudevillian doing a pratfall.

You never think anyone will die in front of you. You never think how it will feel.

"I heard you," she says, and her face is so tight, her mouth stretched like a piece of red string. "I heard you fighting. You had to do it."

"Oh, no," I say, wriggling, trying to lift my body. "You don't understand."

"I do understand. Take it easy."

"It was an accident," I say, up on my elbows now, my head feeling like a bowling ball plugged with sand. I look over at Alex again, the way his hands rest on his chest, his wrists bent. The blood is everywhere, a hot-penny smell.

"Are they coming?" I say, my voice speeding up, catching up now. "Did you call 911?"

"No," she says, and I don't know why she isn't moving. Why she's just kneeling there. Looking at me. "Don't worry. I didn't call. It's going to be okay."

I look at her, not believing her, not really able to line my thoughts up properly or be sure I'm hearing right.

"My phone is in my purse," I say, on my knees now, my sneakers sliding, my ankles streaked red. "Where is it? You have a phone. Call them. The people who come."

The lights pinching my eyes, I spot the phone on the wall by the door, the old one with the blue light no one uses anymore.

"Stop," Diane says. "It's okay. I'll help you."

"Help me? What—"

I'm standing, but my legs won't do what they're supposed to. I reach out for the wall.

That's when I see Alex's face. I try not to see his throat, so I end up looking at his face. His eyes cloudy, a scrim pulled across.

I'm looking at Alex's eyes and the tilt of his jaw. I'm looking at what's happened and how I couldn't stop it.

I scramble to the emergency phone, its blue light, Diane fast behind me.

"No." Diane slaps her hand over mine, pushes it against the wall. "You're not thinking. Your head's full of chloroform."

But it feels like the opposite. That I'm wakening to it, to how monstrous this all is, the body straggled scarecrow-like, and death is so cruel.

"Look at you," she says. "What do you think the police will decide the minute they see you?"

My eyes glide down to my shirt, my jeans heavy with blood.

"It was an accident," I say once more, my tongue thick in my mouth.

She looks at me and I can hear myself breathing.

"I told you to call 911," I say, my voice jangly now. I think of the squeaking sounds, the soft hillock of Alex's Adam's apple. I remember the ABCs they teach you in CPR. Airway, breathing, circulation.

"We can't do that," she says. "I can't let you do that to your-self."

It's only then that I realize it. "You don't believe me."

She pauses. "I heard you two fighting about something. I heard shouting."

The feeling, the way she's looking at me, is unbearable.

"No, no, no," I say. "We weren't . . . it was just an argument. It wasn't anything."

She doesn't believe me. I can see it.

So the words just come, my mouth loose and hapless.

"We were arguing, but it was an accident. He was threatening to . . . he . . ." Then it's as if a shudder of something rises inside me, my hand grabbing for the lab bench, clawing at its edge. "Diane, he was going to ruin everything."

She doesn't say anything, but there's a dawning on her face.

"I told him," I say. "I told him everything."

"About my dad," she whispers.

I look at her and nod.

Both our hands jostle for the phone, Diane grabbing it from me, clawing at me.

"Don't you get it?" she says, voice husky and strained, a new urgency. "He knew something that we both wanted no one else to know. Now he's dead and we're the ones in this room with the body. How does that look?"

"What does that matter? We didn't do anything, we—"

She looks at me. "If he told, it matters a lot."

I don't say anything. I'm thinking of Alex: *It's under control. I got this.* That look on his face, his mouth opening as if he's about to say something but then stopping.

Could he have told someone already? I can't be sure.

"He didn't," I say anyway. Then, scrambling, remembering, "I asked him if he'd talked to Dr. Severin. He said no."

She pauses. "If he told her, we'd know already," she decides. "Dr. Severin doesn't wait. She acts."

I nod wearily, trying to stay upright. Trying to catch my breath.

"But we don't know who else he might have told," she says. Then adds, "What if he told his girlfriend?"

I look at her. "His girlfriend? He doesn't have a girlfriend."

She looks at me and now she says nothing.

There doesn't seem to be any other way. In my chloroform-draped, panic-thick state, I can't think of any other way.

We walk back around the corner, wet step by wet step, away from the sight, the smack of the chloroform, the everything still hovering in the air, and I have to see it all again. See what it looks like from the outside. The blood trail like a wreath, the way he spun before he fell. The red treads from my sneakers fanning through the sludge of blood. The bench, my palm print seared on it. And who knows what hand or fingerprints might be down there? My eyes scattering to all the other places I stood, where my hands and fingertips rested.

I look at everything but him, the dark clump in the center of the room.

"We don't clean up the blood," Diane says, pulling on blue lab gloves and handing me a pair. "We only get rid of your prints."

"How do we . . ."

"Whoever finds him will assume it was an accident. They'll run over and contaminate everything anyway."

"It *was* an accident, Diane," I say yet again, so many times it no longer feels real or true.

"Put on those gloves," she says, looking at me. "And take off your shoes."

Later I'll wonder why I didn't stop her, stop everything. But there was some voice in my head, a low throb that said, *But it is your fault, really, Kit. But Kit, you are guilty. You are.*
     Wasn't I?

I've cleaned up many spills in the lab, but I've never done something like this. In our gloves, goggles, and coats, we move quickly. Wearing only socks and shoe covers, I can hear myself breathing and the sound is strangely soothing. Spraying and wiping, we go through a box of Kimwipes, attacking with great precision the mad scatter of my shoe prints, partial and whole, my bloody hand-heel print on the lab bench. Both our prints on the emergency phone. The nitrogen valve Diane must have turned off.
     The lab is you. It was something Dr. Severin told me long ago, the day she hired me. *You're one of us now. And the lab will come to feel like home. Maybe, if you're like me, more like home than home ever felt.*
     That was all she said, but she was right. The lab did, and does.
     Its lenses and scopes become your eyes. Its buzzing spectrometer, the buzzing of your brain. Its clicks and beeps forever clicking and beeping like your heart never stopping.
     You are everywhere. The lab is you.
     We save this part for last. The most incriminating sight: those shoe prints smack in the center of the great lake of blood, my sneaker ridges like gnashing teeth.
     "I have an idea," Diane says, leaning over the wound itself. "It's old blood, but it's the best we can do."

It takes me a few seconds, but then I see what she means to do. The surest way to obliterate the shoe print is to engulf it.

"I'll do it," Diane says. "You don't have to look."

"No," I say. "We can't. Diane, no."

I'm kneeling now, and Diane is too. The body is dark red from chin to waist, the red weeping into the furrows of his shirt.

Red streamers streaming from the center of his throat. It has a kind of terrible beauty.

Heels of gloved hands to stiff shoulder blades, we tip the torso off the floor, his neck flopping like a doll's.

I do it, but I don't look. I never look. My eyes not on him but on Diane's shoe covers as we lift him. It takes nearly a minute for gravity to do its work, for the pooled blood to seep over the shoe print, effacing it. Or close to it.

His body tilting, the wound gaping, we both feel the last of Alex's heart release itself. Together, we let slip the last of Alex's thumping heart.

"I think we're done," she says.

I don't say anything.

"Kit."

"Stop talking," I say. "Stop talking. Stop talking. Stop talking."

I say it over and over again.

Back in high school, at the Golden Fry, I was always the one to scrape the mold from the bottom of the ice machine, to kneel under the pressure cooker, cleaning the grease traps. I was the only female employee who ever did it. The other high-school girls, their nails gelled, their hands forever damp from the coconut and vanilla buttercream and cherry blossom balms they squeezed from tubes so tiny they hung from their key chains—they were never going to do it.

The nineteen-year-old manager was too afraid to ask the older ones. Justine and Careena, all of twenty-four and twenty-eight, both seemed so brine-hardened by real life. In Justine's case, she'd been sharpened to teeth-baring rage; in Careena's, dulled to sloe-eyed sorrow.

So it was often left to me, and I never minded after the first time. I guess deep down I took a certain pride in going to such places. I was very young and didn't want to be afraid of anything.

Now, before I put a needle into a mouse's quivering belly, I cross myself twice, every time.

We can judge the heart of a man by his treatment of animals. That was what Serge told me the first time he watched, approvingly. *I am sure Mr. Kant meant the heart of a woman too.*

"We have to go," she says, on her feet now. She extends her arm, her gloved hand.

Because I am not moving, crouching still over the red blur my shoe print once resided in.

"Come on."

I look up at her. The fluorescents burning off her.

"Give me your hand," she says, offering hers. "Hurry now."

At the eyewash station, I shove my forearms over the spout.

Diane is stuffing all the used Kimwipes, a pair of mop heads, the shoe covers—rinsed but still red-seamed—into a plastic bio-hazard bag.

"Who comes in on the weekend?" she asks.

"Anybody might," I say.

She's looking at my clothes, stiffening on me like brown paper.

I don't move and don't look at the slumped thing on the floor. Any second, I expect to hear a soft click from the door and see Zell, Maxim, Juwon, anyone. Above, in the ceiling, I hear a scratching and imagine more mice, imagine Serge up there in the crawl space, tracking them down.

When I look over again, she's pulled her old lab coat from her backpack, the scarlet one from Freudlinger's lab, like a flood of blood pouring over her arm.

"Put it on."

She's so much taller than me, it falls to my ankles.

Walking down the long, empty hall, I can hear my clothes rustling under the lab coat. My sneakers, wet from the sink and ammonia saturated, squeak with every step. It's so loud I want to plug my ears.

Beside me, Diane moves with purpose, but the biohazard bag swinging like a stoplight bothers me.

"We need to get rid of that," I whisper.

"Where's the campus incinerator?"

I shake my head. "There's cameras all over campus."

After tucking the bag behind her backpack, close to her body, she presses the elevator button and we step inside.

As we descend, I look at myself in the security mirror, my face stretched, my arms red wings, hoping, hoping the elevator doesn't stop on any floor.

When the elevator chimes at the ground floor and the doors open, I exhale at last.

It's only when we turn the corner and head to the front doors that we see Serge.

Diane touches my arm with her fingertips.

"Good morning," he says, that deep Slavic voice of his. "Good

165

morning to you both." He looks at me. "Are you going to church?"

I stare at him dumbly. He gestures to my ensemble, my body swimming in Diane's lab coat.

"I do not think," he says, "I have ever seen you in a dress before."

THEN

Can you imagine what it might feel like for someone to confess a murder to you? What it means to hear it, to know it, to carry it with you? You have been made an involuntary accomplice. Accessory after the fact. What would you do? Go to the police? Urge repentance? Offer words of understanding? Pray?

Or would you run?

At first, all I could do was hide. I skipped AP Chem, which pained me, so close to news about the Severin scholarship. But even avoiding my locker, our shared classes, I couldn't escape her. She knew my beats. Finally, she found me in the library, on the floor behind the tall stacks, curled over my overheated, sticky-keyed laptop.

She found me anyway.

I saw her feet first as she prowled the stacks like the monster in a movie. Those black flats, shiny as soldier boots.

"Kit," she said. "I don't understand."

I told her I couldn't see her. I didn't ever want to see her again.

"But the AP exam is coming," she said, kneeling down next to me. "We need to study."

"Diane, we're not study partners anymore," I said. I just said it. "We're not anything anymore."

She looked at me, a notch of pain over her brow. It was as if she'd had her first one-night stand without knowing it. She'd shared something with me, something as intimate as if she'd let me between those long, locked legs of hers, and now I was pulling away.

"Oh," she said, nodding almost to herself. Rising slowly, brushing the dust off her knees. Then adding, softly, "I ruined everything."

Watching her walk away, wending through the stacks like a pale ghost, I felt something awful inside, even if I couldn't name it.

That night, I dreamed of Mr. Fleming. His weekend khakis and his funny mustache like a bristle brush. In the dream he was on a gurney, his heart swollen to five times its size. And Diane in her long gored skirt, staring as he thumped his own hands over his heart like his hands were paddles. Like he could will himself back to life.

I dreamed of my own dad calling me, his voice pained and throbbing through the phone. Like the phone itself was quivering with it. *There's a girl here*, he said. *She says she's your friend. She says she has something to give me . . .*

And I dreamed of Diane coming into my house at night, sneaking down the shag carpet of the hallway. Dreamed of waking up to her white face above me.

Isn't this what you wanted? the dream Diane asked me, as if just noticing me there in her dad's apartment, her dad dying on the floor.

Was it what I wanted? Didn't I crave all her secrets, plucking the heart of her mystery?

I wanted to know her secrets, but I didn't want them to be *this*.

Why did you tell me? I asked, and it sounded like a whimper, and I wasn't even sure if I was awake or asleep. *Now it's part of me too.*

That's how it felt, like a tumor lashed to my insides.

I'm sorry, she said, crying softly but smiling too. *You told me your secret. I wanted to tell you mine.*

In the morning, I told my mom I was sick, the sickest I'd ever been. Maybe I was dying. Something inside me, cramps like an animal crawling inside my ovaries.

She let me stay home for three days. I didn't shower or brush my teeth, a mouthful of fur. Finally, the third morning, she dragged me into the shower stall, scrubbed me down like one of her mangy rescue mutts.

"Tomorrow you go back," she told me.

After she left, I tried to study, but the words kept turning into pictures and I kept falling asleep on the afghan or having dark, semi-awake thoughts.

At one point, I guess I started moaning. It got so loud I frightened myself.

I had to get out, go somewhere. My hair full of dried shampoo and my legs hairy, like the down on a baby pig; what did I care?

I looped the collars on Grimm and Fudge, even though it was sure to rain, the sky so heavy it seemed nearly to touch my back. We walked all the way to the highway before it started, slow splotches, warm and thick. Grimm never wavered, the thick hunks of fur on his back glistening, but Fudge yanked free and ran straight for the nearest overhang, the old arcade where my dad once broke his hand playing air hockey.

"Is that Scott's cuz?" a voice came. A tall guy in a Klassic Pinballz T-shirt unloading warm crates of Faygo in the alley.

"Yep," I said, thinking how the rain made my tank top pucker from my chest and what he might see.

"The smart one, right?" he said, petting Fudge with his enormous long-fingered hand. "Wanna have some beers?"

I did, taking a fat little pony of Miller High Life.

He said his name was Lou and he used to play drums for Scott's sometime-band. He'd been delivering slick cans and Slim Jims and vending-machine condoms all day with his friend Jimmy, the friendly fella sitting on the upturned trash can, and wouldn't it be fun to sit in the back on these empty kegs and have a few?

So we did. Lou turned the radio up on his truck, bass-thick grooves and old metal. And we all took turns throwing an old tennis ball to Fudge, and Jimmy showed me the hard white pads on his thumbs from his decade of pinball devotionals. At some point, Jimmy's girlfriend appeared and danced alongside the back fence, doing whirling snake-charmer things with her long dark arms that ended in sharp manicured points studded with blue crystals.

Soon, I was dancing with her, and we were talking of getting our tongues pierced with the piercing kit she'd bought earlier that day from a place called HottyBodyJewlz. Her fingers on my face, she told me I had the prettiest eyes she'd ever seen and kissed me flush on the mouth.

Watching us, Lou and Jimmy kicked the kegs with their sneakers and cheered and hooted as Grimm let out a howl and Fudge was somewhere by the trash cans, licking up foam in long, snaky gulps. And then the piercing kit got torn open and Jimmy brought the needle close to me, Lou holding a cork and dirty cubes from the ice machine. Punching both our tongues and the blood filling our mouths with metal and grit. We couldn't get enough.

The dark swallowed the sky and someone brought over chicken

on a stick from the Chevron and I had long since stopped drinking but the pony bottles became a magnificent monument in Jimmy's hands, an *objet,* his girlfriend kept saying, and she studied art at City Tech, which is how she could see that my eyes were so beautiful that Lou better kiss me before she beat him to it again.

And he did. Lou.

Lou kissed me, his big hands folding around my face, my blood-thick chin. My tongue numb and bold and the strangest kissing I'd ever had or ever would have. Sticky dust on his fingertips, and a whisper in my ear that said, *You, you, smart girl, look at you. Look at you go.*

Oh, it was the warmest place to be.

"I'd like to know, little girl," my mom said when I stalked in at two a.m., my shorts on backward and both dogs shuddering from rain and beer and rain again. A scatter of bottle glass in Grimm's mane from when the monument fell.

The boy Lou had wanted to drive me, but I'd scuttled away crabwise when no one was looking, when Jimmy and his girl were trying to find a broom, or maybe some cigarettes, and Lou was trying to start his car, an angry grinding, and his belt buckle still loose from what we'd been up to.

The walk home had been spooky, and once I thought I'd seen Grandpa Fleming's truck, Diane's halo of hair as she sat behind the wheel, her eyes darting for me.

What would she want from me?

Everything.

"I'd like to know," my mom kept saying, "where you got the idea you could behave like this."

"I love our dogs," I said, still drunk. "I'm sorry."

That's when I started crying, which upset my poor mom a lot.

She rubbed me and Grimm and Fudge with rough towels until our skin burned to dry us and clean off all the sooty rain.

She made me drink four Tupperware cups full of water, which is the worst way to drink water unless you like plastic. Then, trying to get my jellies off my blackened feet, I finally said it. Finally asked it.

Nothing could have stopped the words from stumbling perilously from my waterlogged mouth.

"Mom," I said, "what if you had this friend who told you something they'd done. Something really bad. It's so bad, Mom."

She looked at me, dipping a dishrag into a tub of Vaseline, working out a piece of tar caught in Fudge's paw pads. "What did you do, Katherine Ann?"

"Nothing. It's a friend."

"Katherine Ann, you need to tell me," she said, motionless, Fudge's paw pads curled in her palm. "Just tell me what you did."

"I didn't do anything," I said. "I know about someone who did, and it's bad. Am I supposed to tell someone?"

She wouldn't quite look in me in the eye. I knew she had to guess it was Diane. I knew she'd had a feeling about Diane.

"It depends," she said. "Would telling make it better?"

I didn't say anything for a second, my eyes on Fudge. His eyes looked fearful, his paws clamped between my mother's red fingers.

"I don't know if it would make it better, but Mom"—I looked at her—"it's so heavy."

As I said the word, I felt my voice go high. *Don't start crying again*, I thought, *you'll scare her.*

She set the dishrag down. "Is someone in trouble or in some kind of danger?"

"No."

"Is someone going to get hurt if you don't tell?"

172

I thought for a second. "No. But someone will if I do tell."

"Then don't," she said, grabbing for the dishrag again, Fudge squeaking. "Everybody screws up. And everyone has their reasons."

"I guess," I said.

"You're a good friend, honey," she said, stroking Fudge's puny body, her fingers slick with the Vaseline, her face tired. "And if she needs your help to make it right, you'll give it."

"Okay."

"Kit, you can't fix other people's problems," she said, slapping the dishrag on the table, Fudge yelping desolately, shaking under my hand. "You can't fix other people."

NOW

It's amazing—well, alarming, really—what you can do when you have to. When you're cornered like a rat.

"Look at us. Bright and early on a weekend," I'm saying. My voice is jolly and jaunty, not my own. "Serge, let me introduce you to Diane Fleming."

We're all standing in a circle in front of the lab building, my eyes darting once, twice past the security camera mounted above the door, its red light blinking.

"We have met," Serge says, nodding at Diane.

"Oh, right, right," I say, my mouth unable to stop moving. "Diane, have you experienced Serge's famous multi-hour animal-protocol orientation yet?"

Diane shakes her head.

"We will have to make a date for that," Serge says. "When she has time."

"I'm taking Diane around town," I say. "She hasn't seen much. You know, like the Walmart, the Chicken Ranch and Bunco Parlor, all the important sights."

"Really?" Serge says, his eyes lively, roaming everywhere—Diane, me, the lab coat, my bleachy shoes.

"I didn't know the techs had to work weekends," Diane says, a faint briskness to her tone.

Serge's eyebrows lift. "I will not be here Monday," he says. "I like to be sure everything is in place before I leave."

"He's the one who keeps the vivarium humming," I say, turning to Diane, who is looking at me like I need to shut up, which I do. But I can't. "The mice love him."

I don't know what I'm saying or why I'm talking so much, so promiscuously. My right eyelid keeps sticking and I think there might be blood there.

"I hope the mice will love Diane too," Serge says, looking at her again. There's something in his eyes I can't figure out and my heart is thrumming wildly, my feet cold and my legs quilled.

"Kit," Diane says, "should we take my car?"

I nod, grateful for the cue.

"Good luck in the dentist chair," I say to Serge. "Don't forget about the milk shakes."

"I will not forget," Serge says, but he's not smiling. He's looking at Diane. I turn too and see it, a flash of red, the biohazard bag she's tucked so nimbly inside her backpack, out of sight, appearing like a flare.

"Oh my," Serge is saying, and I can feel a coldness rack me, "what has happened?"

Diane looks down, trying to cover the bag with her long fingers.

"Ceiling mice again," I blurt. "More casualties from the leaky tiles."

He looks puzzled. "Maintenance promised to tape off that room until they repair the ceiling," he says. His eyes are on the bulging bag.

Diane is quick. "I stumbled in there accidentally, and they welcomed me. A nest of them."

I jump in. "More guests from Panda Garden, I guess. Probably drawn in by the smell of MSG in Zell's lo mein." But Serge is looking only at Diane, both of them so tall and dignified, and there I stand, legs bare, blood in my eye.

"You should not carry them out of the building," he says. "No, no."

"We were just about to toss it in the bins," I say.

"I will call pest control," Serge says, shaking his head, nearly tut-tutting. His eyes return to the bag, stuffed full of bloody Kimwipes, red-stained gloves.

"I may have overdone it, Serge," Diane says, the briskness gone from her tone. Softer now, a slight helplessness, her wrist bending under the bag's handles. "I think I quadruple-bagged them."

"You should not have touched them," he says. "But you are new."

Lifting her head, Diane looks him straight in the eye. "You're right. That must be it."

"Here," he says, reaching out for the bag. "Let me."

I watch as Diane helplessly passes the bag to Serge. Her hand ever so slightly touches his.

"We are breaking all the rules now," he says, smiling faintly. "No gloves. Like prowlers in the night."

I look at both of them, trying to understand the strange energy between them. *Is he flirting with her?* I wonder. *Or something?*

Diane smiles back at him, as much as Diane ever can. "Well, we're all off the clock."

"Come," he says, beckoning her, "I show."

He escorts us toward the loading dock. I see the row of red bins every day, but today they look different, like little stumps. A gummy mouth knocked loose of teeth. Dr. Severin's nails tapping on the conference-room table.

Serge presses his foot on the pedal of the one marked BIO-HAZARD; the top lifts and he tosses the bag inside.

Both Diane and I inhale, quick and hard.

The lid snaps shut.

"I hope Kit shows you the prettiest sights," he says to Diane, eyes dancing. "Sights far prettier than this." A grin.

N O W

In the car, we don't speak. She drives carefully. Stopping at all the yellow lights. Every time she turns a corner, her key chain smacks the ignition panel. One of those furry key chains kids used to have swinging from their backpacks. Soft and perfectly white and I find myself wanting to touch it, hold it. Or—*smack, smack*—hurl it out the window.

Her face looms above me once more.

"Kit, you better wake up," she says, her eyes big and grave. "We need to figure things out."

We're in my apartment, Diane's car parked in the lot.

The drive from the lab took less than five minutes, but I threw up once, then twice, into a folded newspaper in Diane's front seat.

"Did I fall asleep again?" I ask. I don't even remembering lying down on the sofa.

"It's the chloroform. Does your head hurt?"

"Like a sack of rocks. Wet rocks." I try to sit up, stomach bending. "Did anyone call?"

"No," she says.

I rub my eyes, look at the light coming in the window.

"Did it happen?" I ask. "Did that really happen?"

She looks at me. "Yes."

What did we do, what did I do?

"He turned up the pressure too high," I say. "The glass already had a crack and I guess it just blew. A piece caught him in the throat. The carotid."

Diane nods. "Jugular. The carotid, you die much faster."

"Jugular," I repeat, something twitching in my own throat. "It didn't spray. The jugular."

Cut the carotid artery, you might die in less than a minute, but cut the jugular, you could make it six, seven, eight minutes with enough pressure. With help.

I've taken dozens of science courses—biology, human anatomy, physiology, systems anatomy, neurophysiology. I've dissected fetal pigs and kitty cats and oily minks. I've stood before cow ovaries and sheep brains. Human spinal cords and brain stems and hearts.

And yet when a body was splayed before me, open on my lap, no microscope needed, no scalpels or probes or forceps or heavy wooden mallets, I hadn't been able to do anything other than, ultimately, pass out.

From the fog of thought, Diane's voice comes like a careening arrow.

"What matters now," she says, "is we need to keep our stories straight."

The way she's looking at me, how close she sits, I feel a chill.

"I shouldn't have listened to you," I say, my face hot. "I should have called the police. Called 911."

"But you didn't," she says. "And that was the right thing."

The right thing, which, I realize now, means the smart thing to Diane.

I can't do the moral math, not yet. Not for myself.

"Why did you tell him, Kit?" she asks. And for the first time since Diane blazed back into my life, her voice wobbles. "About me."

I pinch the skin between my eyes. "I was drinking. We were drinking."

"Oh," she says, pulling back. "Were you two involved?"

"No," I say quickly, my hand falling to my lap. "Once. Only once."

"Oh."

"What? You're surprised?"

She pauses a second. "No," she says. "I don't know that side of you well."

"What side?" I say.

"Never mind. It doesn't matter."

I look at her. "Diane, it slipped out."

"Okay."

"I don't owe you anything," I say.

"No," she says, "you don't." She pauses. "So you went there and you wanted to make sure he didn't tell your secret."

"Yes," I say. "I mean, to ask him if he wouldn't."

"I heard you fighting," she says. "I couldn't hear what you were saying. And then what?"

"And then it happened."

She looks at me. Pauses. There's a glimmer of something in her face; does she not believe me?

"Well," she says, "he can never tell now."

We've taken turns in the shower, Diane's shorn scalp glistening. The floor mat from her car is hanging wetly from the shower bar. Diane's lab coat sits in pink bathwater in the tub, salt and peroxide doing their work. Our OxiCleaned shoes, now marbled white, dry on a bath mat.

"Someone could find him any minute," she says, beside me on the sofa like we are back in Lanister, droop-eyed Grimm on Mom's shag carpet staring up at us. "We need to have our story ready. We saw Alex in the lab, said hello, but we didn't stay."

"After the mice infestation, you were spooked. You wanted to leave."

She looks at me as if doubting anyone would believe she would be spooked by dead mice or anything at all. "You offered to take me on a tour of the area," she says.

"So we left. The cameras show us leaving. We left."

"Today or tomorrow or Monday morning, someone finds him. Runs over to the body, or doesn't. Calls 911 or the campus police: There's been an accident at the lab."

"The police will wonder how Alex could turn off the nitrogen with a piece of glass in his neck," I say. My brain has returned, full force, and I can think of a thousand ways to get caught.

"It probably has an automatic shutoff. No one's going to think about that anyway," Diane says. I'm not sure either of us believes it.

"Our access cards—"

"Our access cards show we left together," she says. "Your Russian friend saw us. The cameras saw us."

"What about our shoes, your lab coat?"

"We're going to dump them. I'll take them. There's some deep storm drains by my place."

"What if they find them? I read once where they found a baby in a storm drain. They'll match my shoe prints—"

"The shoe prints are gone. The blood covered them. The Oxi-Clean will take care of any spots we might have missed and—"

"And it'll interfere with luminol," I finish. Such smart women, we did manage to do a few smart things.

I pause, thinking of G-21. The things we did.

"But Diane, it didn't..." She must know. "It didn't look... natural."

"There's nothing natural," Diane says, "about any of it."

I close my mouth, bite my lip. She's looking at the bathroom's open door. Her scarlet lab coat hanging now, dripping dry.

"Are you worried about the Russian?" she says abruptly.

"Serge?" I blink, startled. We're in a spy novel now. I picture Diane with a pistol disguised as a lipstick tube in her hand. "No. Serge is a good guy."

"Do you think he'll go back later?"

"If he does, probably only to the animal unit. The cage-wash room or the vivarium. He doesn't like Zell, some of the others. He thinks they're slobs." I pause. "I don't think he liked Alex."

He is the political animal, Serge said. *He is the one.*

She looks at me.

"He didn't look inside the bag," I say, my voice speeding up. "And it was sealed."

"How often do they pick up those biohazard bins?"

"I don't know," I say, staring down at our legs, our feet, both of us smelling like my soap. That's when I feel a hot rush up my cheeks, under my eyes. But I don't let it happen. I won't let her see it.

"Kit," she says, very gently, "we need to stick together now."

"I need some air."

"I won't let anything happen to you."

I step out onto the balcony and stay there, alone.

The sun starts to drag down and the sky goes vermilion, smoke drifting from wildfires somewhere. *Calcium,* I think. The flame test just two nights before. His hand holding the wire in the Bunsen's flare. Everything beginning, or seeming to.

But it had begun before, hadn't it? He would push and probe and prod and pry. He would find my weakest spot. He would take what he wanted for himself.

It's easier to think about this than about anything else.

When I step back inside, I don't see her.

For a few frantic seconds, I think she's gone and wonder what it means. But then the bathroom door opens and she appears, newly pale, her eyes red.

"Are you okay?"

"Yes." She walks toward her backpack, sitting on my lone dining-room chair, the plastic one with the crack.

"You were in there awhile."

"I felt a little sick," she says. "I'm okay now." As she reaches for her backpack, her shirt lifts, exposing a small bit of flesh. I nearly flinch at the xylophone of bones on her spine.

"The sun's down," I say, hoping she'll leave so at last I can breathe.

She nods distractedly. "You've been through a lot," she says. "Just remember, it was an accident, like you said. And anyone can have one bad second. The poison wasn't meant for him. It just happened and then it was too late."

"Poison—what?"

Diane looks confused a moment, then shakes her head. "I mean the accident. It wasn't your fault. That's all I mean."

I look at her, the quivering in her hands. She seemed so cool, so self-possessed in G-21 and with Serge. But now I wonder if any of that was real. Was it possible she'd been going through all these motions while her brain was somersaulting back in time? The thought is terrifying.

"You can go home," I say quickly. "I'll get rid of the shoes and lab coat. It makes more sense."

"But no one here knows me. Doesn't it make more sense—"

"I'll do it," I say, even as I wonder if my rust-shingled car will stall in the evening chill, if I ever replaced the headlight. "It's my responsibility."

She nods, sliding her backpack on. Reaches for her keys, which have fallen to the carpet.

"I'll leave, then," she says, looking out the window. "It's dark enough."

The lab coat is dripping with excruciating slowness on the shower bar, the shoes from the tub. Lifting them to my face, I think I can still see the blood, smell it even, which is impossible.

I know I need to get them out of here.

I put them in a garbage bag, and then I put that in another garbage bag.

I grab my jacket. My fingers move strangely on the buttons, as though they're no longer used to routine tasks, only blood and mayhem.

In the building parking lot, I scrape massage-parlor flyers off the windshield of my slowly dying Pontiac hatchback. The only thing I'd ever won, back when I was nineteen. The local used-car dealership held a contest. Whoever kept a hand on it the longest won. Ten-minute breaks every three hours. It took me fifty-six hours, and I got lucky when my main competition, a truck driver with legs thick as propane tanks, fell asleep on his feet. *All this for a clunker with sixty thousand miles on it already*, my cousin Scott said, shaking his head.

These days, I use it only to drive to the big box store once a month for bales of paper towels, coffee tins like barrels. I hope it will start and it does and before I know it my foot is shaking over the gas and the car erupts to shuddery life.

Driving, my SoWest Lab Supplies baseball cap pulled low, I begin to make my way out of town. No one sees me; no one ever does.

But my brain zigzags to dire places. It's as if Diane's brain, so wary, so watchful, after more than a decade in hiding, so wired for vigilance and self-protection, has infected my own.

Why had she been so eager to dispose of the shoes? Why did I listen to her?

In the end, there's only you, my mom always said, sitting me down at the kitchen table to explain about payday loans and title loans and my dad's bounced checks. *And your mom, of course.*

NOW

There are storm drains all over town. And the next town and the next. But somehow I can't stop driving.

I'm at least a hundred miles away when I pull off the interstate and meander a few miles until I find a highway drain that looks deep enough to devour anything. I don't even stop the car, just open my door. The bag slips from my hand into the abyss.

And then I keep driving.

The AM radio broadcasting from another era (Dottie West and Juice Newton and *I want a lover with a slow hand*) and the road black and empty, I drive with my right foot trembling the whole time, it seems. By the third hour on the interstate, the foot is nearly numb and then I know just where I'm going, the sky flattening on the land, the grimy wastewater-treatment plant all lit up in the distance like a great rust-furred wagon wheel on the Lanister marshland.

The chemical smell when I roll down the windows is exactly as I remember, so strong, like pressing my face into my old Pocahontas comforter or my mom's pilled Hickory Hill Animal Rescue sweatshirt. Ammonia and marsh sulfur and pet hair and Lava soap and everything that stifled and smothered me and that now seems as magical and as extinct as a lost land in a fairy tale or the first few years of childhood when everything is fixed by a banana split with Spanish peanuts or a trip to the dusty old petting farm with your mom and dad.

Just before the city limits, I stop.

I pull the car to the shoulder and sit on the hood for a half hour and try to remember things, try to push aside everything else, try to hurl off the hushing breaths of Diane on my face, in my ear, her voice such an insinuation (*We need to stick together now*).

But why would I ever believe her? Can you ever believe a killer?

You're a killer too now, Kit.

My head wasn't right, I imagine telling someone, the police. *I couldn't think at all. I should have called 911 right away. My head wasn't right. I just did what she said. But I never hurt anyone.*

Inside, somewhere, I feel it. That flickering sense of guilt when someone you're at odds with, who's an obstacle to you, who's trapping you, or so it seems, is suddenly gone. Dead.

Except then I start thinking about Alex. Alex as he was, that charming man, that flirty boy, his throat open before me. Did I do enough to stop the flood of blood? To save that wily little heart?

Alex, his hands to his throat, his scraping voice, *You killed me, you killed me, you killed me.*

Oh, Alex, I think. *Poor Alex.*

It's nearly three a.m., only truckers on the road and the sky and horizon making one black sheet. The gas ticker shaking, I stop once, filling my tank and improvising a scattershot path through a very bright Flying J, Cinnabon steaming, pajama pants for sale by the register, the frozen-drink machine overflowing cherry slush into a far corner, red streaking the floor tiles and wall.

I buy beer.

It seems better than crying. I've been crying for hours, my face hot as a firecracker. Thinking of Alex twitching on that floor.

Still twenty miles from home, I take the back route, the lonely night roads, the strip of strip malls. I don't remember how it happens, spotting a police station's green lantern, my brain inexplicably filling with my father's voice, making jokes about cops and doughnut runs.

What would my old man think of me, wherever he is.

That's when I turn into the precinct parking lot. I don't know what I mean to do but I sit there, watching, for a long time.

For a half hour, maybe more, a near-empty bag of ranch-dusted pretzels and a froth-lined forty of High Life next to me, I sit and think and wonder, my mouth aching, feeling the ghostly throb from that old tongue piercing long healed.

You do these things, my mom had said, *and they can't ever be undone. The hole closes up, but the body remembers.*

That's when I spot two officers walking toward the station house.

I step out of my car and call to them, my voice hoarse. "Hey! I need to talk to someone," I say. "I need to tell someone, okay?"

The words aren't coming fast enough. They're too big.

They look over at me. I catch sight of myself in the glass door's reflection. Sunken baseball hat, tank-top strap drooping, flip-flops. No bra. The smell of beer all over me.

I open my mouth again, but nothing at all comes out this time.

"Cabstand's over there," one of them says. "No way that chick should be driving."

"Go home, honey," the other adds, laughing as he pushes the door open. "Go back to your double-wide."

In that second, I can't explain, all my moral conviction slips to the pavement.

I stand there a moment, watching. Only flipping them off once they're safely inside the building, my father's daughter to the end.

The sleep that comes when I get home at last is epic, opiate, endless. Snow White in her glass coffin. Twelve hours or more.

At some point, I feel a grinding inside me, crawling from its deepest caverns, and I know what's happened, the screw–clamp feeling in my spine. I slip into the bathroom, look in the mirror, and take two breaths. When I shove down my jeans, I see the telltale splotch of brown blood.

Back in the bedroom, I stand in the doorway and see what looks like a lump under my coverlet. A stray pillow, something.

A lump that looks like a person, curled up. A man curled, or a woman.

The nausea leaps up my throat as I step closer. Lifting the coverlet and seeing it there. The searing red of yesterday's biohazard bag, slick and wet in my hands. Its insides leaking out.

Then comes the thump like the pneumatic punch of the lab injector, my skull striking my headboard. My body bolting upright, the orange of the sinking sun at my window.

And I'm awake, the bed shorn of coverlet, of top sheet, of everything.

Pushing myself from the nightmare, I pull my panties down; there is no blood.

There is no bag.

There's only me.

*   *   *

I stumble from my bed into the kitchen, my feet spongy on the carpet. Trying to calm myself, the hammering in my chest. But all I can think of is the bag.

The bag. Filled with dirty Kimwipes, mop heads, shoe covers seamed with blood.

So careful in so many ways, we were so careless about that. Diane sauntering out of the lab with it spilling out of her backpack top, with it practically perched on her shoulder like a parrot.

Diane's question comes humming back to me. The only moment she hesitated, unsure.

Are you worried about the Russian?

Serge.

I'm drinking coffee, three cups of instant, eyeing the clock and wondering where Sunday went. It's already dusk.

No one has called. Not even Diane.

And I can't help myself. I grab my keys.

NOW

The lab always looks like it's glowing at this hour. The pale concrete illuminated by ground lights. Those slit windows like shut eyes, black and lifeless. A puzzle box snapped shut.

I don't see Zell's dirt bike or Juwon's sturdy Nissan. Dr. Severin's grove-green Citroën is nowhere to be found. Alex's car isn't there either, and I can't remember if I saw it earlier. I barely recall what it looks like, only that it was the Quietest Car in All the World. Sometimes he bikes, but the rack is empty. Sometimes he walks. You never know with Alex. Never knew.

It doesn't matter anyway, I remind myself. *He's not going anywhere.*

Heat rises fast under my eyes, and I try to stop it. There's no time for it, no time to give myself over to any feeling at all.

Are you worried about the Russian?

Now I am, Diane. I can't stop thinking about how unlike Serge it was to dump what he thought were animal carcasses in the bin when the policy was freezing and then special pickup or incineration. Might he have gone back for the bag?

This is Serge, after all, who cares deeply about the rules,

about the order of the lab, at least his portion of it. The way he walks through the vivarium, headphones on, tending to his flock, like a bygone aristocrat strolling through his private gardens. Even when he must take the green-tagged mice to the carbon dioxide machine, he is so gentle and always gives them the iso first, sliding the needle into each one's still-beating heart, no bigger than a kidney bean. Especially then.

You alone understand the heart—that's what Serge told me once, watching me scruff one of the mice and insert a needle into its tiny, bean-size ticker. *The others are made of darker material.*

But maybe that tenderness he reserves only for lab mice, his lab mice. Not dark, slippery rodents from the Chinese restaurant across the street, which can be tossed in the bin like he'd tossed the others through the incinerator door.

Or maybe, when he took the bag, he was too entranced with Diane to care. There was that way he was looking at her. So intently, those long-lashed eyes blinking slowly.

But I'm not sure. I'm not sure at all. Thinking of the bag sitting in that bin—do you see?

What if Serge went back for it? What if he looked inside?

Are you worried about the Russian?

She poured the poison in my ear and now I am inflamed.

Cameras are everywhere. They always are when your job is to flatten animals on tables, punch toxins deep inside. There have been protests, occasional vandalism.

There's one in the lobby. Several in the parking lot.

And there's a camera on the loading dock by the heavy iron door, which is where I'm heading. The tidy row of biohazard bins, those red stumps, their sides stamped with spiky symbols. Sharps, human fluids, liquid waste, mixed chemicals.

If I stay close enough to the right wall, the camera won't find me.

Walking quickly, my arm scraping against the concrete, I arrive at the first bin, SOLID WASTE, the one that counts. I put my foot on its pedal; its lid pops open, the smell of bleach and plastic. Something else, sweet and strong. It seems to me the creak of the lid rings as loud as cathedral bells on an Easter morning.

Inside, it's empty, gaping red, its molded plastic like bony tonsils.

No soiled and tugged gloves and bench paper, no clotted slides and caking petri dishes, the sealed bags of dark matter tossed daily from labs everywhere. And no large red biohazard bag, puffy with our sins. It's not there.

They're all empty, every one, lids snapping one after the other.

It's not there, the bag.

They picked it up, I tell myself, walking away fast. *It's in the campus incinerator, burning to soot.*

"Hey there!"

The high voice snaps like a rubber band. I stop midstride at the foot of the parking lot. A slender figure flits around one of the concrete pillars and heads toward me.

"I'm sorry!" A pitch of mild panic. "Can I ask you a question?"

For a second, I think it's Maxim's pale, neck-tattooed girlfriend hunting for her workaholic lover again. But this is a younger woman, a tall blonde in a cloud-colored sweater that drifts past her wrists—the kind of sweater you want to touch because it will feel like the ears of a bunny rabbit—and a moss-green scarf and ballet flats, a heavy diamond stud jabbed through each ear.

She approaches tentatively, then more swiftly.

"Oh, thank God," she says. "You're not Ted Bundy."

I blink twice. "Pardon?"

"Sorry," she says. "Isn't Ted Bundy the one who prowled campuses, killing coeds?"

"Don't they all kill coeds?"

She smiles, a nervous smile, the smile of someone who's unused to being nervous. "Do you work in there? The lab?"

"Sorry," I say. "Students can't get in here on the weekends without an access card."

"Oh, I'm not a student," she says. "My fiancé works here."

I look at her. She's gripping her phone in her hand, her fingers red and tight.

"We had plans, and, well..." She can't stop smiling, color soaring up her face. "I feel silly. I'm not that kind of fiancée."

"What kind?"

"The kind who shows up at his job," she says, showing more of her fine orthodontal work. "It's just that he isn't answering his phone. We were supposed to meet hours ago."

The evening wind is whipping around the building now, our heads ducking beneath its shade fins. Up close, I see she's maybe twenty-two with that kind of milky skin where any bit of pressure, any touch shows, blooming pink. I'm imagining art-gallery assistant, business-school student, fashion marketing.

"Who's your fiancé?" My mouth is dry; my eyes too. My ankles tickle as if still speckled with blood.

She smiles again, a dimple emerging. "Alex Shaffer. He works in the Severin Lab. Maybe you know him?"

I pause, and, for a pulled-loose second, the wind cocooning us, I think I can hear both our hearts beating, hers like a little sparrow caught in a chimney, mine like an earthworm's, wrapped around its own throat.

"Alex, sure."

Her long sweater sleeve slides back as she reaches for her phone. That's when I see the ring, its diamond fat and insistent.

"He left for work so early, part of me was afraid he was hit by a diesel truck or something. And what's your name? He doesn't talk much about the people at the lab. Except the Dragon Lady."

"Dragon Lady?" I say, jaw tightening. "You mean Dr. Severin."

She grins. "Sorry. That's what he calls her. Alex is, you know—he doesn't stand on ceremony."

"Well, he's probably just caught up in something," I say. "I'd let you in, but I don't have my card."

"Oh," she says, shoulders dropping slightly, her magnificent teeth disappearing. "So why are you here?"

"Just heading to the library," I say. "You should go home."

She nods, wilting further. A buttercup. For all her height, those long legs, and those long, bolt-bright locks, that's what she is.

An impossible mix of feelings floats through me.

"I guess you're right," she says, sliding her phone into her pocket at last. "What's your name again? I'm Eleanor."

"You know what, Eleanor?" I say, not answering, swinging my backpack over my shoulder. "I bet he's on his way home now."

At home, I lie in the bath for an hour, adding hot water every fifteen minutes.

A fiancée. A fiancée.

Ms. Owens, you can see how this looks. That's what the police would say, wouldn't they? *You have your rendezvous with Shaffer, then—what, you found out he was engaged? Or did you know all along, demand he break it off?*

But that's only if they find out about Alex and me. And no one knows about that. Well, two people. One is dead. The other is Diane.

*   *   *

I turn on my phone for the first time in hours, fingers shaking. But there are still no calls, no panicky voice mails, no lab text alerts.

But there is an e-mail. It's from Dr. Severin, who has never e-mailed me, ever. It says:

Make sure you're in by nine tomorrow. We need to get started.

(Yes, that's a hint.)

Maybe it's a moment of relief from the shock and tremors of the last two days, maybe it's the churn and froth of last night's beer still roiling through me, or maybe it's the eternal mystery of the neurons firing scattershot in my head, but I can't help but feel something lift inside of me.

I may be smiling, just for a minute. A long, long amoral minute.

All my life, I've only seen as much as a keyhole allows, side glances, small corners of something larger, some massive vision. But Dr. Severin—whose brain is immense and, it seems to me, very beautiful; no, sublime, beyond my reckoning—is able to see things I long to see, overarching networks, grand symphonies of the body, the brain, the genes, and the blood. Reproductive hormones and serotonin, stress hormones and neurotransmitters. The whole rickety biological pathophysiology of our women. The PMDD women, maybe all women. She sees the dangerous relays in the suffering body. She understands the mad pulses of the blood.

But to understand, you need to see so much more. Because everything affects everything else. One small speck in one narrow recess and everything else is dark with its shadow. And working with Dr. Severin, I know I'll see it all. And I'll be a part of the grander seeing, the illumination of darkness.

The hand outstretched to all those women in the shadows. *Come with me, come, come.*

Dr. Severin beckoning me so that we both may beckon them.

And I think of my mom and one of our last conversations, in the dusty hospice room, the skin under her fingernails darkening.

I always knew you could do important things, big things. Anything at all. I always knew.

I just wasn't sure you did.

Mom, I didn't know. But now I do. And Mom, I can do this. I can. I can I can I can.

THEN

"This is Monday morning, May the eighth, and you will be taking the AP Chemistry exam. You may now remove the shrink-wrap from your exam packet and take out the section one booklet, but do not open the booklet or the shrink-wrapped section two materials. Put the white seals aside..."

The gym, waxed and silent, high windows streaked with dirt, and it was like we were all afraid to speak, to move, to turn our heads.

The proctor, a man with short furred arms and a thick wrist-watch, spoke from a script and examined all our calculators.

Diane's hair was shining. She didn't turn around, but I noticed an odd odor from her. Something earthy, even animal.

"Now you may open section one and begin."

The page was momentarily mysterious and then, in a flash, completely familiar. My pencil felt hot under my fingers and then began moving. And once it started, it never stopped.

There was nothing but a roar, and then a blur.

Everything else—the room, the teacher, the pressure, the way my left sock was sinking into my sneaker, the grunt and sputter from a tree-removal truck idling in the parking lot outside—disappeared.

Because, immediately and then ever after, my mind was doing things. Like up there in my head, I was pushing through overgrowth and far reaches of cheatgrass and hoary knapweed, and those reaches stretched themselves to points and the points became spears, and the spears were in my hands, and nothing could stop me.

Something had happened. Something was firing inside me now, and nothing could stop me.

Ever since Diane had told me, I'd been lost, a lost soul floating, but suddenly I felt myself again. In an instant, I was back and I didn't need her. I didn't need her gentle nudges, her shining example, to fire my ambitions. Maybe, I told myself, I never needed her at all.

After I finished the exam, long before anyone else—three hours, which was three minutes, so much blasting through my brain— I walked straight into the girls' room and banged my fists on the sink so hard I split two nails, tearing one loose, a tender pucker slick with blood.

"Goddamn, goddamn," I said under my breath, then louder, then louder, the echo making me feel godlike. "I killed it. I killed that motherfucker." Like my old man used to say whenever he hit his number, waving his five-dollar scratch-off.

Running down the near-empty hallway, running to get outside and kick my legs and run and run and run.

I know things, I know everything. I'm smarter than anyone ever thought I could be. Even with my dad's swiney genes mingling with my mom's kindly ones, from that briny stew of cunning and weakness, I have something important inside me.

Something extraordinary.

When Diane called out after me—*Kit, wait, Kit*—her voice wobbly and plaintive down the long, empty corridor, I didn't turn my head.

That night, my mom made brownies with Kahlua, and we danced to her dad's scratchy Waylon Jennings albums.

It was only very late, coming down at last, the propulsive, fist-pumping, masculine thrust of the day collapsing in on itself as I crawled into bed, that bed, the bed of the blood confession, that I started to feel it all come back on me.

Staring at my split-nail finger, the flesh laid bare like a little baby's tender skin, the spot where the cord stump finally fell free, I thought, *I am not afraid of this, or her.*

And: *I never needed her anyway.*

Then my mom in the doorway today, holding a check in her hand, waving it.

"Will wonders never cease," she said. "Your dad sent you twenty-five bucks for high-school graduation."

"Cash it fast," I said, sitting up. "Cash it today."

The next few weeks, the lurch and panic of final exams, graduation, the acceptance from State. Yes, State would allow me into its ranks, but without funding, it was just a piece of fancy bond paper, a taunt. I still hadn't heard the official decision from the Severin scholarship people, but it seemed impossible. It was Diane's to lose.

"Don't worry about that," my mom kept saying. "City Tech is so happy to have you. You can live here as long as you want. Maybe I could get you a job at the clinic. No more smelling like chicken fat."

Thinking then of all the things my mother sometimes smelled

like, wet dog or hot cat or far worse, those smells she scrubbed so hard to remove they made her hands look like raw hamburger.

"You don't know until you know," Ms. Castro kept saying every time I passed the guidance-counseling office, eyes on the Severin scholarship flyer.

But I did know.

Because there was Diane lurking under the dark scrim, Diane's voice in my ear, a worm wriggling. *I'm taking your scholarship, and leaving you with* this.

Because whenever I paused a moment, whenever I let my imagination overtake me, Diane's confession would reappear, sitting on my chest like a succubus.

In the morning, running, I'd sometimes imagine her chasing me through a thick forest, all the trees with big fat veins blackened from soot, from untold things. Behind me, I could always hear Diane.

The miles-long strides of those colt legs of hers, the slow breathing whirling through my ears. There was no way she would not catch up.

We were matched runners, and she had a will as iron-soldered as her heart.

Her blood ran cold and merciless.

The girl who could do anything.

Who had a rage in her like a bomb in her chest.

Those breaths on my neck now, I readied myself for anything, her arm, a scythe, her perfect doll teeth.

Small but sharp, they'd never stop tearing.

NOW

At five a.m. Monday, my phone clatters like wind-up teeth.

"Have you heard anything?"

"No."

I can almost hear Diane's mouth pressed against her phone. It feels like there's some tunnel made of breath and skin connecting us. An artery blown to life more than a decade ago.

I nearly tell her about going to the lab, opening the bin, about the girl, the fiancée, but I stop myself. *Why*, an animal part of my brain asks, *should I tell her how foolish I am twice over. Alex has a fiancée. How foolish and fooled.*

"We shouldn't be doing this," I say. Which could mean anything but in this case means only talking on the phone.

"Kit," she says finally, "it'll be fine today. Just remember what matters."

What matters, I think.

After I hang up, an ancient phrase from the back of my thoughts floats forward:

You don't have a self until you have a secret.

*   *   *

It's hard to wait, but I need to be sure I'm not first. That I'm not the one to find him.

I sit on the edge of my sofa and drink coffee after coffee, running new water through the old grounds.

It's just after eight thirty when I make my way across the parking lot.

The chug-chug of the soda trucks, the diesel pickups lined up behind the Flying J.

There's a funny feeling in my chest, an odd exhilaration, like the time I finally sat down for my AP Chem exam or when I spent the hour before my oral exams eating a maple glazed at the Donut Hut instead of reviewing my notes. The sense that the dread is about to come to an end and no matter what happens, at least the dread will be past.

My access card in hand once more, I push through the building's heavy front doors at eight fifty. Past the security guard with the intricate braid snaking down her back. Past random gray-hoodied students, past the biohazard bins, into the elevator and up to the fifth floor.

When the doors open, I expect to see something. An agitation, a knot of hysterical researchers, a pair of departmental secretaries with grim faces, phones out.

But I don't see anything, and for a second, I'm worried no one's arrived yet.

My eyes land on G-21 in spite of myself. I expect to see biohazard tape across it, or police tape. The bloody chamber. But there's nothing.

"Caught!" The voice like a drill in my ear. It's Zell in his

Motörhead T-shirt, headphones round his neck, a curl of toothpaste on his lip.

"Look at you," he says. "Slinking in after eight like you're one of us and not Kit Owens, Super Lab Rat."

"I haven't been feeling well."

That's when I see Maxim walking toward the lab rooms, coffee and notebooks balanced expertly. He nods at me as he approaches G-21, and I think, *Please not yet, please not now, I'm not ready.*

"I get it, Owens," Zell is saying as if we are having a conversation. "Why come in early like the good little girl when what's done is done? Severin must've known who she was going to pick on Friday. Making us dangle over the weekend is classic Severin, though. Shiny-shiny, shiny boots of leather."

I watch over Zell's shoulder as Maxim steps into G-21, shuts the door behind him.

Here we go, here we go, ready or not—

Time snaps and unsnaps.

My hand reaches for the wall, knees buckling. I feel my head crack against the baseboard like a busted marble.

"I'm sorry," I say. "I didn't faint. I just..."

The bank of fluorescent lights, acid yellow, flyspecked, shudders into focus.

"*Faint* is a pretty ladylike term for what you just did," says Zell, extending both hands down to me. "You been sniffing toluene again?"

"I haven't eaten," I say, sliding back up the wall on my own. "I..."

My eyes are on the door to G-21 when something flickers in the periphery: the golden bowl of Diane's head as she walks toward us.

"Here," Zell says, hoisting a grease-thick bag of cinnamon-roll holes in front of my face. "Gobble a few of these and get it together."

My eyes shuttle back and forth between Diane approaching and G-21. I'm waiting, and hasn't it been far too long? Shouldn't Maxim have seen—

The door to G-21 shushes open.

My heart folds in on itself as Maxim emerges, head down, looking at his phone.

The door closes, and Diane reappears behind it, her hand dropping from her chest where, momentarily, it must have lain. Her face goes ashen. She pauses a moment, her lab coat around her like moth wings.

"You're gonna eat tile again, aren't you?" Zell says, shaking his soggy sack of holes at me again. "You girls and your diets."

"Get that out of my face," I say, smacking the bag.

"Conference room, folks," Maxim says, approaching us. "Dr. Severin is in the building."

But Zell's gaze has drifted to Diane. She sees him looking and begins walking toward us again, her gait funny now, stilted.

"I gave Alex five-to-one odds that it's her and him on the team," Zell says to me under his breath. "Guys like that never stop winning."

"Where is Alex anyway?" Maxim says, a tsk-tsk lip twitch. "He'd be late to his own funeral."

"Is it time?" Diane asks, reaching us at last.

I look at her and then at the door to G-21. *Maxim was just in there. He was there.* The expression on her face like a child's fright, eyes big and mouth small.

"D-day," says Zell, nodding toward the conference room.

"At last," Diane says, smiling strangely, too widely, showing all of us all her teeth. "Let's get it over with."

*   *   *

The ceiling fan skitters dust, pencil shavings, potato–chip crumbs into the air.

Juwon, who's already staked out the good chair, the one with padded arms that Dr. Irwin donated when he got his Eames, is typing away on his laptop, trying to look busy, unconcerned.

Zell has pushed his headphones back up over his ears, a buzz-saw fuzz escaping into the soundless room.

Maxim is tap-tapping his pen. I can almost hear his anxious thoughts: *I'm the one who's put the most time in with Dr. Severin. All these years, sixty hours a week or more, thousands upon thousands of hours recording cell activity, running gels, tracking supplies, managing the grad students, all for a sad little stipend. Five years ago, I was her darling, her anointed, but then, one after another, came newer, shinier—*

"I can't believe Shaffer is gonna miss this," Zell says loudly, over his music. "Maybe Severin'll change her mind if he can't bother to show up."

Maxim looks at him, clenches his jaw.

Juwon just keeps typing as if we're not there. I wonder if he's typing the same sentence over and over again. The look on his face is like the time someone spilled Mountain Dew all over his cell cultures.

"Why would she pick Alex?" Maxim says. "He's a light-weight."

Zell shrugs, drumming the table with meaty pink fingers. "I heard he has an in."

"Who told you that?" Juwon says abruptly.

"Serge."

My hands knotted, I look over at Diane.

"Well, you know Serge," Maxim says.

"True."

Diane's eyes lift toward mine.

"I'll never catch up with all your lab intrigues," Diane says, so smoothly it makes me think of Dr. Severin. Of how Diane aspires to be like Dr. Severin. The nice shoes, the chic haircut. Except Diane will never, ever be like Dr. Severin. Dr. Severin is cool and Diane is one of those people who appear so cool, icy, but touch the surface once, you'll realize they're aflame.

"Serge is a strong believer in the rules," Maxim explains to Diane.

"He favors compliant souls," Juwon adds.

Diane nods and looks away, her shoulders hunching in a way I haven't seen since high school. *Diane*, I think. *No, Diane.*

Everyone is quiet. There's the distant sound of heels on sealed concrete.

I tuck my feet under the chair's bottom spindle to keep from shaking. There's no chance Maxim could have been in G-21 and not seen everything.

So I must have lost my mind. But Diane lost hers first.

The door claps open, and with it comes a cloud of that perfume she sometimes wears—figs and soft leather.

Unwinding a long, slender scarf with a pair of red lips painted on either end, Severin walks to the table as we all watch, turning our heads one by one.

"Well," she says, the scarf still unwinding, Isadora Duncan–like, until it wafts to the table, its lips pursing at me. "I imagine it was a long weekend for all of you."

No one says anything; a few weak smiles.

"Where's Shaffer?" she asks, surveying us.

Shrugs, silence. I look intensely at my hands folded before me.

"Should I text him?" Maxim, ever helpful, asks, rat-a-tatting his pen again.

"Doesn't matter," she says. Her head swiveling like an exquisite lizard's, she faces Diane, then me. "The PMDD team. It's going to be Fleming." She looks at Diane, who lowers her eyes to the pen in her hand. "And Owens." Her eyes rest on me, dark and crackling. "You two up for it?"

Diane nods, eyes darting to me and back down again. "Yes."

I don't say anything or even blink, but Severin seems not to notice. It wasn't really a question, after all.

The men's gazes are heavy on us. Heavy and pointed, three dull sabers to our chests. They would be high-fiving if it were them. Crowing and banging tabletops. We don't move or even smile.

"Gentlemen," she says, "Dr. Irwin is very glad to have you join his hypogonadism team. He's just received pharma funding for the oral-testosterone piece." She pauses. Is there a whisper of a smile there? "Heady stuff."

Juwon nods without looking up from his laptop. Zell nods too, twisting an old brown Band-Aid on his thumb.

"Glad to help wherever needed," Maxim says, tossing his pen onto the table, the closest he's ever come to showing disappointment.

My fingers press hard into the heel of my hand.

"Dr. Severin," Diane says, turning to me, "we won't let you down."

Severin swishes a pair of forms across the table at us.

"I would be surprised if you did."

After, Juwon snaps his laptop shut and leaves without a word. Maxim is watching me but says nothing, fingers now tapping on his phone.

"Well, hell," Zell says. "I guess Shaffer missed his shot." Walking past me, he palms the top of my head, his hand hot. "Lucky you, Owens."

Diane is watching.

Whatever's in her eyes, he sees it and drops his hand to his side.

"Hey, congratulations is all I meant," he says, backing away from us both. "It's gonna be gangbusters. PMDD. Its day has come.

"Blood will tell, right?"

"What happened?" I whisper to Diane, my face nearly on hers at the far end of the hallway. "Maxim was in there."

"We shouldn't be talking here," she says, low and cool, unblinking. She nods to the door and we duck into the stairwell.

"He was dead," I say. "He was deader than dead."

I felt his heart under my hands.

"He's still dead," Diane says. "He was bleeding from his jugular for five minutes, ten minutes. It took us maybe twenty minutes to clean all the blood up. He's not Rasputin."

"Well, he didn't get up and walk away."

She pauses. "Do you think someone else came to the lab?"

"No," I say. "I mean, I don't know."

"We have to wait, then," she says, her eyes on me like we're two of a kind, partners, collaborators. "This is how it works."

She places a hand on my shoulder.

"Don't," I whisper, pulling away, instinctively covering my shoulder. Suddenly, I don't want to be near her or her saint's haircut and her whittled-down body and her silky, insinuating voice. I open the stairwell door and step back into the hallway. "Don't touch me. Never touch me."

The look on her face is stunned and sad.

"I should never have listened to you," I say. "I should've called 911."

She pauses before saying, "Then why didn't you?"

"You know why. The chloroform. I passed out."

But there's a hot flush on me then. A feeling of being stripped clean before the world for an instant. Because it couldn't be only the chloroform, could it? What took me so long to act when it was happening? And after, emerging from my stupor, why didn't I insist? Call myself, despite Diane's protests?

"I...I don't know," I blurt, not meaning to say it aloud. "I don't know why."

"That's how it was for me too."

"For *you*?" I say. "Diane, we're not the same. I didn't push the glass into Alex's throat. *I* didn't kill him."

Slowly, she nods. "But somehow," she says, "it still feels the same."

I look at her and have that same feeling I had in my apartment when she started talking about poison. When that razor-sharpness that is Diane's brain, that precision, dulled into something formless, strange.

"There you are," someone says, somewhere. Turning, I see Dr. Severin watching us, head tilted.

"Look at you two," she says. "A study in dark and light."

Diane's face—it's like a sheet has fallen across it.

"Meet me downstairs at noon," she says. "I'm taking my new team to lunch."

I have to blink twice; the whiteness of the lab's clean stainless everything nearly blinds me.

I'm in G-21 for the first time since Saturday. Since I scurried away like a lab rat, trails of blood instead of a tail. Since I watched Alex die.

And there is nothing to see.

Maxim is cleaning glassware at the sink. Juwon sits at his lab bench, laptop open again. I think I spot his CV on the screen.

Walking briskly to my station, I let my eyes drop to the floor. The spot where, forty-eight hours ago, Alex lay split open—a deer ready for dressing, limbs still twitching but dead as earth—now gleams bare. It is as clean as a car showroom, as my mom's slop-mopped kitchen floor.

As if reading my mind, Maxim looks over at Alex's bench.

"Did anyone call Shaffer?" he asks.

Zell and Juwon both look at me. It reminds me of when Zell came upon Alex and me in the lounge a few weeks ago. We were laughing, our heads bent over our ramen. Later, Zell teased me about it. *You and your lab husband, canoodling over your noodles.*

"I can call him," I say, taking my phone from my pocket. And then I begin a ridiculous charade: pushing his number, holding the phone to my face, which still feels hot and throbbing, waiting for the outgoing message.

"It's just voice mail," I say. This ridiculous dumb show.

I listen: *Hey, you've reached Alex, which is me . . . I guess that's it, right?* Slightly stuttery and that quality he had, so it always sounded like he was smiling when he talked.

I hear it and I hear him, and I can feel a tug of something dragging me to a place I don't want to go. Juwon is looking up from his computer, and Maxim is watching me, head cocked. Zell, headphones on, purses his lips. The phone is wet in my hand.

"Hi, Alex," I say into the phone, my own voice tinny. Like a recording of my own voice. "It's Kit. We're just wondering where you are. You know."

There's a long second where I can't seem to unstick myself. To push the button, to end the call. I can almost hear, like the old answering machines, a great and horrible tape whir.

"So call us, okay?"

As I move the phone from my face, my jaw aches.

The door opens and Diane steps into the room with another woman.

I let my arm drop and look at the two of them. The two elegant blondes. Diane, with her eyes blue and glittering, and Eleanor, Alex's fiancée, her pink face like a corsage, crushed.

I almost don't recognize her. Gone is the deft, levelheaded young woman I met last night. Instead, she's crying, weeping openly, the sleeves of her sweater—pale green today—wilting over her long fingers. Weeping long tears like a drowning Ophelia, the glassy stream, her muddy descent.

Diane has one hand floating a few inches above the girl's shoulders, but she doesn't touch her. Diane never touches anybody but me.

"I can't find him anywhere," Eleanor says. "It's just—he's gone."

We all surround her, but at a distance.

"You," Eleanor says, her face lifting, eyes like great gray puddles, "you're the one I saw on Saturday."

Everyone turns to look at me.

"Yeah," I say, "on my way to the library."

"Kit and Alex are pals," Zell offers, a whiff of provocation in his eyes. Even more provocation than usual. "Joined at the hip."

"What does that have to do with anything?" I say, too abruptly. He looks at me, twirling his fingers around the soft cushions of his headphones.

"He was here in the morning, at least," Diane says, calm but forceful, nearly stepping in front of me. "Working."

"That's right," I say. "He was still here when we left."

Zell's eyebrows lift and Juwon folds his arms. "We?"

"Kit gave me a tour of the town," Diane says.

"The Walmart or the Sav-a-Lot?" Zell asks.

Eleanor looks back and forth at all of us, her chin trembling slightly in a way that moves me. How does a sweet girl like this—a New England blonde, fisherman's sweaters and golden Labs, the kind with adoring parents and grandparents and nice jobs in nice offices where all anyone wanted from her was her winning smile, fine manners, and untroubled efficiency—end up in our wolves' den?

Our *nest of vipers,* as Alex called it.

Zell smiles at her, twirling his headphones across his knuckles like a card trick.

"I'll take you to the administrative offices," Maxim says. "They can help. If he was here over the weekend, they'll be able to confirm it."

"Did you know?" Diane asks me under her breath, standing close to me over the sink, our glassware clanking.

"Know what?" I say briskly.

"About the girlfriend."

"The fiancée, you mean." I turn the water on harder. "No."

Diane nods carefully and says nothing. But I feel some kind of judgment passing across me like a dark tide. Diane, who seemed never to have had a sexual urge in her life. Once, I used to think of her as a Barbie, and now I wonder if, like a Barbie, there is a smooth spot between her legs instead of a vulva.

She doesn't say any more and I don't say any more. I'm remembering something.

Years ago, back in high school, I'd told Diane about the first time I ever made out with a grown man, not a boy. Stevie Shoes. I'd been dog-sitting his bloodhounds so I knew he had a girlfriend. Her clothes were all over the house, gold-ringed sandals on the patio, filmy aqua panties hanging in the laundry room where the dog food was kept. One night we got to talking and he told me all about his failures as a husband, a dad. How his little boy drew a picture of his family that made him look like the ice king from his favorite cartoon. That was before I ended up making out with him, doing things with him in his car. I can still remember the smell of the detergent on his jeans, how the scar groove on his forehead pressed against my thigh.

It just sounded so awful, Diane had said. It made her *never want to do anything like that, ever.*

Ilene, Dr. Severin's lab administrator, pages through my grant paperwork with grim precision.

Behind her, Dr. Severin's office looks dark through the marbled glass, but that's not always a sign. Sometimes she meets with graduate students without turning on the light. We think she does it as some kind of test. Do they dare to suggest the setting sun has shrouded the room in eerie darkness? Dare to reach over and snap on the desk lamp or rise and turn on the sizzling overheads?

No one has yet.

"Are we supposed to meet her here?" I ask, my voice low. "For lunch?"

Ilene does not reply, merely continues to count, collate, and double-check. Ilene is humorless in a way we all find very humorous. Her hair swept into a perfect chignon—a Hitchcock-blonde chignon, only brunette—her nails always meticulous half-moons, she is as severe as her boss, and, in place of Dr. Severin's skunk streak, there's a distinctive beauty mark on her cheekbone, like Serena on *Bewitched*.

For a second, I think I see a shadow behind the glass, a dark thing.

"Is someone in there?" I ask. "With her?" I wonder if it's Eleanor, the fiancée.

Still sorting through papers on her desk, Ilene looks up at me from under the thick velvet rim of her perfectly shaped hair.

"You didn't sign this one," she says, pushing a paper at me.

While I sign it, I see something flickering on her computer screen. An open document with a dateline and a headline: *Severin Lab Awarded Major NIH Grant for "Potentially Groundbreaking" New Study Aimed at Severe PMS.*

I'm trying not to stare.

Dr. Severin will collaborate on the two-year, renewable study with Dr. Harkness (neuropsychiatry) as well as her own team members, including . . .

And if I squint, I can see my own bullet point, my own name. Boldface, all caps.

KIT OWENS

And Diane's, of course.

"Is that a press release?" I ask, not even caring how foolish I sound to Ilene, who finds nearly anything any of us ask about foolish and, *quite frankly, not your affair.*

"It is a press release," she says, sliding my papers into her file folder and capping her pen. "You're done."

My name. Mine.

With the same brisk movements of her boss, Ilene rises and strides into the copier room, but I linger. On the desk, I see the new file folder: FLEMING, DIANE.

So I open it. Look inside.

There's a personnel form, several long co-authored articles, sparkling letters of recommendation, a research proposal; my fingers dance quickly through all of it. The curriculum vitae, though, is the star.

I try not to think of my modest twelve-page CV, toner low, content limited, its staple crooked.

Even printed double-sided on copier paper, Diane's feels substantial. Turning the pages, I wonder at it, its heft and ballast.

The steady drone of Ilene's copier behind me, I can't help but look more closely. Just a quick scan—overseas conferences, Phi Beta everything, more laurels than I can count.

But then, flipping the pages, I stop. Because I see the name *Severin*.

It appears in one item of a half a dozen under the heading "Internships."

Severin Summer Program, June–August.

The date is eight, nearly nine years ago, back when Dr. Severin had her old, smaller lab. Back when Diane and I were both finishing our bachelor's degrees.

I have to read it twice and even then, the letters blurring, I doubt myself.

But it's there.

The hum of the copier ceases and Ilene appears, swooping around me, snapping the papers from my hand, and giving me the same look Serge used to give Alex when he meandered around the vivarium asking questions loudly and jostling the cages.

"I was just curious," I tell her. "Sorry."

Ilene does not reply, or even look up.

Diane and Dr. Severin, they have a history, those two.

But Diane hasn't told me. And Dr. Severin never said.

Didn't I somehow know anyway? Didn't I feel the closeness there, hovering?

In the end, my mom always said, *there's only you.*

Walking through the parking lot, I see them. Black head, blond head. Both in their trench coats, swaying in the breeze as they stand by Dr. Severin's car.

"Hey," I call out.

Both heads turn.

"There she is," says Dr. Severin.

A cigarette in her dark mouth, she opens her car door. Invites me in.

NOW

The perversity of woman is so great as to be incredible even to its victims.

I remember that quote from college. The great philosopher Caro. Deep in the stacks of the State U. library, I found it in a dust-gilded book from the nineteenth century, its leather slipping from its cover like old skin. *Sexual Aberrations in the Criminal Female.*

It was filled with revelations. For instance, the most intelligent female criminals favor poison. And the blame for women's crimes must sit squarely on the shoulders of their mothers. *Want of maternal affection,* he called it.

But what I remember most is the story of an epileptic tattooed prostitute who murdered her lover, then embroidered his epaulets on her own shirt, declared herself "chieftainess of the brigands," and terrorized her small Italian town.

Women have always been far less violent than men, the author conceded. *The facts speak for themselves.*

But why, then, he asked, *are women so much more ferocious in their violence?*

It has always seemed to me that the answer lies in the question.

*   *   *

Here we are, snug in a corner booth. It's a restaurant like in old paintings, crimson-flocked wallpaper, heavy drapery with dustless fringe. Round, red booths like tight cherries and pristine white tablecloths with napkins so heavy they feel like a psalm book across your lap. And no sound from outside or anywhere. That must be the thing when you have money, I think. You never have to hear anything you don't want to, ever.

Across the table, Diane is asking smart-girl questions in her low voice. About the first round of study participants, about which of the neuros will be participating and did she see the article on brain-derived neurotrophic factor and stress paradigms in the latest *Biological Psychiatry*?

"Look at you. Straight out of the gate," Dr. Severin says, smiling and not answering any of the questions. "We won't waste your time like Freudlinger did. Is he still hot on the ASR?"

"We used it on his cocaine study," Diane replies. "But only with animals."

"Giving foot shocks to rats," Severin says, raising one long hand for the waiter. "Sounds like Freudlinger."

I sit there, mindlessly flipping the pages of the thick, bound menu, *crêpes Suzette* and *chicken à la champagne* and *iced cracked crab*. The hushed room, the passing waiters in their black waistcoats and glossy black shoes. I keep thinking about Diane's internship with Dr. Severin, what it means. Maybe nothing. Maybe not.

At the next table, a trio of white-haired businessmen are hunched over steaks quivering on their plates. Instead of sawing, all of them seem to stroke the meat toward themselves, never switching hands, never scraping the plate, never doing anything I'd need to do to make eating happen.

219

Their plates pooled red.

It makes me think of when I was little, my dad had that job selling watermelon at the county fair. He'd dig a chunk out to show passersby how red its meat was. *Plugging,* he called it. *Tender as a . . . well, you know,* he'd say to the men, and I'd always ask him, *Tender as what? As what?*

Tender as your mama's heart. He'd wink.

"I have to wash my hands," I say abruptly, rising.

Diane and Dr. Severin look at me, surprised.

At the gilt-rimmed sink in the ladies' room, I run the hot water over my hands. A sweet-smelling older woman stands in front of a gold-rimmed tray of colored tonics, lotions, mouthwash, tampons stacked like cigarettes. When I turn the water off, she gives me a hand towel, soft as a baby blanket. It smells like lilac.

I stand there another minute, drying my hands laboriously, and the woman never says anything but never stops looking at me. I have a feeling she knows all about me.

I peer into the dining room, my hand holding back the tasseled curtain.

You couldn't miss them, Diane's golden hair and Dr. Severin's sable black, skunk-striped. Diane's head is down, and Dr. Severin is speaking to her, her wine-colored lips dancing.

There is, between them, a feeling of something I can't put my finger on. Neither one is smiling and Diane lifts her hand to her neck, a nervous gesture I remember from long ago, her hand always to her throat, her earring, her necklace clasp.

There is definitely something between them. Something I don't have with Dr. Severin.

I walk toward them, soundless on the thick tongue of carpet.

They are chatting, both looking intermittently in my direction.

What lies behind two such expert poker faces? I wonder. For different reasons, for reasons professional or emotional, they likely have spent most or all of their lives wearing masks, cool and aloof and impenetrable. It serves them in the lab, in the research community, in our profession. It serves them, period.

Not me. Not me.

"Did I miss anything?" I say, too loudly, tugging back my chair, where I find my napkin tidily refolded into a perfect seashell shape.

I look up, both sets of long-lashed eyes blinking at me.

"No," Diane says. "Just talking about the study protocol."

"You'll get up to speed fast," I say, sitting down, determined. "After all, you've worked with Dr. Severin before."

Neither one flinches.

"Yes," Dr. Severin says, turning to Diane. "When was that?"

"Years ago," Diane replies. She looks at me. "But I didn't work with her. It was just an internship. Dr. Severin was gone most of the summer. I just did scut work for the grad students."

"But you remembered her," I say to Dr. Severin. Bold—I, who've never had a conversation with Dr. Severin lasting longer than three minutes that didn't involve supply orders or lab data. "All this time later."

"I'd like to say it was my keen foresight and elephant memory rather than the petty desire to pillage Dr. Freudlinger's finest booty." She pauses. Then: "In fact, why not say that?"

Dr. Severin lifts her hand for the waiter.

"And you, Kit," Diane says softly. "You have a history too. You were one of Dr. Severin's scholarship recipients."

Hearing her say it aloud feels strange. I wonder if Dr. Severin knows Diane and I were competitors. What a tangled history we all have with one another, knots upon knots.

"I just got lucky," I say.

"You both had very strong reports," Dr. Severin says, opening her menu. "And I'll tell you both something: Banish the *just*s from the way you speak about yourself. It's tedious and not productive."

"I'm sure Kit was very deserving," Diane says, looking at me.

Dr. Severin looks at me too, as if waiting.

"I was," I say, firmly. Then, even more firmly: "I really was deserving."

Saying it out loud, and seeing the look of satisfaction on Dr. Severin's face, it changes things. It gives me a burst in the chest. It is maybe the greatest feeling I've ever known.

And then, as if on cue, champagne arrives in a dewy bucket, for-real French champagne in a sleek black bottle, and Dr. Severin leans back, looking first at Diane and then at me.

"Do you two know why I brought you here?" she asks.

Then we must wait as the waiter pours champagne into glasses shaped like long tulips.

"I'm the daughter of two agrochemists," she says. "I've been working in labs since I was twelve years old. I've lived a long time in that world, the world of oil and commerce, and in this one. The world of scientific discovery and, well, commerce. And I've been hustling for my work for going on two decades, the last hooker in the hotel lobby every night.

"So I can tell you this: It's important to honor these moments, because they are few."

She lifts her glass. We follow suit.

"This is the beginning for both of you. A grand beginning. And for me, the culmination of so much."

She leans that dark, shimmering head of hers back and takes a long sip. Again, we follow suit.

She looks at us both, her eyebrows so immaculately arched, her lips so dark, she reminds me, fleetingly, of the queen in *Snow White*. Except Diane and I are the ones with the poison apple in our hands.

"And you two didn't get this because you're women," she says. "You didn't get this because of institutional politics, or optics, or because you bleed every month, because of *pussies* and *tits*—"

Heads turn slightly at the table beside us.

"Or whatever any of the less competent boys might say behind your back or in the lounge when they think we can't hear."

It is nearly impossible for me to imagine any of our group, even Zell, saying *pussies* or *tits,* but it makes me wonder how it was for Dr. Severin twenty years ago.

"And you didn't get this because you work longer hours than anyone else or play by the rules or can be counted on to do the grunt work or clean up your lab bench immediately and maybe your neighbor's too."

Diane has her eyes on her hands, folded. She is nodding and her face is trembling.

"You got this because I wanted you. No. Scratch that. I wanted your brains. Young and fat and juicy. I intend to feed off them mercilessly. So, in the coming months, plug your ears to all the rest. Including any voices in your own noisy heads."

She looks at us, then adds, "You must never be fearful when what you're doing is right."

Both Diane and I nod. Those words. Marie Curie.

The champagne hums madly inside me. All around the room, the dark suits and bobbing white heads of white men.

"Because this," she says, pressing one manicured finger on the tablecloth, freshly scraped clean with a thin silver wand by the waiter, "what we're doing, what I'm doing, will *make* you."

She lifts her glass. "And I'd hate for you to blow it."

She turns from me to Diane and back again. "Got it?"

Then she leans back, spreading her arms across the booth in a way that reminds me of the way John Wayne, in old movies, would lean against a corral, rifle balanced on his shoulders.

I can't deny that I desired her in that moment. Anyone would have.

By the time our entrées—some kind of diaphanous butter-swirled fish—are cleared, everything is glinting pinkly before me. A future grand and limitless. I can see myself, age forty-five or even older, with my own lab, a windowed office overlooking a warren of benches. There I am in chic eyewear and a sharp-shouldered blazer, leaning back in my Italian leather work chair, observing my team of grad students and postdocs buzzing silently below, leaning over centrifuges and chromatographs.

It's amazing, the brain, isn't it? What it can do? How we can make ourselves forget anything? Because in that moment, three glasses of champagne and the sun-struck pleasure of Dr. Severin's delicious forecast of a life of professional achievement and acclaim, I forget everything. I forget the blood and the chaos and Diane's slithering return even as she sits across from me, and I even forget my mom being gone, her body having sunk slowly and then suddenly into her hospital bed like a beautiful ghost.

"Get ready for the inane questions once this goes public," Dr. Severin says, holding her empty champagne glass up to the light as if looking for a spot. "Everyone will ask you why you chose to study PMDD. And you will tell them how underfunded research into women's conditions is. You will tell them there are five times as many studies on erectile dysfunction as on PMS and that you're happy to play a role in changing that."

"Is that why you do it?" I say, my voice slipping out like warm balm, like we are best friends day-drinking, spilling secrets.

Dr. Severin pulls a small pack of cigarettes from her purse, removes one—short and wide like Frenchwomen smoke in movies. Though I'm sure it's not permitted, no one stops her.

She fumbles in her purse for a light. I nudge the candle between us toward her. That flicker of a smile as she bends down to light her smoke.

For a moment, I think she isn't going to answer my question, which wouldn't be unlike her.

Leaning back, she runs a few fingers through her dark hair.

"My mother was a very, very brilliant and difficult woman. The only female chemist wherever she went, and consumed by disappointment. She always used to say she'd be better off in the Soviet Union, where forty percent of chemistry doctorates were awarded to women. No one would hire her, especially—as was always made clear—once she became pregnant with me. Then, at last, she won a position at a plastics lab. I was in second grade and it was the only time I ever remember her laughing from happiness. She bought a new hat for her first day." Dr. Severin smiles, wryly. "Sunshine yellow, with a wide brim. After school, I rode my bike all the way to the lab, four miles, to see her finally in her rightful place.

"But when I got there, no one in the office seemed to know who I was talking about. They kept saying, 'There's no Dr. Severin here, go home to Mama.' At last, a filing clerk overheard. 'She means Marina,' she said, pointing me down the hall. And that was where I saw her. My mother, scrubbing beakers, loading them into a sterilizer in the washroom."

Diane and I look at each other.

"What did you do?" I ask.

"The only thing one could. The only thing she'd have wanted. I snuck out the back way before she could see me. And never mentioned it once." Severin taps her cigarette onto her china plate. "She worked there for years. Laid off during cost-cutting in the eighties. Lab aides are always the first to go."

I take a breath. Such an intimate confidence, and she's shared it so freely. Because we are close now, I think, taking one last sip of the last of my champagne, the bottle upturned in the bucket. We are close because we are embarking on this monumental project together.

But Diane is not even looking up. Staring at her hands folded before her—those red hands of hers, like the rough husk of a pomegranate—she does not appear moved or struck or anything. It makes me think she already knew this, though I can't hold on to the thought, the champagne fizzing in my head and Dr. Severin mashing her cigarette onto the plate with a great flourish.

"But I would never tell anyone that," Dr. Severin adds, leaning forward once more. She smiles ruefully. "You can never tell a man or he'll think, *Ah! That's what drives her. And that's a way to weaken her.*"

She pauses and I wonder if she's a little drunk too.

"Many of these men, and the women too, sometimes even more so, would like to use your heart against you," she says. "They think it's a ticking time bomb in your chest, waiting to explode."

"Maybe it is," Diane blurts out. I look at her.

Severin smiles. "Maybe that's our strength."

And with that, a small tray arrives with a trio of petite amber glasses, each barely more than a thimble. The waiter does not blink at the crushed cigarette on the fine china.

"Ladies," Dr. Severin says, "one final toast before we get to work. The real work. Harder work than you have ever known."

She lifts a glass and gestures to us to do the same, one hand opening and closing as if performing a magic trick: *Your future is under one of these two hands. Choose carefully!*

Leaning forward, her face lit by the candle, she grins at us.

"Remember this," she says, glowing, her skin golden and life-marked, "you will have to fight your entire life. And that's why you'll always be better. Because you wanted it so much more."

We both nod and we all lift our glasses and knock them back.

Whatever's inside tastes like a Red Delicious, both tart and very sweet, and it goes right down.

You will have to fight your entire life.

It's the champagne, Dr. Severin's sonorous voice, the amniotic warmth of our high-walled booth. For a half hour, the past two days seem to disappear.

My future unfurling like a great golden spool as Dr. Severin speaks. The three of us achieving a breakthrough, changing lives, grinding our heels hard into the thick earth of history.

It could happen. I feel it now, and the rest doesn't even seem real. This is real.

My head is so full of plans that it seems aflame. Marie Curie working furiously, ceaselessly, radium tubes glowing in her dress pockets, slowly killing her. She would not be stopped.

Both Diane and Dr. Severin look at me and I realize I've said it aloud.

Dr. Severin taps the side of the empty champagne bottle and winks.

We're gathering our purses, our coats, when Dr. Severin's phone buzzes. Then buzzes again, and again.

"Well," Dr. Severin says, looking at it, "interesting."

Diane and I both stop.

"This business with Shaffer, who's gone rogue—the security log shows he was in the lab on Saturday. Arrived at six thirty a.m."

"Yes," Diane says. "We saw him."

Dr. Severin's eyebrows lift. "Really? Both of you?"

"Yes," I say, hard and quick. "On our way out. Diane wanted a tour."

Dr. Severin glances at her phone once more. "The fiancée's not going to like this."

"What?" I say, my voice like a cough. "What won't she like?"

We both look at Severin expectantly.

"The log says he left at nine thirty-six a.m.," she says. Diane's head jerks ever so slightly. "When did you two see him?"

"Nine," Diane says quickly. "Around nine."

"Did he say anything about leaving soon?"

"No," I say. "He didn't."

"This girl, this Eleanor," Dr. Severin says, shaking her head, "is apparently the take-charge type. She's contacted the police."

I look at Diane, who quickly looks away.

Dr. Severin shrugs. "If there's something to be found, campus security has eyes everywhere."

She slides on her trench coat. Neither Diane nor I can manage to say anything, the silence awkward, unbearable. Severin turns to me. "Kit," she says, "you were friends with Shaffer?"

I pause, jacket half on, my hand resting on the white tablecloth. "No. Yes. I mean, lab friends, sure."

"Did he have a wandering eye?"

"Pardon?"

"You know," she says. "Maybe he's ducking the ball and chain?"

"I don't think so," I say.

Dr. Severin, eyes on me, pulls her trench-coat belt taut.

"I mean, maybe," I amend. "Aren't they all?"

"Clever girl."

As we walk away, my eye catches Dr. Severin's napkin on her chair, oxblood lips smiling at the fold.

Walking from Dr. Severin's green Citroën, battered and unbearably cool, to the lab, I have the fleeting notion that the police will be waiting, a ring of uniformed and plainclothes cops, batons in hand.

Then a darker thought strikes: It'll be Alex himself who's waiting, a thick bandage tied rakishly around his ruined throat and that crooked smile aimed straight at me. Milky coffee in his outstretched hand. A niggling, irrational fear scratching in the back of my brain: Is it possible that Alex didn't die? That his heart leaped to life again and he rose, cleaned up his own blood, walked out the front door, and disappeared?

"We need to talk," Diane whispers as we go in the building.

"Why didn't you tell me you knew Dr. Severin from before?" I say, pushing the elevator button.

Diane looks at me. "But Kit, you never told her you knew me from before."

I don't say anything, watching the lit numbers: *1, 2, 3, 4.*

It never crossed my mind to tell. Alex was the only one and it was a mistake. Telling meant something, seemed to suggest something. That me and Diane came from the same place, shared things.

In the elevator doors' reflection, I catch a glimpse of myself, small and crouched.

"Does she know about us?" I ask. "Does she know about you?"

"No," Diane says, her face paler than ever. In the door's reflection, she is a ghostly smudge stretched. "She can't ever find out. If anyone else found out, I would—"

The doors jolt open to the busy hallway and a swarm of grad students, backpacks heavy as infantry rucksacks, enter.

We are swallowed.

THEN

My mom pressed her best dress, sky blue—a*zure,* she said—and sat near the front, clapping and clapping, her eyes bright as streamers.

Almost like she was trying too hard.

It was Senior Achievement Night, and I'd already stepped onto the stage four times—for chem honors, for calculus, for National Honor Society, for the yearbook.

Each time I set my jelly sandals—the same ones my mom threatened to throw into the bushes after my wayward night with Lou and Jimmy and all the beers—onto the shiny wood lip of the stage, I felt sure it would be the end. I can't explain it. I felt sure that it would be the end of me. Some catastrophe unguessed, some pig-blood prank gone to red mayhem. But it just kept going.

"Class salutatorian," cheered Principal Oaks, and that was a special one indeed. There was so much clapping I could barely hear my mom's whistling cheer.

Grave and striking in a long lace dress and pearls against her neck, Diane followed me onto the stage as class valedictorian. She'd already been up there for six, seven, eight other honors, each time returning to a seat beside her grandfather, looking frail in a checked blazer that hung on him, his shirt pressed like for church.

By the time she took the certificate in her long hands, the audience was on its feet. All the clappers seemed to feel this was the climax of a gripping and moving story in which they had played some part.

Settling back in the worn velveteen seat, I watched. Her tasteful pumps, her empty eyes, the shine of her hair, the way she walked, like something unreal and untouchable. Even my mom, fingers looped in mine, seemed to have a choke in her throat somewhere for Diane.

Because—and this was the first time I understood this—everyone always likes the best, wants the most, admires deeply, the girl who's just out of reach. The girl no one can touch, really. We don't know why we're drawn, but it's unstoppable.

I could see it in their faces: *This lovely young girl, so modest and sweet, arrived newly to our town just nine months ago and look what she has done, and we are somehow a part of it. We've given her this. Ah, our special girl.*

"Congratulations, young lady." It was Diane's grandfather, frailer still up close, that blazer of paper-soft linen flapping off his frame. "Diane speaks very highly of you."

He bent slightly at the waist to shake my hand, like an old-time gentleman.

"We're lab partners," I said, feeling myself sweating under my dress. Wishing my mom would get back from the ladies' room. "And we both run cross-country."

A flash of recognition in his watery blue eyes; he said he'd seen me running before, out by the highway.

"And just what are you running from, young miss?" he said, winking.

Suddenly, I was laughing, even though I wasn't sure why exactly.

"And do you know where you'll go to college?" he asked. "You must have your pick."

It was all so normal, and I just started talking about how it'd probably be City Tech right here in Lanister, but they had a Podunk chemistry lab with no gas chromatograph and no spectrophotometer.

"Well," he said, "I bet your mama would like to keep you close."

"Maybe that's what I'm running from," I said, laughing nervously at my own dumb joke.

But Mr. Fleming matched me full-throatedly, as if I were very charming.

And then, before I could stop myself, I kept going, talking about how Diane and I were both waiting to hear about the Severin scholarship, and that would mean I could go to State, and they had a great cross-country team there too.

"Diane's better than me, though," I added.

As if on cue, over his shoulder, I saw Diane approaching us slowly, cautiously.

"At running or science?" he asked, reaching his arm out for Diane.

My eyes on Diane, I lost my words in an instant.

"Two marathoners, either way," he decided, smiling. Diane's eyes on me.

"Well," I said, backing away. "I gotta go." *This*, I thought to myself, *I cannot do*. To stand here with Diane and the father of the father she killed. *This I cannot do.*

"And you, Diane?" he said, turning to his granddaughter with a grin. "What are you running from?"

Diane looked at me, then looked away.

At the reception, Principal Oaks, who'd never said a word to me in four years, pinched my cheeks like you might a prize pig, and Ms. Steen pulled me into a freesia-scented embrace, and Jed Malinkowski, the bushy-haired yearbook editor I kissed once at a ninth-grade party, our foreheads banging, making me see stars, whispered in my ear: *A genius with dimples like cut glass.* And I felt like a star, a special person for the first time. Back then I knew so little.

"Mrs. Owens," Ms. Castro said, "watching Kit bloom this year has been a great joy. We always knew she had it in her."

My mom nodded, smiled, unable to speak, brushing the bangs from my face with trembling fingers.

"And I never said this," Ms. Castro adds, leaning close to my mom, voice low, "but I hope she gets the Severin."

After, we sat in the car for a long time, both of us breathing hard, ragged.

"I didn't really know until tonight," my mom said finally.

"What?"

"How it was. Is. How you are. What you can do."

"Mom," I said, hand out, because I didn't want her to cry.

"Listen to me, honey." But she wasn't looking at me and her jaw was set, locked. "You listen to what I'm going to say now."

"Mom."

"You must do for *you,* okay? That's what matters here. You must do everything you need to for you."

I knew then that even though she couldn't know what Diane

had done, she knew what it all meant, Ms. Castro buzzing in her ear all night.

I didn't say anything. She turned to me, her face dark in the dark car.

"Do you promise me?"

"Okay, Mom."

She made me say it again, and then one more time.

"You're going to be fighting your whole life," she said. "You have to take the chances you've got."

And we were both crying by then, her hands damp on the steering wheel, yet both of us stronger than we had ever been before. Or would be again.

NOW

It's a relief to be away from Diane, to be in a room of men, a lab stuffed with them, and everything so bare and simple and plain, including the openly jealous glares Irwin's postdocs are giving me: *She's one of the chosen ones, the one on the grant five times the size of ours.*

I'm standing at my bench, earbuds in, looking at my cell cultures through the microscope. Behind me, Zell and Maxim are talking. They haven't stopped. They no longer care about work now that the competition has ended, now that they have *lost,* so why not talk?

"So did you see him on Saturday?" Zell asks Maxim. "Don't you usually come in?"

"Not this weekend," he says. "Family wedding."

"So it was just Kit and Shaffer here," Zell says.

I look up. "And Diane," I say. "Don't forget Diane."

Zell nods, lifting his eyebrows. "I never even knew Shaffer had a girlfriend," he says, eyes still on me.

"Fiancée," Maxim corrects. "Knowing Shaffer, she's some big shot's daughter."

I expect it from Zell, but this is new for Maxim. Or is it? I wonder. Now that the team is in place, the mask comes off, and the gloves.

We're a nest of vipers.

I reach down and turn up the music louder, my fingers pressing my earbuds hard into my ears. So hard I can't hear anything but my own neurons firing, like static on an old radio.

There is no hiding in the ladies' room today. When I walk out of the stall, Eleanor is at the sink, touching her face, like she doesn't quite understand what's happened to it. That look of fear, panic. It's as if she's never felt it before.

"Hi."

"Hey," I reply. "I didn't know you were still here."

"I'm not going anywhere," Eleanor says. "Not until I find Alex."

There's a new firmness about her now. And a chilliness.

"Do you have family here? Someone to . . . help?"

"They're back east. It's just me and Alex." She looks at me. "Didn't he ever mention me?"

I turn the water on, glance away from her. Shake my hands dry. "We don't really do that here," I say. "Talk about our home lives."

She nods. "Mano a mano. With an emphasis on *man*."

I pause and then can't stop myself. "Did he talk about us?"

She looks at me distractedly, both of us moving to the door. "A little. Just little things."

"Well, there's not much to—"

"He said you were Dr. Severin's favorite."

I stop. "He did?"

She nods again. "And he told me this story about how you won a car once. Some kind of contest for who could keep their hand on it the longest. You made it something like three days."

"Fifty-six hours," I say. I'd forgotten I'd shared that story with him.

"He told me that said everything about you he needed to know."

I swing open the door, trying not to look her. *A hard worker, a good little worker bee.*

"Well," I say, "last man standing is sometimes a woman."

She tries for a smile. "My lab was the same way. Mano a mano, like I said."

As we step into the hallway, I try to recover. "You're at a lab?"

"Not right now. I'm on fellowship."

"Really?" I say. So much for gallery assistant, jewelry designer, trust-fundee, whatever I'd imagined. "I mean, studying what?"

But Eleanor is distracted, looking up, her eyes catching on one of the mounted cameras. Staring into it. This is something some people do when they visit the lab, so I've gotten used to it. It has to do with all the cameras, the age-specked convex mirrors like bug eyes. The buzzing and sibilance and the slow shimmy-shimmy of centrifuges, the constant hush. All the visitors fear they're being watched. Because they are.

"Theoretical physics," she says finally. "Dark energy."

"Dark energy," I say. "We don't really know what that is, right?"

Eleanor nods, eyes still fixed on the camera. "I had a professor once who called it the bone in our throat. But that's what I like about it. We keep trying and trying, and getting everything wrong."

"All those eyes on the sky," I say, my voice small and breathless. Thinking about the cameras and everything that's been seen and everything that's hidden.

"There's so many questions we try to find answers to. We lead studies, we get these grants, like your grant. All these little steps. But it doesn't really change anything."

"I don't think I agree," I say. "Our grant—"

"But dark energy," Eleanor continues, finally looking at me, eyes glassy, sleepless, "we have to figure that one out." When she talks, I can see the pink inside of her mouth, full of health. "Before it swallows us."

Back in G–21, no one is getting any work done. Diane, now returned, is filling out her paperwork at her bench. If I squint, I can see her pen shaking slightly in her hand. Juwon has been making phone calls in the lounge, even taking one at his own lab bench a few moments ago, his laptop hot and charging.

"He'll have a new job by midnight," Zell says to me, playing with his phone, which keeps making small explosions. "I heard him tell his wife he sure as hell doesn't intend to spend the next two years shooting ferrets full of testosterone to see how long it takes to make their dicks hard."

I've never heard Juwon say anything like that, or even complain once, but now it seems all our masks have fallen, and do I really know any of these guys?

They surely don't know me.

Maxim returns from his supervision meeting with news.

"They looked at the lobby camera from Saturday," he says. "They can't find any footage of him leaving the building."

Juwon shrugs. "That's not that strange. I don't always go through the lobby. Fire exit, loading dock. It's hard to get inside the lab on the weekends, but it's not hard to leave."

This is true. Fire doors are often propped open by smokers. Sometimes, when I'm over in the more lax academic wing, I exit there. Sometimes, following someone else, I don't bother to swipe my card.

"Well, they'll have to look at all the cameras," Maxim says. "But they're pretty old. I suggested last year that they replace them. Some are still coated in dust from the last renovations."

"You see that one in the neuro wing that hangs funny?" Zell asks. "I heard someone bent it so they could have sex in the lab."

I swear, he looks at me as he says it.

"But what do you suppose he's up to?" Maxim wonders. "What reason does a guy like that have to fly the coop?"

"Sidepiece," Zell says. "Old story, ain't it? Weekend sex jag."

Talking hard-boiled, like a pair of skells, rather than two post-docs whose only crime is likely Zell's regularly absconding with Erlenmeyer flasks for his home brew.

Zell grins. "I heard the girlfriend—the fiancée—talking to the head of security. That guy with the mustache that always looks wet."

"Yeah?"

I can feel Diane looking at me now. Watching.

"She went to Alex's apartment. His mail from Saturday was still stuck in the slot. There were still old grounds in the coffeemaker. Everything's untouched."

"Is that supposed to be a sign he's gone?" Juwon says, rolling his eyes. "Three months here, guy hasn't cleaned a beaker yet."

"Well, the fiancée had a lot to say about it, to the guard, to Severin. You could hear her *concerns* all the way down the hall. Guess Shaffer likes a big mouth. Or lungs."

"He's a lung man, yeah."

"Maybe he's one of those guys with two lives," Zell says, practically rubbing his hands. The lab has never been so exciting for him as it is today. "Back in New Haven, my PI got caught banging two underage Russian girls in a parking structure downtown. They found two hundred thousand dollars cash in his trunk. Turned out he'd been selling trade secrets to the Chinese for years. Sneaking antibodies out of the lab at night in Styrofoam containers."

"Is Serge off today?" Juwon asks, ignoring Zell. "I need to see if my new embryos arrived."

It's hard to believe no one's asked about Serge yet, but he's a tech and postdocs don't think of techs until they need their logs, their tail biopsies. Or unless there's mice falling from the ceiling. I look down at my cells, cloudy and maybe contaminated, and pretend not to hear, but blood is roaring through my brain.

"Maybe he and Alex ran away together," Zell says.

"He's at the dentist," I say quietly as Diane passes, heading for the door.

"You mean Serge wasn't Alex's sidepiece?" Zell says, grinning at me. "I wonder who it was, then."

It seems like he's going to say more, but at that moment, Diane drops all her papers onto the floor.

"Sorry," she says as Zell bends over to help her. Maxim does too. I watch them.

"Zell, if any of your Alex theories are true," Maxim says, "it'd be a surprise to me. He doesn't seem half smart enough."

"Yeah," Juwon says, grimmer by the minute. "He's much smarter when he's not here."

Afternoon gives over to evening and everyone scatters. I head for the vivarium wing. Through the windows, I spot two of Serge's techs closing things up for the day. One of them sees me and waves forlornly.

We miss Serge too, he mouths. At least that's what I think he says. He knows how often I make excuses to be here. To follow Serge on his rounds. To sit in the quiet, enjoy the classical music Serge pipes through the cages.

But I'm not there because I miss him. I'm there because of that red biohazard bag, that unfortunate meeting, my ankles stippled with blood.

I picture him in the padded dentist's chair, paper bib and rubber mask. The *shush-shush* of the gas tank, the narcotic haze darkening his dark, dark eyes. Serge, who gently anesthetizes his brood before tail biopsies, or euthanization. I imagine him leaning back into the starry expanse of the nitrous oxide and worrying about his mice, the fleecy legions of them, and even the rats.

It's only when I'm sliding my access card into the elevator again that I hear the low, husky whistle. And, out of the corner of my eye, see him. The dark, slender figure, an aristocratic vampire, or the Cat, as Alex dubbed him.

"Serge!" I call out, turning fast.

But it's a trick of the light, my own reflection on the elevator doors. No one's there.

In the ladies' room, in the smeary mirror, my eyes are bagged, saggy pillows, my pupils pinned.

I can smell the chloroform again, even though it's nowhere to be found.

I sit down on the vinyl bench, a throwback to another era when ladies' rooms were powder rooms, salons, places where women made and remade themselves over atomizer huffs and confidences.

I close my eyes.

When you're in the sciences, when you know about things like neuronal biochemistry and the complex interplay between, say, hormones and emotion, you might imagine you have a deep understanding of the mind. *Explain to me why I feel this way, think this way, dream this way, am this way.*

But consider it: Would you really want to know?

When I open my eyes again, Diane is at the sink, just where Eleanor stood a few hours ago.

"I thought it was gone forever," she murmurs, her fingers to her face at the mirror. *Just like Eleanor,* I think. *Am I dreaming?*

"What? Diane, I—"

"Who told you that I worked in Dr. Severin's lab before?" she asks, as if we've been talking a long time. "I need to know who told you that."

I look at her. "I saw it on your CV."

She holds my gaze a minute. Something seems off. Or more off. The odd way her fingertips keep touching her face. The blackness of her eyes, so black no white could squeak through.

"I have to go," I say, rising from the bench.

"Kit, you have to understand: I was fixing it for you, for both of us."

"I never asked you to fix anything," I say.

"You've always been scared to say what you want," she says, the words coming slow and deliberate. "To admit all the things you want."

"You don't know me—"

"And when you finally do, you hide from it. You deny it. You think it doesn't touch you." Her face fills with something like feeling. "But Kit, it does."

"Don't talk to me like this," I say. "I never killed anyone. We are not the same. You're a killer." I almost gasp with pleasure from saying it aloud, something so big and final.

She looks at us both in the mirror, her eyes like two dank

caverns. I get the feeling I used to have when I opened my grandma's cellar door, the smell down there, the smell of earth, mushroomy, ancient, and stinking of mortality. I used to cover my mouth the whole time I was in it. *She buried all her ex-husbands down there*, my dad used to say. *Watch out for the bony edges.*

"You do something bad," she says. "Very bad. You can't even really believe you did it. You wait for your punishment for a long time. You expect it. You wait every day."

She looks down at her hands, then up again. From the hallway, I can hear the elevator's ding. Its doors open and shut.

"But then nothing happens. Your life continues. Except you're not a part of it, really. You go forward, you have experiences. But they don't touch you. You're watching them from the outside. It's like you're a ghost haunting your own life."

"Don't try to make me feel sorry for you, Diane," I say. "Because I don't."

She gives me a funny look. "I hope you never do," she says softly.

I reach for the door handle.

"Kit, wait. I need to ask you something."

"What?"

"Alex. He's the only one you told, right? About me."

"Why," I say, my voice with a funny shiver in it, "would I want anyone else to know?"

The door whooshes shut behind me.

Turning, I think I see a shadow at the far end of the hall. Hear the slow *click-click* of expensive boots.

THEN

"I shouldn't be here," I said, standing at the guidance-office door. "I just didn't know what to do."

After ushering me in, Ms. Castro asked me to sit down, turned her chair to face me, told me I could tell her anything.

"What if someone told you something they'd done," I said. "A secret that no one else knows."

"Well," she said, her eyes bright, "what *kind* of thing?"

You could smell the excitement on her, the batwing sleeves on her shiny blouse shuddering.

"It's really, really bad."

"What might feel bad to *you*—"

"Ms. Castro, I told you: I'm not talking about myself. I'm talking about someone very close to me."

"Okay." She pursed her lips and I felt sorry for her. "Can you tell me what it is?"

"Ms. Castro, I think this person is very unstable. Maybe dangerous. Well, definitely dangerous. Look at what she did."

"Who are you talking about, Kit?" Ms. Castro leaned forward, her whole body seeming to swoop over me like she might take me under her rayon wings, like she might eat me.

"Oh, Ms. Castro, I can't tell you who, but what she did is worse than anything you'd ever guess."

I had to do it. I swear I did.

I'll always remember her listening and nodding, gripping her pen tightly in her fig-lotioned hands. Her tidy manicure. Ms. Castro's world was so tidy. Her paper clips, green and purple, in a clear plastic box. The sparkly bottle of hand sanitizer. Look what I'd brought her, deposited like a bloody organ in her lap.

Like that time I'd proudly carried home the heart and lungs of the fetal pig I'd dissected in biology. I wanted to show my mom I'd done it so perfect, nickless, that I could use a straw and inflate the lungs. Little pink bags swelling obscenely, squeaking blood. She smiled like a proud pageant mom.

Ms. Castro did not give me any smiles.

"And now I can't stop thinking about it," I said. "About what she told me."

"She did something to her dad," I said, the exact reversal of the gravest conversation Ms. Castro prepared herself every day to hear. "And no one ever found out."

I never said how she did it or when or where. And I never said her name.

"Ms. Castro, I can't," I said. "I can't ever tell. She..."

"It's okay," she said, patting my arm, which was shaking. "It's going to be okay."

Her eyes filled with worry, and calculation.

But I never said her name. It could have been anyone. Any girl, any woman I knew. I never said *Diane*. Even though I felt the name, its sound, its weight, like a pressure in my mouth.

I was right to do it.

She had done this thing to me, burdened me with this vile, howling thing. And now it shuddered in me always and I'd felt I might have to live with it forever.

I was right.

NOW

That night, unable to sleep, I remember a dream I used to have, years ago. Diane's dad in my apartment, standing on my carpet. The purple swell, the sweat-slick mustache.

Beside me this time, though, is Diane's mom, her long white scarves, the smell of lipstick.

He's watching us both, his eyes filled with surprise. His hands clutching his throat, his chest.

Did he ever know what was happening or who was responsible?

What is it like to die from your own heart bursting?

Two, three a.m., I'm lying in bed wakefully, my phone in my hand like a flashlight.

I find myself doing strange things, dragging from the hamper the bedsheets from the other night, looking at them, bringing them to my face and nose.

Where is Alex? I mean the body, not the man. Or do I? None of it seems precisely real any longer. Saturday, he died. Today is Tuesday and he's still missing. There is no logic to it.

Could Zell or Maxim have found him? Or both of them? But why would they do something with Alex's body? To blackmail us?

Would someone—anyone—really use blackmail to get a PMDD slot? That's a question I don't dare ponder. I don't even want to think what I'd do for one. What I, in some ways, have done.

At five a.m., the apartment still thick with night, I take my coffee and sit down in the plastic chair, the one with the crack that Diane sat in three days before. I feel something beneath me. When I reach down, my fingers touch something soft.

Diane's furry key chain. It must've come loose from her keys and fallen here. I see now that it's a tiny rabbit's foot. Just like the one she had all those years ago, dangling from the keys to her grandfather's enormous truck.

I hold the foot, rub it with my thumb. Now I know why Diane was always stroking it.

I put it in my pocket, thinking I might need it today.

Two police detectives are in Dr. Severin's office when I arrive. A ruddy-faced young man and a petite woman, both in raincoats. It's not because they are movie detectives, as Zell whispers to me, faking a dramatic cigarette puff, but because it's been raining since late last night.

Dr. Severin emerges from the office, shuts the door behind her.

"They want to talk to everyone," she mutters to Ilene, standing over Ilene's immaculate desk, forever gleaming with lemon polish. "They have a list."

Ilene looks at Severin over the top of her glasses, shaking her head.

"This is very obstructive," Dr. Severin adds.

"It is," Ilene says. "It really is."

Several feet away, I'm at the copier, Xeroxing log sheets. *This is bad*, I'm thinking. *But how bad is it?*

"And the dean's idiotic champagne toast for the grant award is today." Dr. Severin plucks at the stiff leather pleats on her collar. It's the first time I've seen her fidget with her clothes. The only time I've ever seen the shine of sweat at her temples, on her brow.

"Yes, at three."

"Three o'clock so the dean can go straight from his martini lunch to his cocktail hour," Severin says. Then, voice lower: "How long do they intend to be here?"

"They wouldn't say, Dr. Severin."

"I'm not letting some postdoc's runaway-groom routine distract us."

"No, Dr. Severin."

"Did you guys talk to them yet?" I ask as I walk into G-21. Maxim shakes his head.

"And Juwon called in sick," Zell says, rubbing the flocked front of his favorite fluorescent-green YEAH, SCIENCE T-shirt. "We're dropping like flies."

"My bet is Juwon's interviewing across the river," Maxim says, walking toward the supply cabinet. "Or maybe he's on a plane to Freudlinger, gunning for Diane Fleming's old job."

With Maxim's back turned, Zell beckons me over.

"Maybe Maxim figures if he can wait it out," Zell whispers, the smell of ethanol and salami coming off him, "you or Diane might disappear into the ether too and he can get your slot."

I look over at Maxim, who's staring at something on the floor by Alex's lab bench. It's a long stare, intent and specific.

"And then there were none," says Zell with a wink.

My eyes on Maxim, I feel something twist and buck inside me. For a moment, his head tilted, his shoulders slightly hunched, Maxim seems about to duck down to look closer. *What is it...is that—*

Or am I imagining it, all of it?

But then the door opens and Dr. Severin appears and Maxim snaps straight as a pole. We all do.

"They'll want to ask each of you a few questions. Please cooperate," Dr. Severin says, tapping her boot on the floor of G-21. "But do it as efficiently as possible. I'd like to have this over before the dean's dog and pony show."

She's wearing her black lace-up boots with crimson insets. Heels that could gore a toreador. Every time her foot hits the floor—so near the spot Maxim's eyes landed moments before—I think of the red pool, a lagoon now in my head, a swamp, that had been there a few days ago.

Every time her heel hits, I imagine it puncturing the smooth white, and a red fountain spouting from the spot.

"We have a great deal to do to facilitate the transition, reconfigure the lab space for the new study," she says, looking around the room, the benches crowded with work, with slides and crusted glassware, a rainbow of Post-it notes, pipette tips like star points.

"The detectives are using my office," she adds. "Fleming's in there now."

I look up with a start and see Severin watching me. Now I have to say something.

"But is Alex...," I say. "Do they think something happened to him?"

Severin lifts an eyebrow.

251

Was no one going to ask that? I think. *I'm the only one who knows and I'm the only one who asks?*

"I don't know what they think," she says. She moves toward the door, her eyes on me. Everyone's eyes on me now.

"I'm just concerned," I say, unable to banish the *just.* "For Alex. I mean, he was one of us."

Severin gives me a funny look.

"You mean *is,*" she says. "He *is* one of us."

Diane is in there with the detectives.

I haven't seen or heard from her since the ladies' room the day before and, against all logic, I feel a strange tug. The tingle of a missing limb. *We share this thing. We share this.*

But when I imagine her talking to the police, when I imagine her under the hot lights, I start to feel a dull dread slowly sharpening.

After all, do I have any idea what she would do in the face of police?

Does she know what I would do?

I know what we're supposed to say. What we've been saying: *Left at nine, left to do a tour of the town,* just a regular welcome wagon, I am. *And, yes, we saw Alex. And, yes, walking out, we saw Serge.*

Serge. The only person who saw Diane and me at the lab on Saturday. The only witness. What will he say to the detectives? About the biohazard bag, my odd attire, a lab coat subbing as a dress.

Serge has always liked me, I think. *Serge would never—*

The vivarium is quiet, tomblike as ever.

"Serge?"

I think even just seeing his face, I'll know if something's wrong.

As soon as I pass the cage-wash room, I spot him sitting down on one of the benches, his head in his hands.

I hold my breath.

"Serge," I say. "Are you okay?"

When he looks up, I see it, the great puff of his cheeks, like a cartoon chipmunk's.

"Oh Jesus," I say, "does it hurt?"

He shakes his head.

"Can you talk?"

He nods, then whispers, his voice even lower than usual, curiously sultry. "I can, yes. How are you, Kit?"

We are going from cage to cage, looking at the mouse pups, determining which ones are ready to be weaned.

"How old are they?" I ask.

"Nineteen days," he says, his voice even more muffled now by the masks we're wearing. "If we wait too long, they may end up mating inappropriately."

Or, as Zell once put it, *they might get plugged by Papa.*

"Serge," I say, "you heard about Alex?"

He nods. "It is unfortunate."

"It is."

"But he is a capricious young man, so."

He can't suspect anything, I think, *or he wouldn't say that.*

"Did you know the police are here?" I ask, trying to play it cool.

Serge nods again. "I have spoken to them."

I look at him, wanting to pull the mask down, so hot against my face.

"It was very routine," he says.

Inwardly, I sigh with relief.

"But I waited a long time," he adds. "I thought they would never be done with her."

"Done with . . . her?"

"Diane Fleming."

I turn my head, adjusting the mask, the loops pinching my ears.

"Oh," I say. "And she was with them awhile?" He nods. "Did she seem okay? When she came out?"

Serge pauses, standing over one of the cages, thinking.

"I cannot say," he says. "She would not look at me."

There it is again. That curious tension when Serge talks about Diane.

"But," Serge says as we move to the next cage, an even more wrinkly mass of pups, like rosy pearls, "I do not take it personally. Some people are very focused on themselves."

I look at him, and he looks at me. I can see only his eyes, which seem to be telling me something. Just as, a few days before, he told me about Alex, the *political animal*. A warning. One that came too late that time.

"Do you see what I mean, Kit?" he adds.

I nod, the mask sucking into my mouth now. Would Diane say something to the police? Would she take that chance, given what she knows I know? And why?

But did I really know what any of her motives were, ever? And she had lied to me about her history with Dr. Severin. Lied by omission.

"These had been fighting," Serge notes, looking into the cage, "so we removed the dominant one. It will be better, don't you think?"

I nod thoughtlessly. He guides me to the next cage.

"Did you know," I whisper, watching Serge place his hands

on the cage top, "that Diane worked for Dr. Severin before, years ago?"

"Of course," he says. "I was there."

I look up at him, my mouth opening behind the mask. I don't know what to say.

"The most accurate test for weaning," Serge says, lifting the lid on the cage, "is this."

We both look down into the open cage.

Inside, the bitty mouse pups, like pink eraser stubs, do not move at all. Instead, they seem to stare up at us.

"They are not ready," Serge says, closing the lid firmly.

NOW

I saw it. This is what Diane could say to the detectives. *I walked into the lab and saw it with my own eyes. Kit killed Alex. Three days ago, in this very lab.*

If she wanted to save herself, she could say that. It'd be a risky move, given what I could say about her, but who could know what drove Diane?

Didn't you know? Diane could say. *They were involved. Alex and Kit. They had, recently, been intimate.*

I could imagine the whole thing.

I don't know why Kit did it. Maybe she found out about the girlfriend. The fiancée. Because she certainly didn't know before.

Women are complicated creatures, after all. All those hormones raging inside. And with women, isn't it always a crime of passion?

Kit's always been a passionate person.

I saw it. This is what I, in turn, could say to the detectives. *I walked into the lab and saw it with my own eyes. Diane killed Alex.*

Didn't you know? I could say. *He found out about her past. About how Diane killed her own father.*

A crime of passion. Diane's always been a passionate person. Most women are.

I could say all these things. And she knows it.

Diane and me, partners in crime. A Mexican standoff, both our guns poised, ready for the head shot if we must.

When it's my turn, I tell myself, *I will be ready.*

Back in G-21, Zell and Maxim are packing up glassware while two of Irwin's postdocs—matching wire-rims, khakis one infinitesimal shade apart—supervise, clipboards in hand. Juwon is with the detectives.

"They're moving you to Irwin's already?" I say.

Zell rises from his crouch over the box, stuffing the top of his errant boxer shorts back into the waistband of his jeans.

"Herr Severin doesn't waste time."

"Don't you mean Frau?" one of the Irwins says, grinning.

"No," Zell says, not looking at him, "I don't." He seems more subdued by the hour, as if yesterday's disappointment is finally sinking in.

"The blonde was looking for you," Zell says.

"The blonde?" I walk toward my bench. "Diane?"

"No, the civilian. The fiancée. She seemed like she really, really needed to see you."

Zell faces me, cocking his head. There's a mean look in his eyes.

"Okay, thanks," I say, not moving.

I had no idea until today just how much he dislikes me. And there he is, standing just a few feet from where Alex stood. I look right back at him, at his doughy skin, his ruddy throat, uncut. I do not blink.

For a second, watching my expression, he seems to shrink from me.

Maxim covers a beaker in bubble wrap and says nothing, but his eyes are on me also. And Irwin's men. They're looking too.

"Congratulations, by the way," one of Irwin's postdocs says to me. "Cheers to you and all that."

All four of them looking at me like I just ate their cherry pie.

I'm the very last one called down the hall. I've watched as Juwon, Maxim, Zell slipped in and out of those doors. I've imagined every self-serving or insinuating thing they might say.

But worse still is what Diane might have said.

It's strange to be in Dr. Severin's office without Dr. Severin. Strange to see a police detective, holster on, sitting in that high-backed leather chair.

Detective Harper is petite, small-boned, neck like a baby starling's. Still, she looks strong, arms folded across her blue shirt. Shoulders squared. And her hands are big for her size, nails cut to the quick. Her black hair is smoothed flat and pulled back with combs like a Spanish dancer's. When she turns I can see the pins crisscrossed in the braided bun.

I bet it takes her a long time each night to untangle those braids, to pull free all the combs and pins put in place for her job, her world, another world of men. I picture her standing at the mirror, dropping them into the sink. I wonder who she takes her hair down for. Or is it just for herself?

Every morning for the past decade I've dragged my hair— what color even is it? *The color of spring mud*, like all the Owenses', my cousin Scott once said—into a ponytail. It gets in the way even like that, strands sliding loose, the humming ventilators blowing on me all day. You can't really use hairspray in the lab, unless you want to set your head on fire.

It would be easier to cut it all off. Maybe that's why Diane did it.

I've always kept mine long, though I've forgotten why.

You, Alex said that night after Zipperz, his fingers sliding under the elastic, pressing into my scalp, *your hair smells just like you.*

Solvent? Cell cultures? I'd laughed, the ends tickling me, slipping into the hollow of my throat.

Like a match, he'd said, *just lit.*

"So," Detective Harper says, "you've known Alex Shaffer how long?"

"A few months. Since he started here."

"You work together?"

I shift in my chair, so close to the window, the sun's glare in my eyes. "We all work together."

She looks at me and blinks once. "So that's a yes?"

"Yes." I curl my fingers under. *Keep it simple,* I tell myself.

"And you say the last time you saw him was here three days ago? That's Saturday?"

"That's right. Well, down the hall. In the lab."

"He was working?"

"Yes."

"Was that typical? On a weekend morning, so early?"

"Not that typical, no."

"Was he behind on work?"

"Maybe. I don't know. I focus on my own work."

"So what kind of guy is he?"

"Nice. Easygoing."

"Smart?"

"Of course. I mean, yes."

"You're all smart," she says, a hint of a smile lurking there.

"Yes," I say, matching her gaze. "We are."

And so it goes. *What was he wearing? What was his mood? Did you notice anything unusual about his behavior?*

We circle around and around and around as I try not to stare at the detective's small spiral notebook on the desk, a pen tucked inside. Each time, I give the briefest of answers—*I don't know, jeans, a shirt. Fine. Nothing unusual, no*—my eyes fixed on Dr. Severin's desk, a thunk of wood that looks like barn boards. That framed picture to the right, the one I always assume is Severin herself when she was young, a little pigtailed girl in a cowboy hat, fried rattlesnake in her stubby hands, her grim, flat-line mouth. Dr. Severin, a once and forever cowboy, frontierswoman, pioneer in pursuit of her destiny, the research she was born to do.

It's one thing to be smart, brilliant even, but something else to be able to do all that Severin does. Always in motion, eyes on the horizon, wrangling all her cattle, all her work oxen and beef makers and errant postdocs, branding them, driving them long across hard country, never losing sight of something she sees even if no one else sees it.

If she came to believe that one of us might hold her back, bring her down, what would she do? What would it take for her to cut one of those steers loose? If she saw one go slack, turn lame, froth rabid, would she send it to the killing floor?

"And you said you left around nine with Diane Fleming?"

"Yes."

"Did you see anyone else here?

"Just Serge. Like I said."

She looks down at a piece of paper in her hand. "You exchanged greetings—you, Diane, Serge. That was it?"

"That was it." I don't say anything about the biohazard bag. She does not ask.

"What kind of guy is Serge?"

"Serge?" I say. "He's an animal guy, you know. Very dedicated, very protective."

"Protective?"

"He's great at his job. That's what I mean."

She taps her pen on the pad. "Does Alex think he's great?"

I look up, surprised. "I don't know." I have only a second to decide, or at least that's how it feels. "Serge thinks Alex is ...messy."

Her right eyebrow lifts. "Messy how?"

"Just not careful with his equipment. Not clean. Serge is particular. A lot of techs are." *Has someone*, I think, *said something about Serge? Has Diane?*

She looks at me. "Are you friends?"

"With Serge?" I say. "We're friendly. The postdocs—we don't really hang out with the techs."

"Got it," she says. "Caste systems all over, right?"

I look at her. "No," I say. "The vivarium is in another part of the building. That's all I mean."

She looks at me, nodding slowly. "Sure."

I begin to think it's nearly over. It's nearly over and Diane must have not said anything to cast suspicion on me. *Why would she?* I remind myself. *Everything is fine.*

"One last thing," she says. And I ready myself for the old *Columbo* move, another of my dad's favorites. "You and Alex Shaffer, you socialize much?"

"Sorry?" I say. "Socialize?"

She pauses, studying me, or so it seems.

"Do you eat lunch together?" the detective asks. "Does he bring you coffee?"

"Who told you that?" I ask. Immediately, I want to roll the words back into my mouth.

She squints at me. "Is the light bothering you?"

"No," I say. "Coffee. Sure, yeah. We all drink a lot of coffee."

"Maybe go out for drinks?"

"Drinks?" I wonder how long I can keep repeating her questions back to her.

What did she tell them? I think.

"After a long workday," the detective says, leaning back, adjusting the blinds on the window behind her. "Happy hour, five-dollar pitchers, free wings, that kind of thing."

"We work pretty late."

"So is that a yes or a no?"

Breathe, breathe. "A few times."

"When was the last time?"

"I don't know," I say, trying not to stutter. "Last week, the week before."

She narrows her eyes.

Diane, Diane, Diane, how dare you.

"We work a lot, Detective," I say, as evenly as I can. "The days can blur together."

"And when was the last time you heard from Alex?"

I look up. "I told you. I—we saw him here on Saturday morning. Just for a few minutes, but he was working."

"Right. But you two texted occasionally, right?"

"Sometimes," I say, the sick feeling returning.

"How often?"

"Sometimes," I say again, my hand on my phone in my pocket. "We all do."

"So have you gotten any texts from him since seeing him on Saturday?"

"No," I say, truthfully.

"Did he talk much about his home life?"

"No. None of us do. We're here a lot."

"Were you friendly with his fiancée?" she asks.

"No," I say, pinching my fingers against the sides of my chair. "I'm sorry. What does this have to do with Alex being missing?"

"Not at work parties, that sort of thing?" she asks, not answering my question.

In my head, I am picturing Diane: *Kit didn't even know he had a girlfriend. They had a flirtation. Well, a little more than a flirtation—*

"No, I'd never met her. Not until—you know."

"Did he talk about her, about getting married?"

"No," I say.

I'm looking at the blinds instead of her face.

"Have you two ever been romantically involved?" she finally asks. She asks it lightly, flicking her eyes up to watch my reaction.

There it is. Diane. It can only be Diane.

"No," I say. "We have not."

She looks at me very closely. I can see a small vein at her hairline. A wiggly wormy little vein that I think is her tell. I just don't know what she's telling.

"Okay," she says.

"Did someone say that?" I ask.

"We're looking into all the possibilities," she says. "Sometimes, if there's trouble at home, it can feel like a lot of pressure. Maybe they leave town for a while."

"Maybe," I say. "Maybe some people do."

She smiles. "Some men. Runaway grooms."

I look at her, the echo of Dr. Severin's phrase humming back at me.

"Maybe," I say, and trying to recover, trying to be light, I shrug. Then, remembering something my dad used to say in his spooky nighttime voice, I add, "Who knows what evil lurks in the hearts of men?"

Harper smiles again, laughs even.

"We're done?"

"That's all for right now," she says, closing her notebook, her eyes drifting to the press release about the PMDD study on the desk. "So you're an investigator too," she says.

"In a way," I say. "I mean, yes. We're trying to solve a different kind of mystery."

She grins. "So let me ask you: Where do you think Alex Shaffer is? What's your hypothesis, Miss Owens?"

I look at her, thinking.

"Sorry." She corrects herself. "*Dr.* Owens."

"I don't know where he is," I say. "Hopefully not far." I rise, smoothing my lab coat. I am careful. I say it just right. "He's one of us, after all."

Is, is, is one of us. After all.

Ilene glances up at me from her desk as I leave Dr. Severin's office. Lips pursed, she jiggles her computer mouse and says nothing.

But when I move past her, I can feel her eyes on me. Dark and narrow, like little arrows.

Shoving my hands into my lab-coat pockets, I begin walking. My fingers touch fur, and for a second I start. One of Serge's mice?

But no, of course, it's Diane's rabbit's foot, too late to bring me luck. Or just in time to bring me something else.

I walk the hallways for ten, fifteen minutes looking for her. I'm afraid to call or text, afraid to use my phone, so I move to the large windows at the front of the building and perch on the sill. Waiting.

Why would Diane point a finger at me when she's the one who helped me to begin with? Accomplices in a cover-up. This is what I'm wondering, my head heavy and throbbing.

If it weren't for her, I'd have called 911, I'd have rung for campus security.

Unless, I think, something heavy sinking inside me, pulling me down, *that was her plan all along.*

Some people, Serge had said, *are very focused on themselves.*

Did she stop me from calling, did she push me into this byzantine cover-up not to protect me but to put a target on my back?

These had been fighting, Serge had said, looking into the mice cage, *so we removed the dominant one. It will be better, don't you think?*

When she came to my apartment that first night, when she told me I was on the PMDD team, I'd reminded her over and over again what she'd done, what she was.

Did she decide to get rid of me when she saw she had a chance? The last viper in the vipers' nest. *Look at you,* she'd said in G-21, Alex's body on the floor. *What do you think the police will decide the minute they see you?* Convincing me not to call 911. Convincing me to join a cover-up. Making me look guiltier and guiltier.

Why, I think now, and it's like a blow to the chest, *would you keep around the only person who knows who you really are? What you really are.*

*   *   *

The staircase door beside me swings open, a cloud of smoke emerging.

Dr. Severin appears behind it, hand to her mouth, wiping a stray bit of tobacco from her lip.

"Kit," she says. I can't remember her saying my first name before. "How did it go?"

"Pardon?" I say with a start.

"With the police." From her lab-coat pocket, she takes out a makeup mirror, a silver clamshell burnished like a sheriff's star, and opens it.

I clear my throat. "Fine. I mean, I wish I could have been more helpful."

"I'm sure you were just as helpful as you needed to be," she says, clicking the mirror shut. "We must keep our focus on the work. That's what's gotten us this far."

I can't stop myself.

"You and Diane?" I say. "You go so far back." There is something in this. The fact that neither of them told me, mentioned it at all.

She pauses, then sighs, stepping closer to me, very close.

"Is this workplace paranoia?" she asks. "Or is it impostor syndrome? *That* is the real female malady. Perhaps we should be studying that."

I can smell the cigarettes on her for the first time. We are that close.

"You're smarter than this, Kit," she says, her hand on my arm for a fleeting second. "I'm the only one in the world who knows just how smart you are."

It means something to me to hear this from her. I think she's probably right.

Down the hall, Ilene appears, looks at Dr. Severin, and points at her watch.

"That goddamn dean's champagne toast," Severin mutters.

"I'll be there," I say.

"You will," Dr. Severin says, turning away. Waving good-bye over her shoulder.

I watch her walk down the hall, the long dark skirt like an exclamation point.

Though we're both heading in the same direction, I wait. Catch my breath.

"We're lucky, our kind, if we get one shot," she's saying as she walks away. "Even one. We may only get one."

What would it take for her to decide one of her team members was more of a liability than an asset? What might Diane have told *her?*

You would think that in a lab, with its key cards and protocols, its hazardous materials and rules, the walls would be thicker. But the lab is old, dropped ceilings that sag and bellow, belching steam heat, furring pipes, rodent-gnawed spray foam. A lab is supposed to be sleek, immaculate. A building-size brain whirring with activity. Not a place for human sounds, the quivers of the heart.

And so, when I hear the noise coming from the lounge, I feel a fumble in my chest.

"What is that?" I ask Maxim. Cleaning his bench methodically and grievously for the last time. The act for him is sorrowful and wrong. Zell just took one arm and swept everything on his bench into a mail bin.

"It's the fiancée," Maxim says, looking up as the bleat returns. "The lament of the fiancée."

It sounds like she's talking on the phone and crying.

No one's ever cried in the lab before—not in front of anyone, anyway. Once, after a trying day and the awful realization that I'd lost three weeks' work to mysteriously contaminated cultures, I'd hidden in a stall in the bathroom and flushed the toilet four times to conceal my crying. With only a handful of women in the whole building, who would have heard me? But I didn't want to hear myself.

Zell's fiddling with his phone. "Isn't she looking for you?"

I need to talk to Diane. I need to find out what she's done. But Eleanor finds me first, opening the door from the lounge just as I try to pass, hurriedly.

"There you are," she says. Her hair is lank, a forlorn banana peel, and her face, pink and tender. But her jaw is set and there's a new coldness in her voice.

"I'm sorry," I say, "but I'm late already. We have to be in the auditorium for the—"

But she pulls me into the lounge. There is no stopping her.

"I think something bad's happened to Alex," she says, her hands wrapped around each other, a diamond poking angrily between her fingers.

"No," I say firmly. "Look, it's only been a few days. It—"

"I was just telling his parents. The police pinged Alex's phone," she says. "It's either turned off or the battery ran out. This is the last known location."

"The lab?"

"Or nearby."

"Cell towers," I say, as dismissively as I can, trying not to ponder what they can find out next. Texts between Alex and me? *I've been thinking a lot about it and I have to tell Dr. Severin. Alex, you*

CANNOT *do this.* "That's junk science. It doesn't mean anything." I pause. "I don't have to tell you that."

But she will not be stopped.

"There's something else," she says, blocking me as I try to pass, leaning against the hard casement corner into the next wing. "Thursday night, I was supposed to see Alex, but he never called me back. And when I talked to him Friday, he said he forgot, but now the detectives keep asking about it."

Thursday night.

"You know cops," I say, averting my eyes, fighting off a vaulting panic.

"We had plans, a lecture I wanted to go to. I drove by his apartment a few times." She looks at me, jaw tight. "I don't think he ever came home."

Zipperz Thursday-night specials. Long Island Iced Teas, two for one.

She looks at me, head tilted. "Did you see him Thursday night? Were you all working late or something?"

I move to the door. "No. Sorry. I left early."

She doesn't say anything, her mouth opening then closing.

"I'm sure it's nothing," I add.

"Why are you so sure?" she asks after a moment. The chilliness chillier.

I glance at the clock on the wall. Two fifty-seven, thank God.

"Eleanor, I'm sorry. I have to go," I say, not quite pushing past her. "It's later than I thought."

NOW

GRANT AWARD CEREMONY says the hastily written sign, Sharpie on posterboard, an easel in the auditorium lobby.

I'm looking for Diane.

Glass-walled and teeming with people, the space reminds me of a greenhouse I once visited on a class trip in first grade. It was exotic, like a jungle in a book, but there was something wrong and I kept telling my teacher that there was a smell of dead things.

That's how greenhouses smell, he said. *That's how nature smells.*

But it turned out the place was filled with spring-loaded rat traps and we found a dead cat in one of them and most of the girls and two of the boys screamed. I knew I'd smelled the dead thing, even if no one believed me.

Through the crush, I see Dr. Severin. You couldn't miss her. She'd made a quick wardrobe change for the occasion. The woman in red—red stockings, to be precise. And a black leather shift with long, vented sleeves like tent flaps. Booties with gold at the toe. Soft and hard. I can't take my eyes off her. Who could?

The auditorium is swollen with university bigwigs in pinstripes, with white coats from the medical school, with grayish lab rats like me. Everyone so eager to be pulled from their routine at three o'clock on a Tuesday.

All of it feels faintly ludicrous. *Let's toast female hormonal madness! Let's raise a glass for menses! Isn't womanhood a dark and mysterious thing? Will we ever penetrate its surface, fathom its depths, dissect its enigmas, lay bare its witchy power?*

I'm stuck behind Maxim, who's nearly a foot taller than me and, texting furiously, barely notices me. Juwon and Zell don't appear at all.

Scanning the crowd, I spot Diane standing over by the door, under the exit sign. Her usual poise gone, she leans against the curtained doorway, neck thrown back, arms hanging stiffly like an unposed mannequin's.

Before I can move toward her, the ceremony begins.

Dean Baker presents Dr. Severin with a novelty bottle of champagne that is nearly half her height. Six liters, he announces, "a size known as the Methuselah." It is bigger even than the novelty check behind her. The grant funds themselves, confetti-shredded by administrative fees and overhead, wouldn't appear for months.

But the champagne bottle, wrapped in an enormous ribbon, looks oddly right in Dr. Severin's slender hands. The way she holds it, like a club.

"I'm not going to give a speech," she says, that sweep of her hair like smoke emanating from that leather dress, the red slash of her stockings. Chosen, I have to believe, for this occasion. Blood and the woman. And the woman waiting for the blood to come. "Instead, I just want to say a word about Shakespeare."

I feel my lips part. I see Diane's head turn. It swivels side to side. She finds me. I can feel her looking at me.

"My favorite character has always been Lady Macbeth," Dr. Severin is saying. "And my favorite moment is when she's trying to get her nerve up to kill the king. She calls upon the darker spirits and demands, *Unsex me here.*

"Make my blood thicken, she says.

"Make it come to a halt. Stop my blood. Stop me from feeling anything womanly, or human."

I look down at my hands, which are pale. Blinking twice, for a second I see Diane's hands there—gray-red, like a piece of meat left on the counter.

"Unsex me," Dr. Severin repeats. "It's a plea I've heard countless times. From Tania, who hid under her desk at work so no one could see her crying. From Ayoka, who dug a razor into her arms every month and became afraid to pick up her children. From Iris, who had a total hysterectomy at age twenty-four because the week before her period she couldn't stop vomiting. From so many others."

Looking up, I see Diane's eyes on me again, direct and unblinking.

"Make my blood stop. Stop that unbearable push of feelings, feelings gone out of control. For these women, womanhood feels like a wretched curse, and they seek relief, would kill for it, some of them. And no one will help them. Not even the darker spirits.

"But the fault for these feelings, this monthly horror show, does not lie with uteruses, their sex. It does not even lie with their estrogen and progesterone. Not with their bodies at all, much less their minds. The problem lies with science. Which has failed them. We have. We've failed these women.

"But no more. We are only beginning, but we are, in fact, beginning."

The clapping gathers loudly, thunderously, as Dr. Severin steps back, that face stage-lighted and luminous. In seconds, the crowd surges forward, moving toward the doorway, toward the lobby and the discount champagne.

When I look up at the microphone again, Dr. Severin is reaching out for someone, pulling someone close to her to share the applause. She is even smiling.

I see the blondness first, the back of her long neck. Diane swept up by Dr. Severin's silken arm, its winged sleeve long and shining. Diane steps inside it. She nearly disappears.

What might Diane have told Dr. Severin? I think again. *About me, about Alex. And what might it take for her to cut me loose?*

In the lobby, plastic flutes are stacked into high pyramids and someone has pulled out all the decorations from the science-achievements dinner last month: the double-helix-shaped table runners, the test-tube flower holders, floating candles in beakers. *Where are the ovary gravy boats?* Alex had joked to me. Oh, Alex . . .

It's too much. All of it. The crush of the bald-pated well-wishers, the red-faced scientists and Adam's-appled students encircling Dr. Severin.

As everyone pushes forward, I push harder. I don't care; no one knows me, no one even sees me, ever. These men never do. And I need to reach Diane, at the center of everything. At Dr. Severin's side.

I push through the lab coats, the shiny blazers and yellowing collars, all the white-haired white men with gray or flushed faces, and reach for Diane, whispering her name in her ear.

"I need to talk to you," I say, pulling her near the windows, out of the scrum.

"Kit," she says, her voice even lower than mine, "did you see him too?"

"See who?" I say. "Diane, you told the detective things. The questions she was asking—"

Diane's eyes widen. "No," she insists, our bodies pushed closer together with each wave of men behind us, "Kit, I would never do that."

"How else would they know about Thursday night?" I say, trying to be discreet.

Behind Diane, a few feet away, a loud bearded man is talking animatedly to Dr. Severin, touching her shoulder over and over again with hairy hands. Sweat shimmers on her brow from the hot lights.

"I didn't say anything," Diane says, again, shaking her head over and over. "But I've been looking for you. To tell you about what happened."

"You're lying," I say, and her hand is on my arm, pulling me against one of the cold, fogged-windowed walls. "You're lying again."

Her fingers slip around my wrist. "Kit, I saw him. Over in the vivarium."

She is so close now. I can smell her, a whiff of something unclean.

"Serge?" I say, yanking my wrist free.

"No. No. I saw *him*."

In that instant I know who she means and there's a stiff feeling across my chest, my heart.

"That's impossible," I say.

Her eyelid twitches, and then again. And the smell from her, earthy and sharp.

"He was walking and holding his throat."

"Diane, stop," I say, turning away, pressing my hand against the cold glass. "We were there. We know."

But she can't hear me, her fingers to her own neck. "He was moving so slowly, but I'm sure it was him. I called out to him."

"You were imagining—"

"He didn't have a mustache anymore," she whispered. "But I'd know his walk anywhere."

"Diane." *His mustache.* It's just like in my apartment, that telltale slip: *The poison wasn't meant for him. It just happened and then it was too late.* "Are you okay?"

She looks at me. "Of course I am. But we need to be careful, Kit."

"What do you mean? Diane, I think you—"

"I'm not sure we can trust Serge. I don't think he likes me. I know he doesn't. I—" Her face tightens. "She wants us."

"He doesn't like…" I turn, following her gaze, and see Dr. Severin summoning Diane from her circle of admirers. She doesn't seem to see me. Only Diane.

"Don't go," I say, my voice reedy and insistent. "We need to talk. You're not okay, Diane. And what do you mean about Serge?" But Diane is already moving toward Dr. Severin, slipping between all the old men to her mentor's side.

"Lena, dear!" The plummy tones of Dean Baker, his face Rudolph-red and shiny amid the flashing cameras, the energy. "I have so many people you need to meet." He gets an eyeful of Diane, matching him for height. "Why not bring your lovely protégée?"

Through the white coats, the dark-flanneled arms, Diane looks at me, and then the crush of men temporarily overwhelms us, an enormous silver tureen of wan shrimp set down center table, an impossible wheel of cheese, and the *pop-pop* of the Methuselah, all heads turning to watch.

"What about Kit?" Diane is saying, the dean's shiny arm around her, her voice small and far away now. "Kit?"

The smile on Dr. Severin's face is fixed, a mask. Her eyes move right past me.

NOW

Everyone is leaving or gone.

I wonder if it's wise to stay in the lab with the detectives still here, with Eleanor still lurking, closer and closer to a mad Ophelia, her drooping sweater sleeves like water-weighted hems.

But it seems too dangerous to leave. With Diane and what is going on in her head. And Dr. Severin is still here.

When I return to our floor, the first thing I see is the bright yellow security tape crisscrossed across the door to G-21. In the dark hallway, it nearly glows.

I start walking faster and faster.

All I can think of in that moment is the floor by Alex's lab bench. Maxim's eyes drawn there. What did he see? A fleck of browned blood? A bit of tissue? The tail of a washed-away spatter? A shirt thread or strand of hair? Was it mine or his or even hers?

Or any of the hundreds of samples—blood, semen, urine, tissue cultures, cells of humans and animals—that pass through the lab every day?

And then all I can think of is that I must leave. Now.

But as I reach the elevator, I hear someone call my name.

I turn and see it's Detective Harper with her partner, a rooster-breasted young man who missed a spot shaving, both of them with coats on.

"What's going on in G-21?" I ask. My voice sounds woozy to my own ears.

"We'll see," she says. "Maybe nothing."

"Or maybe something," her partner says, and I can't tell if he's speaking to her or to me.

"We were looking for you," she says, her police radio crackling.

"You were?" I say, and the elevator doors shuttle open. My heart suspended in my chest.

"We have more questions," her partner says.

"Oh." Nodding, nodding.

"Just a few," Harper says. "We were hoping you might come by the station later."

"The station? I ... why there?"

We all watch as the elevator doors close again. I look at myself in the mirror, a white blur.

"It's easier," she says. "Alex Shaffer's parents are arriving tonight and meeting us there so we can take some DNA samples."

I push the elevator button again.

The male detective looks at me, shifting his weight from one leg to the other.

"Okay," I say. "Anything I can do to help."

The elevator doors open and I walk inside.

"Great," Detective Harper says. "We'll see you soon, then."

"Right," I say, and both of them watch me as the doors tremble closed.

*　　*　　*

It's a trap, I think. *They'll ask to look at my phone; they'll ask for DNA samples.*

In the parking lot, walking briskly and close to the curb, I try to avoid seeing anyone.

And maybe, I think, my mind racing, *they found something on the cameras too.*

I spot Juwon and Zell ahead of me, walking to their cars.

I slow down, hang back. Catch my breath.

"They didn't ask me much," Juwon is saying, his voice lifting in the evening air. "It was quick."

"Fleming was in there a long time," Zell says. "But Owens was in there longer than anyone."

"See you tomorrow," Juwon says, stopping at his car, "unless I get a job offer tonight."

Zell waves and keeps walking toward the bike rack.

My head down, I try to veer the other way so he doesn't see me. But as he walks under the golden cone of one of the parking-lot lights, I find myself stopping.

Zell, his back to me, is tugging off his messenger bag.

That's when I see it, like a warning flag, a hazard sign. That YEAH, SCIENCE T-shirt, so neon it glows in the growing dark. Burn-your-retinas green against the pink of his thick arms.

With his lab coat off, I finally see the back of the T-shirt, the word BITCH! emblazoned there.

Where did I—

A week ago—less—my Long Island Iced Tea nearly knocked from my hand. The careless shove of a passerby in a BITCH! T-shirt. Zell, in the crowd that night at Zipperz. Elbowing me, spilling my drink. Watching Alex and me.

How I'd turned, thinking I'd recognized him. *Wait*, I'd thought, *I know*—

Zell at Zipperz, like a bad joke.

"Zell," I call out. "Zell, you son of a bitch."

When he sees me looking at him now, he smiles, mean as dirt.

"What did you tell them? The detectives. About me and Alex."

My hand on that rubbery arm of his, his elbow crooking, Zell looks surprised, but only for a second.

"Only the truth," he says, squinting at me. "Except I didn't tell them how you can't hold your booze. Or keep your hands off—"

"Shut up," I say, releasing his arm, pushing back. "You saw us at a bar—so what? We had a few drinks. What's it to you?"

He touches the spot on his arm my hand had clasped. A coolness drops across his face. He turns to his bike, making me wait.

"You and Alex, always laughing together, thick as thieves," he says, popping his U-lock, shoving the key into his pocket. "You know what he said to me once? That he could tell he was gonna get into trouble with you. How you just screamed trouble to him."

His face scrunches; he seems suddenly fragile and nasty at the same time. A little boy with a lit firecracker in his hand.

"Alex never said that," I say. "I don't believe you."

"Look, I told the detectives the truth. You two were at the bar. You were all over each other, making out on the patio."

I won't let him see a wince.

"If you have nothing to hide," he says, pulling his bike from the rack, "you don't have anything to worry about. Do you?"

He's not smiling at all. He has never looked so serious.

"By the way, enjoy the new gig," he says. "Win that Nobel for the ladies."

*   *   *

I don't remember the walk back to my apartment other than the hard wind, my hands clutched to the edges of my jacket.

I can't put any of the pieces together.

At home, I sit on the plastic chair and scroll through my phone, pointlessly deleting old texts from Alex, from Diane. I don't read any of them. I just delete them all.

It's not until I tug my jacket off that I realize I never even took off my lab coat. Diane's rabbit's foot slides from my pocket to the floor.

I look at it. *Lots of luck you gave me*, I think.

Once, my dad's second wife, Debra, gave my mom a Mother's Day gift: a sackful of crystals and coins and other pocket pieces and a few things that we couldn't figure out—dried-up things that might have been old feathers or bug wings. Debra called it a jack bag and said she'd made it personally to bless her. Two days later, my mom started bleeding even though she'd had a partial hysterectomy years ago. It went on for days and she hated going to the doctor. Finally, she took the bag, drove out to the salt marsh, and tossed it in, which she said was the only way to make sure it stopped. Later, I'd wonder if it ever did.

I pick up the rabbit's foot and toss it across the room, watch it skitter across the pile of papers, articles, case studies on the floor.

There's a sharp hum in the back of my head, the downy hair back there, tingling.

Rabbit's foot. Rabbit's foot. Then I remember.

Moments later, I've heaped all my PMDD files on the coffee table, the pages fluttering. I know it's in here. I read it only days ago.

Journal Articles, Pharma, Case Studies. My fingers flipping through the folders.

And there it is. The folder labeled, in my inconstant handwriting, *Severin Studies 2005-2009.*

Case Studies (Unpublished)

I'd even circled the paragraph:

At age twelve, Nina's mother, who Nina believes also suffered from undiagnosed PMDD, gave her a rabbit's-foot key chain. Nina notes that when "the feelings came, I'd stroke it and stroke it, hoping they would go away."

I sit down on the carpet, my elbows on the coffee table, and begin reading:

Case Study
(see also: Exclusion Criteria: Rejected Subjects)

Nina, a twenty-year-old college student at a large university, enrolled in the first round of the PMDD and GABA$_A$ receptors study. During intake, she described feelings of extreme moodiness, anxiety and despair that frequently overwhelm her. In recent years, she states, her symptoms have become a source of great distress. While Nina cannot point to connections between her "dark moods" and her menstrual cycle, she has read about PMDD and feels certain "it explains what has gone wrong in my life."

And farther down:

Nina reports that her mother suffers from heavy periods and, through Nina's childhood, marked the number of tampons she used on index cards. When asked for more information about her mother, Nina refuses to give any.

"I have disordered thoughts," she informed the interviewer more than once. When told she didn't seem disordered but in fact seemed calm, Nina noted she had learned not to show her feelings because of childhood experiences.

When asked to articulate those experiences, Nina declined to go into detail. Her survey responses show that she did not live with the same parent in the same home for more than a few months after she was seven years old. When asked about these responses, Nina again declined to elaborate.

And then:

Nina reports feelings of aggression that she struggles to control. When asked if these feelings had affected her personal relationships, she stated that she had never had any. "I don't want to burden anyone with my problems," she says. "And I have never had feelings like that." Nina reports no sexual experiences.

Finally:

Outcome/Recommendations: After three months of the symptom calendar and weekly consultations, it was determined that Nina did not meet the diagnostic criteria for PMDD. Her symptoms (emotional lability, irritability and anger) are not confined to her luteal cycle and persist during and after her period as well. While excluded from this study, she was strongly encouraged to undergo further gynecological testing as well as psychiatric treatment for anxiety, feelings of aggression, psychosocial difficulties, possible sexual dysfunction and development issues.

The date on the case study is nine years ago, when I was an undergrad at State.

Diane was one of Dr. Severin's test subjects. And neither one has said a word about it. Just as neither one noted that Diane had been one of Dr. Severin's summer interns a few years later.

Dr. Severin and Diane. Mentor and student. Researcher and rejected subject. Doctor and rejected patient.

I don't know what any of it means. A clue to a mystery I didn't know I was in.

But I do know this: It's time to open that cellar door myself and climb in.

In the end, my mom always said, *there's only you.*

Remember this, Dr. Severin said, *you will have to fight your entire life.*

NOW

Why didn't you tell me about Nina?, I type, my fingers shaking.
   What?
   About Nina. The case study. You were one of Dr. Severin's test sub-jects. You told her you had PMDD.
   Kit. No. You've got it wrong.
   What is going on with you two? What are you doing to me—
   We shouldn't be texting.
   Meet me at the lab now.
   She doesn't reply.

Within twenty minutes I'm back at the lab, hunting for her.

   The hallways empty and echoing, I look in the lounge, the prep room, the ladies' room, Dr. Severin's darkened office. I don't dare break the tape to G-21.

   The only place left to go is the vivarium. The animal unit and its honeycomb of rooms, cage wash, prep, necropsy, freezer.

   I don't see Serge. It's after six and the last junior lab tech is leaving. He waves to me through the glass, swinging his backpack.

   When he is gone, I step inside, slide on a paper coat, a pair of shoe covers, as if Serge is there, nodding and smiling his approval.

Walking through the space, I can feel my phone buzzing in my pocket.

Where are you?

The only movement is the constant scurrying and scampering from the cages. I stop at the feed room, which I haven't set foot in since Serge scooped clumps of Panda Garden mice from the floor.

Vivarium, I text back. *We need to talk.*

Standing at the feed-room door, I hear something, a movement. A shuffle. The *shush-shush* of shoe covers on concrete.

I step inside.

Everything is whirring. The ventilation system, but also a trio of standing fans that someone—Serge, or the maintenance staff—put in there days before, to get rid of the mouse carcass smell.

At the center is Eleanor, her back to me. The heat screaming up the pipes and the trapped, fetid air blowing everywhere, yet she's wearing a thick wool coat.

Paper flapping, window blinds shirring, everything is moving, her straw-colored hair pirouetting around her like a ballerina's tulle.

All I can think of, seeing her, is the undergraduate who died a few years back, her long locks catching in the lab's metal lathe, spinning her around tighter and tighter, her neck pressed against the machine until she could no longer breathe. (*Rapunzel, Rapunzel,* Zell snarked. *That's why the ladies shouldn't be in the labs.*)

"Eleanor," I say, walking toward her. "Eleanor, are you okay?"

Back still facing me, she doesn't move, her shoulders hunching higher in some odd, animal way. Like the wiggle of a garter snake.

"You shouldn't be in here," I say. "We had an infestation. The smell..."

Finally, she turns. All that prettiness is gone, knotted tight in the center of her face. Her fingers tug at her coat's winking buttonholes.

"I was leaving—Alex's parents land in an hour. But I got turned around. Then I saw someone," she says. "Or thought I did."

"Probably the junior tech," I say. "I can show you out."

She looks at me, blinking twice, three times, like she can't focus. "They're bringing the dogs in," she says. "The state police. There's only one reason they bring dogs in."

Suddenly, I feel painfully sorry for her. Because she's right and because it's only going to get worse.

"Let's get you out of here."

I move toward her, trying to direct her to the door.

"They asked me something," she says, not budging. "The detectives. They asked if I thought Alex might be involved with someone." She's still looking at me, wiping her face on the rough wool of her coat. It's a statement that's also a question.

"I don't think he was that kind of guy, Eleanor," I say, my voice a magnificent deceit, so magnificent it frightens me. "Alex, he—"

"He was always drawn to people who were weak. Maybe that's what happened here."

"What?" The fan whirring past us again, Eleanor's hair whipping wildly like some comic fright wig.

"Even unstable. Maybe he thought he could help her."

For a strange, fleeting second, I find myself wondering if this is true.

"Her?" I say. My phone starts buzzing in my pocket.

Her bright eyes are fixed on me, big and spiraling. "And this person," she says. "This unstable person. I think she may have done something to him."

"No, Eleanor, I'm sure that's not——"

"So was it you?" she asks, so suddenly, so plainly I think I've misheard.

"What?"

She's staring at me intently now and I'm afraid to move my eyes, to look at anything but her.

"I heard them talking. Those guys, your coworkers. Saying you were Alex's lab wife."

"That's a joke. That doesn't mean anything."

"That you were at a bar with him on Thursday night."

I don't say anything. The fan lashes past once more, thunderous now.

"I just need to know," she says, her voice low and desperate. "Please. Was it you?"

"No," I say, so easily I surprise myself.

She doesn't say anything, her face gleaming with sweat, her coat gaping open, its silky purple interior glaring at me.

"It wasn't me," I say. "And I don't think anyone's done anything to him. I really don't."

I say it as firmly as I can, as firmly as a doctor might, as Dr. Severin might, firm and resolute.

"I don't know," she starts, her fingers to her temples. She backs away, one step, two. And in that moment, I see the large fan behind her oscillate, its blade catching one wheaty hank of her hair.

I grab her so hard that she cries out as I pull her toward me. It's after she stumbles forward—knocking the cord loose, the fan shuddering to silence—that I hear the sound. The groaning above us, the fan no longer drowning it out. It seems to be coming from the ceiling, the dimpled panel from the infestation, its edges shorn, a hole in its center leading to some dark interior. I think of the mice plummeting from there just a few days ago. Serge's dutiful care of their remains even though they weren't his mice, or even lab mice at all.

I look up and that's when I see it, my heart halting.

"You need to go," I say.

Because I don't want her to see what I see, which is the thing hanging from the narrow space between the sagging panel and the wall. The pale blue flap of Alex's linen shirt.

"There you are," a voice says. It's Diane, pale as a cadaver in the doorway. "Your taxi is here, Eleanor. To take you to Alex's parents."

We don't say a word to each other until Eleanor's steps have faded on the concrete, until we hear the elevator chime and carry her away.

"Diane," I say, and my eyes lift again to the ceiling.

Her eyes lift too.

III.

Present, I flee you: absent, I find you again:
Your image follows me in the forest's night
...I search for myself: and yet find no one there.

—Jean Racine, *Phèdre*

NOW

"I told you I saw him," she whispers, her fingers to her mouth like a child. She even seems smaller, seems to be shrinking.

"Diane, you didn't see him."

"I did," she says. "But his mustache was gone."

I take a breath. "Did you know he was up there?"

She shakes her head, a gray film on her face under the light.

"Why would I ever believe you?" I say. "You've lied about everything."

"No, Kit," she says, the ceiling groaning again above us. "You've got it wrong."

"Could Dr. Severin know?" I ask, my head aching.

"About my dad?" she says, her eyes dark, stepping forward now.

"What?" I say, impatient. "About *Alex*. Could she know?"

But Diane doesn't seem to be listening to me. "No one else can ever know. You're the only one. The only one who knows what I am."

What I am. What are *you, Diane?*

My hand shoots out before I can stop it. The slap is almost a punch, a hard clapping sound, so hard she stumbles backward. My palm print on her cheek, a scorch.

"I never wanted it," I say. "I never asked for it."

The groan is more than a groan this time.

We both look up at the ceiling panel. Swollen like the belly of a whale.

It seems to take forever, the panel peeling loose like a zipper unzipping.

"Kit." Diane's hands are on me, hard, the only time they ever felt hot to the touch.

Pushing, both of us leaping against one wall, her arm around my waist. The scatter of particle dust, the ceiling panel splintering, like the hull of a ship torn loose by an iceberg. The sudden hard thud against me, knocking my feet out from under me, seeing Alex's blue shirt billowing, hearing the awful thump. Everything falling.

My right hand aches. I'm holding something tight between my fingers.

I'm lying on the floor of the feed room. My face is wet, and my legs, and there's a coldness all through me. I can't see from one eye; something's caught between my lashes.

I blink it loose, look down at my hand, see what is pressed between my fingers: the blue linen of Alex's shirt. Next to me, the soft limbs of Alex himself. His shirt lifting like a cloud each time the fans pass.

Then what looks like a half-sunken carnival balloon, green and twisted.

Shifting myself, turning, I know it's no balloon but Alex's arm curled around itself, the rigor long past. Bloated and blistered and meaty. And something delicate, the poke of a leg, the body folded in on itself. The pants fabric straining, stiff with brown blood, and popping from it a calf, the delicate, almost feminine turn of an ankle.

Alex. Poor Alex.

In that moment, I know if I see his face, I will die.

But there's no face to see, his body wrapped tight around itself like a Christmas present. The soft black of his soft hair, hair I stroked with my nail-bitten fingers a few nights ago.

You saved her, a voice is saying, deep, male.

No, she saved me, says Diane.

Diane's face looms above me, that halo of hair lit by a bank of fluorescent tubes hanging by a pair of shredding cords behind her.

The only friend I ever had, Diane is saying.

"There she is." That male voice again, thick, throaty, familiar. "It would take more than a few pieces of wet fiberboard to knock that brain loose in its skull."

Serge's face hovers above me, his cheeks even more distended, an earthy smell coming from his dark mouth.

I try to move, but my neck bends like a plastic straw, and for a second I see stars. I'm on a sofa, itchy and low-slung, in Serge's pocket-size office, just off the vivarium. The walls are white and bare, a laptop humming on his desk beside a tidy stack of file folders.

"How did I get here?" I say. "You carried me."

"It was not so impressive as it sounds. I give my choreography a C minus."

All the lights are off except one plastic gooseneck lamp. Classical music murmurs from a tiny glowing speaker. Through the door, I see the tech kitchenette, barely big enough for a dorm fridge, a narrow sink, a burnt-orange percolator warming itself.

"I should take you to the hospital," he says, sitting on the sofa arm, "but that is not possible."

I feel the back of my head, soft and spongy. The smell.

"So you did it?" I say to Serge. "You found the body. You put it up there."

Serge nods slowly, the snaky trails of a hanging plant dancing behind him as the radiator hisses. "It was not meant to be a long-term solution," he says. "I pride myself on always finishing my work. The cleaning, the sterilization, swiping his access card so it appeared he left. But this job I could not complete. Some tasks are too objectionable."

Serge's words don't make sense and I wonder if it's his swollen mouth, the medication from the teeth extraction.

"Disposing of the body as if it were lab waste was more than I could tolerate. I had a crisis of conscience. Surely you understand that. You of all people should understand."

"I don't understand anything," I whisper, trying to sit up. "Why would that be your job?"

"That is my point," he says, helping me upright on the sofa. "I have sealed off the room. To give us some time to consider things. It's ten p.m. No one will be here until six."

"And...Diane?"

His face darkens. He leans back against the wall, one knee up on the sofa arm. I sit up taller, holding the back of my head, which feels like it might peel off.

"She is here as well. She has cleaned herself in the ladies' room."

On cue, Diane appears in the doorway, her hands clasped in front of her, a brush of blood on her brow.

"The front of her head, the back of yours," Serge says to me.

"Together, we've got one whole brain," I murmur.

Serge points Diane toward the only other seat, a metal folding chair with bright red foot caps like painted nails. "Excuse my manners," he says. "I do not have many guests."

"Do I smell jasmine?" Diane asks, taking a seat. There's a look in her eyes I can't name.

There is something between them. Something fresh and nasty.

"Good nose," he says. Then smiles. "Look at me. As I say, I don't have many guests. I've been having tea. Would you like some?"

We sit for a moment in silence as Serge moves around in the kitchenette, his hands like long-necked birds. I can't figure out what's going on, but something's happened between them.

"We must let it steep four minutes," he says, resuming his perch on the sofa arm.

Diane is staring at the floor intently, a look I do not like. It reminds me of long ago, the shag carpet of my bedroom, her dark words. I wonder what they've been talking about.

I feel a rush of heat to my eyes. *What are we doing here?*

Serge reaches for his phone and raises the volume on the music, which suddenly fills the small space.

No one says anything for a moment, and Serge closes his eyes. He's humming to the music, making little *pit-pit* sounds, his voice rising from a near whisper to a full-throated hum.

"What is this?" I say, a feeling in my chest as the music soars mournfully. "I know this song."

"Saint-Saëns," he says. "'The Swan.' It is, I suppose, what some call kitsch. But I find it appealing."

"I never knew what it was called," I say. I must've heard it a thousand times through the bathroom door when I was little. My mom used to play it on the shower CD player when she took her long baths, Jean Naté and Mr. Bubbles after days full of cancer-rattled collies or tending to her girlfriends Reena and Rae who had to take that second mortgage on their hair salon.

The music purrs and swells with such melancholy, and, half sick at heart already, I find myself swaying, caught up. Wanting to shut my eyes and sink into its sweet harbors.

Smiling at me, Serge holds out his hand.

I swear this happens: I rise, and for a brief moment, we are dancing. Just one, two, three twirls around before we stop, and Serge's warm hand releases mine.

Diane is looking at us both and saying nothing.

"The tea," Serge says, lifting a finger. "Just a moment."

Maybe, I think, against all logic, everything will be okay. Maybe it will all work out. Serge likes me and he will understand and help us. And maybe Diane will pull herself together again.

"This is just like before," she says, barely a whisper. "It's the same as before."

"Diane," I say. "Are you okay?"

She must have fallen too, her head hitting the floor or wall. A hard knot is faintly visible beneath her smooth, wide forehead, the blood-brush framing it.

"This is what I used to listen to when I worked in a pathogen unit," Serge says from the kitchenette. "We gassed hundreds of mice every day. I cleaned the container after each batch. The new ones can smell the pheromones. It is very distressing for them."

I look at Diane, then back at Serge in the kitchenette, his head obscured by the open cabinets.

"It must be so hard," I say, just to say something. "To do what you have to do."

I remember the rumor about Serge's sister. That she'd died of leukemia at age ten or twelve. His eyes blinking behind the kettle steam, he looks at me, and I can feel the music rise again, bittersweet, with each string pluck felt keenly and left vibrating through me.

"It is hard, in a way," he says, returning with a tray holding an enamel teapot, mugs of smoked green glass, and a small jar of seedy red jam. "But if we do it, you do not have to."

"My mom worked at an animal-rescue clinic," I say. "I don't think either of us ever got used to it."

I don't know why I'm talking this way. Why I'm pretending what's going on isn't really going on. The music, the strangeness of everything.

"Well, Kit," he says, setting the tray on a makeshift table, a wastebasket he overturns, "you need to be more like Diane."

We both look at Diane, who is staring at the tray, the steaming mugs, the bruised-looking jam.

"What?" I ask, thinking I misheard.

"Let's just say," he says, sitting, "she has a deeper view of life. I learned that years ago."

"What do you mean?" I say. "When Diane interned with Dr. Severin?"

Serge smiles in that way of his, weary-eyed and vaguely charmed. I see him trying to meet her eyes. She will not surrender them to him or to me.

"You did not tell her?" Serge says to Diane, who lifts her head, her face now eerily calm, as if she has quickly stitched it together again from whatever antic state it was in.

"The internship, yes," she says, talking to me but staring at Serge, lips moist, crossing her legs. "The summer between college and grad school—Serge was a junior lab tech."

The music stops, the speaker clicking.

Serge dips a small spoon in the jam dish. "Fruit, yes?" he says, spoon hovering over our cups. "It is the Russian way."

"Yes," we both murmur at once, thoughtlessly. Polite. The way we'd long ago learned to be. Everything feels so strange that nothing does.

Steam dampening his face, he sets his cup down and leans back.

"I will not forget it," he says. "One of the mothers needed to be put down, and all her babies too. Usually we have to send students home after. The first time, at least. Not Diane. She destroyed them all handily."

I look at Diane, who is so very still. The knot in her forehead, though, seems to pulsate, as if flooded with blood.

"And then she sliced and diced them, as you say," Serge continues, folding his long spider arms, crossing his long spider legs. "The best necropsist Dr. Severin ever had."

My eyes dart between them both. I know I'm not understanding something, or anything, and the speaker keeps clicking.

"Look," I say, "let's all just—"

"It was the job," Diane says, softly, barely audibly. "We've all done it. Countless times." She turns to me. "Haven't you?"

"Well, yes," I say. "Yes. I mean, not that way, but..."

Serge leans forward, hand resting on top of the teapot.

"It was Diane's job," Serge says to me. "But I have never seen anyone do it with such composure. One might even say gusto. The only one who came close was a young man whose family was in the slaughterhouse business. But Diane. Her preferred method was decapitation with heavy scissors."

Diane's voice goes tight. "That was protocol for newborn mice. I was told they were less than seven days old."

"I would have told you they were nearly twenty days old," Serge says. "But you did not wish to wait. As we have seen."

Diane shoves her hands in her pockets and turns in her chair, away from us.

"Whenever she finished the necropsy," he says, "the skin removed, the organs, the head detached, she looked so...how do you say it? Afterglow?"

We all sit for a moment, Serge's eyes dancing with something like pleasure.

"You wanted me to cry," Diane whispers. "Like a girl. I should have cried."

We can judge the heart of a man by his treatment of animals. That was what Serge told me the first time he watched me handling the mice. *I am sure Mr. Kant meant the heart of a woman too.*

Serge shakes his head. "A crocodile cries only because it has not eaten its prey."

"What do you want?" Diane says. "Tell me what you want from me."

The speaker clicks and "The Swan" returns.

"What do I want?" he says. "I want people like you banished from my world." His voice is hard, relentless. "Those born with a splinter of ice in their hearts."

Serge looks at her in that way he has, the same look he has when a postdoc hasn't put on a gown before entering the vivarium or when he doesn't separate the mouse litters. Under his invasive gaze, so sure of himself, so acute, Diane seems to shrink. It makes me feel sorry for her in a way I can't explain.

"Is it money?" Diane says, softly now. "Is that what you're looking for?"

"What makes you think there's money enough in the world?" His eyes hot on her. "To make me unknow what I know? I saw what you did to that young man."

What you did to that young man...

"Serge," I call out, realizing it at last, "you've got it wrong.

Diane didn't do anything to Alex. It was an accident. I was there. He was running a flash column and there was a crack—"

But Serge is not listening to me.

"Diane, why did you have to involve her?" he says, flicking one finger, resting on a knee, toward me. "She doesn't know what you are."

"You don't know what you're talking about," Diane murmurs, recrossing her legs, foot shaking now. Swinging like a metronome.

"I have done some investigations these past few days," Serge says. "I have uncovered some questionable things. Your father, a heart attack at forty-two?"

No, Serge. Diane, white and waxy as a cake of soap, looks at him. Inside, I can feel everything falling apart.

"No history of cardiac trouble," Serge continues. "No one asked for an autopsy. Tell me, was he your first?"

"Stop!" Diane pitches forward, her knee hitting the makeshift table, sending spoons to the floor and blobs of jam skittering. Hot tea splotching us all.

"I'll get towels," Serge says, rising, rushing to the kitchenette. And there I am, bending down to scoop spoons and jam from the floor. The veneer of civilization we cling to amid chaos and carnage.

"Diane," I say, sitting up again, setting the spoons down, "please, just..."

Immediately, I know something is wrong. Her eyes are glistening strangely, like animals right when they go under or like my mom those last days at the hospital. My heart catches a moment.

Serge returns with tea towels. "What has happened?" he asks.

Because my eyes are on Diane, who now has one hand balled into a fist against her knee.

"Did the water burn your hand?" I ask, squinting.

"We'll be here forever," she whispers. "We have no place else to go."

"Diane," I say, eyes on her clamped fingers, red and insistent. "Diane, let me see your hand."

But she's looking at Serge and he's looking at her. "Was he some kind of threat to you?" Serge says. "Do you just go around killing any man who gets in your way?"

"Diane," I say. "What's in your hand?" Because now I know something is.

She isn't listening to me. No one is.

"I knew what you were, all those years ago. The way you handled those mice," Serge is saying, fingers touching his neck, leaving pink spots. "I cannot abide it any longer. This is where it ends."

"You think you know things about me?" Diane says finally. An odd dreamy tone, her balled hand opening and closing now. And I know I see something in it. "You think you know because of the way I euthanized those mice?"

Serge looks at both of us, touching his cheek with the palm of his hand. His face is newly pink, pink as a Pink Pearl eraser.

It comes to me in that instant, the thought, the panic.

This is just like before, Diane said, just a few moments ago. *It's the same as before.*

"Don't!" I say, reaching for Serge, knocking his teacup from his hand.

"What?" he says. "What?"

"Diane, what was it?" I say, grabbing her hand, her palm sticky and white.

Head wobbling, Serge reaches down and lifts the teacup to his face, under his nose.

"How did I miss it?" he asks, nearly smiling. "How did I not realize?"

"You shouldn't have done this," Diane says to Serge, her voice so delicate, vaguely mournful. "I'm so, so sorry you did this."

He lifts one hand to his cheek, rests it there, as if puzzled by everything, by life. By the darkness unspooling at his feet.

"You killed me," he says, a rattling gasp.

Those words, the very same words Alex spoke to me.

"You killed me."

There's a thin band of white at his hairline, but the rest of Serge's face, his long graceful neck, has bloomed cherry red, redder than the jam, as red as poor Alex's hot blood.

"Oh, Diane," I wail.

But just as I reach out for him, Serge tumbles to the floor, his chin smacking the carpet, his arms and legs zigzagging. Froth hangs like lace from bluing lips.

Sinking to the floor, a blur of things: my hands on his curled-in chest, the sickly sound of his receding breaths, leaning over, my mouth open over his.

"Don't," Diane calls out. "Kit, don't put your mouth on him!"

And I can smell it then, what's inside him. Cyanide. The same scent drifting from his smoky teacup. Like an apple core gone to rot.

"Oh no," I say. I say it over and over, reaching into my lab coat pocket for my phone, hoping it's still there. But just as I shake it loose into my palm she slaps it from my hand, sending it careering across the room.

My arm flies up at her; the heel of my hand shoves her, knocking her back into her chair.

The sound from Serge's mouth is terrible. The death rattle like in an old horror movie, but more plaintive, more lost.

I place my hand on his chest, which is utterly still, as I knew it would be. The heart so big, it burst. It's almost as if a wave of cold passes from Serge over me and I know he's gone. I know it.

"It's just like before, and no more real," Diane is saying. She looks like a frame of film paused, her body halfway between sitting and rising, her hands gripping the seat.

Then, looking at me: "Is this really happening, Kit?"

That's when I see the shadow on the floor. Turning, peering up, I see her in the doorway, her face somber and full of woe.

"Oh, Diane," Dr. Severin says, looking down at her, a look of infinite sadness, "what have you done?"

NOW

You alone understand the heart, that's what Serge told me once. *The others are made of darker material.*

The smell of vomit is everywhere.

"We need to get out of here," Dr. Severin says. "The fumes are dangerous."

But Diane won't move, still seated on the metal folding chair, its red foot caps clamping the floor. Dr. Severin clasps her shoulder, her arm, but Diane doesn't move or lift her head.

Everyone moving around her, she couldn't move at all. Maybe she was made of wood too. A wooden girl. Watching Serge on the floor, was Diane thinking of the last time, her father twisting and twitching on the carpet, his face swollen, his throat inflating like a football?

Freud wrote about it a century ago. How we rummage through the armory of the past to retrieve the weapons needed to repeat, repeat, repeat past traumas. He said it was primitive, instinctual, destructive. Like a demon inside us all.

And now we know it's true. The brain itself is built with the battered beams of our early years. What the conscious mind forgets, the neurons remember.

I know what Diane would say. What she did to her dad came from a fleeting impulse in an unsound state. What she did to Serge, however, was about self-protection, survival.

But science knows better.

I'm running through the vivarium, foraging for amyl nitrate, for anything.

There may be a Cyanokit somewhere. That's what Dr. Severin said, reaching for her phone.

We both know it's too late, but still, I'm looking, my breath ragged, and hard sounds, something animal, coming from my lungs.

When I return with the kit, I can see just how late it is.

"This is what we're going to do," Dr. Severin says. There are damp whorls under her arms, staining her silk blouse. "You two found Alex. And then you came down here looking for help, and you found Serge."

"Dr. Severin," I say, "what is it you plan to do—"

"They had a quarrel over protocol," she says, her face moving forward, into the light from the gooseneck lamp. "Things got out of hand. Serge killed Alex. Attempted to hide the body. Consumed by guilt, Serge took his own life. Workplace violence."

"That's not what happened."

"You think I don't know that?"

I pause. "I'm not going to do that," I say. "I'm not going to say those things."

Dr. Severin looks at me with surprise and maybe a whiff of relief.

"Okay," she says, taking a breath. Looking down at Serge, scarlet-skinned. Her fingers touching her mouth, she won't meet my eyes. "Okay, then."

I hear the elevator doors open down the hall. The *beep-beep* and noise of arriving paramedics.

"He wasn't real to me," Diane says suddenly, jerking to life beside us. We both look at her.

"Nothing that happened seemed real." She turns and looks at us, her hands shaking before her, her eyes widening. "My God, my brain."

That's when we hear the walkie-talkies, the hurried feet, the gurney wheels.

"What is wrong with my brain?"

"It's cyanide," Dr. Severin tells them. "Don't put your mouth on him."

"Jesus, we all gotta get outta here," one paramedic shouts. He and a partner hoist Serge onto the gurney, then push the gurney through the office, into the vivarium, and out to the hallway beyond.

Diane, her face unchanged, remote, in some kind of marble-struck shock, nods.

My hands are on her now, lifting her to her feet.

"I had to do it, Kit," she says softly. "I couldn't bear for anyone to ever know what I was."

"Diane."

"But I knew," she says.

"Miss," one of the paramedics says, pushing past me.

When I turn around again, Diane is drifting through the office door and into the vivarium.

When I was little, I saw a scary old movie about a woman who remained in a permanent stupor from a long-ago tropical flu. At night, she walked the corridors of her grand house, face blank, body moving as if on strings. *Does she suffer?* a nurse asked her doctor. *I do not know*, he replied. *A sleepwalker who never wakes*, he called her.

That's how Diane walks. That's how Diane is. Something missing from the center of her, a piece never put in place that now roams loose inside her, never finding anchor.

Pushing past the paramedics, I follow her. All the animals seem to be moving, unsettled, disordered, the feed tubes clacking against the cages, the squirm and squall of thousands of rodents straining.

"Diane," I call out, running now. I can hear Dr. Severin behind me, heels clicking.

Weaving past the cage wash, feed barrels, and mop racks, between the aisles of cages, the endless maze of them, I finally spot her, light catching on that shorn hair, halo white, moving through the doors.

The red exit sign, the light from the hallway beyond, and she is illuminated, her profile turning, that pale down on her cheek.

"Diane!"

Through the open doors, I see two policemen approaching from the hallway's far end. The short one with a rain smock looks at her.

The other, very tall with fuzzy brown hair and a mustache, is saying something I can't hear. Diane sees him too and suddenly begins running toward him. As if he were a finish line she must tear through.

"Careful!" I shout, though I'm not sure to whom.

Like an arrow, Diane thrusts herself straight at the policeman, so fast he nearly reaches for his gun. The startled look on his face as she presses herself against him, her arms curled in front of her, like a child finding a lost parent at the mall.

I stop and watch, struck, Dr. Severin behind me.

The mustached cop doesn't seem to know what to do, tentatively touching her arm, patting her back, looking at his partner with confusion as she burrows against him. Not a hug, not an embrace, but a kind of effacement, disappearing into him, his bulky jacket, his stiff arms blotting her out.

"It's okay, miss," he's saying. "You're okay."

Her head turns slightly toward him, bobbing back like a wounded animal's. The sleepwalker who has woken up.

"No." The voice is a child's voice too, her body sinking, holding on to him for dear life. "No, I'm not."

NOW

Once, in a neurobiology class in college, our professor showed us an MRI of a man's brain that was covered with white blobs. He asked us what we thought they were. Everyone guessed tumors. I was the only one who got it right.

"Tapeworms," I said. I'd seen them countless times in my mom's clinic, in the slurry excrement of the strays she brought home. They start out as ribbons, unwinding to a dozen, two dozen feet, loping around the intestine. But before that, they're larvae and they can drift effortlessly into the bloodstream, find their way to the brain. Burrowing in. Getting trapped in its cavities, sprouting like grapes. They can thrive there, live there for years. Pressing against the membranes, swelling the pinky-gray tissue like a tissue-paper pom-pom.

If I sliced open Diane's beautiful, extraordinary brain, I feel certain of what I'd see: a swarm of worms, a cluster of sickly grapes, pushing against the chambers of her brain, inflaming it.

She didn't ask for it, but it's there. Maybe she can't help it, a fatal combination of nature and nurture, a derelict upbringing, a feckless parent.

Maybe she can't help it, but can't we all say the same?

*   *   *

We're in Severin's office, waiting for our turn. Diane will take a long, long time, I think. She's been waiting quite a while to talk. Maybe forever.

Severin brings us both coffee from her secretary's machine and slugged with a shot of brandy from her file-cabinet drawer.

"I can't decide about you, Kit."

The voice, like smoke-heavy curtains rustling behind you.

"Can't decide what?" I ask. The lights so low. The blinds half shut as in some lost film noir. The room is gray, or white, or no color at all.

"Whether you're the luckiest or unluckiest person in the world."

She shakes a cigarette loose from a small pine box shaped like a miniature coffin on her desk.

"Let me know if you figure it out," I say, rubbing my neck.

Cigarette in mouth, she feels for her lab-coat pocket on instinct, but she's still wearing her party costume, the sleek leather dress of a winner.

"Don't suppose you have a light?" she asks, maybe smiling a little.

I shake my head: *Not this time.*

She opens her desk drawer and fumbles around until she finds a box of safety matches. She lights up and takes a drag, leaning back in her chair.

"Oh, Serge," she says, cigarette dancing between her lips. "So he just tucked the body away, eh?"

"Yes. He said he couldn't finish the job. The job was for you?"

She nods slowly. "He told me he'd taken care of it. The campus incinerator. *It took eighty-five minutes,* he told me. He lied."

"So he's the one who told you about Alex? All this time, you knew?"

"Certainly," she says, surprised. "It's my lab."

"But Serge got it all wrong," I say. "He thought Diane killed Alex."

Dr. Severin looks at me, blinking twice. "Didn't she?"

Her face impassive, she nods slowly as I tell her what really happened.

"And you let him run the flash column even with the crack in the glass?" she asks once, then twice.

"I told him to stop," I say. "Over and over."

The look she gives me is one I will feel for a long time. It's a cold thing under my skin.

"You know how he was," I say. "He was never careful. He didn't have to be."

She squints. "Maybe he did."

"What about you?" I counter. "Look what you did. Look what you made Serge do."

"I'm not proud of it," she says, her voice clipped. "Who could be proud of any of this?" She sighs, looking at her hands, which I now see are shaking. "I loved them both."

I look at her, startled. "Why, then? To protect yourself? The lab? The work?"

"Don't moralize with me, Owens. Not now. None of us is off the hook."

"I didn't—"

"There's a reason, after all, you feel so comfortable in that vivarium," she says. "With the mice, and the rats."

Rats. The word stings, rings in my ears.

"So you know everything," I say. I take a breath, thinking of sitting across from Ms. Castro all those years ago. "I should've gone to the police."

"But you didn't, did you?" she says. "Clever girl."

I reach for the pine box, take a cigarette.

"Well, everyone has her weaknesses," I say. "Is Diane yours? First she's your case study. Then she's your intern. And once again you found her."

"If you prefer to phrase it so romantically."

"Are you lovers?" I ask, taking a long drag, my first-ever cigarette. It smells like my dad.

Severin crosses her legs, black leather dress like an oil slick catching the light.

"Oh, Kit," she says, smoke swarming us both, "you are still so young."

NOW

This is how she tells it.

It was more than eight years ago, before she had this lab, her own lab, when she was still climbing hard, knuckles pressed against rock.

She was recruiting participants for a new intramural study on possible genetic factors and PMDD. All day long, her grad students interviewed potential subjects, mostly undergrads drawn in by flyers posted across campus promising UP TO $800 for taking part in the diagnostic testing and interviews. Students were so easy. They'd come just for wax-cup coffee and orange Milanos. And it seemed nearly every college girl who'd ever read Sylvia Plath, which was nearly all of them, longed to be told she suffered from PMDD.

She sometimes watched the interviews through the one-way mirror like a police inspector on a television show. None of the students ever seemed to notice as they nibbled on their cookies, or pretended to. Talking about their bodies and their blood. Their feelings and the heat of them. They were all the same, with their oversize sweatshirts and downy cheeks. Their uptalk and their *justs* and their *I guess, I mean, maybe* and their equivocations (*I don't know, maybe it's just normal to feel this way? To cry all the time for days and days and eat and eat until I'm maybe just gonna die from it?*).

Eased into comfort by the female grad students in their crisp shirts and stylish eyewear, the cool and measured tones she'd trained them to use when interviewing, the undergraduates opened up like loose-hinged clams. (*Ice the muscle first*, her father used to tell her on summer trips to Mustang Island, *and they'll pop like a prom date.*)

But Diane was different. She came on the last day. Everything about her was reserved, even the way she held the proffered cookie, fingers barely touching its edges, like it was a foreign object. She never took a bite, never drank any of the coffee or aromatic tea. Back straight, her head high, her voice low, deep, thoughtful, she spoke clearly, sparingly. She never shifted in her chair, twirled her hair, or tugged her sleeves over her hands like all the others did, girlish and coy. She never spoke in anything other than a low purr.

Yes, anxiety. Tension? Yes. Mood changes? Yes, those too. Yes, hostility. Hostility and other feelings as well.

Because there was a music to it, like a hypnotist's voice. Or like someone who spent most of her time talking to herself, talking in her own head.

Urges that I can't seem to manage. Often, I have this feeling of . . . disorder inside.

When she spoke, she faced not the graduate student interviewing her but the mirror behind. The only one of dozens those first few days who understood what it was all about.

But, after all the tests and interviews and forms, Diane didn't meet the diagnostic criteria for PMDD and so her name did not appear on the list of chosen subjects posted outside Dr. Severin's door.

But I need help, she insisted to the departmental secretary, her fists clenched at her sides. *I must be chosen. I need to be chosen.*

Watching from her office door, Dr. Severin, for reasons still murky to herself, ended up inviting Diane inside. She said she was sorry but there was nothing that could be done. Diane's symptoms did not align with her menstrual cycle.

Simply put, she said, *there's no evidence of a connection between your blood and your feelings.*

But there is, Diane kept insisting, her voice never wavering. *There absolutely is. You're wrong about me. Everyone's wrong about me. I have it.*

It has me.

Dr. Severin listened to her, overcome by a wave of feeling. *This is someone,* she thought, *who has learned something very troubling about herself and does not know what to do.*

That evening, the experience kept humming in her head. The name, it was familiar. *Diane Fleming.*

It wasn't until she, somewhat unethically, looked up Diane's student record that she began to put it together. Diane had graduated from one of the high schools in her scholarship pool.

Had she applied? Indeed she had.

She turned to her scholarship files and found it. That odd letter forwarded to her by the committee chair two years ago. The confidential missive from some guidance counselor at one of those chem-chugging, dying towns by the state line.

It pains me to have to tell the scholarship committee members this. A student has come forward with some upsetting information about Diane Fleming. I cannot confirm the details, but I find this student to be very trustworthy. I do believe her. I realize that the scholarship awards are based on academic excellence but a key guideline is the "in-

tegrity and ethical values" of the applicant and these areas are very much in doubt.

Attached was the obituary. Diane's father. That brush of a mustache and gloomy expression. Medical examiners in those parts don't have elaborate equipment. No mass spectrometer, which could run you a hundred grand. But they do have assumptions, and they assumed. If no family member asks, they assume. Cardiac failure. His heart stopped. Sad, really.

Her first thought had been: *Skip it. Who knows if it's even true? This could be the poison-pen letter of a jealous competitor. Maybe even the other scholarship finalist.*

But her committee chair seemed concerned. *We can't afford to cast a pall over our women-in-sciences scholarship. Our mission is too important.*

And so no one had done anything. And no one told anyone either.

It's not our business, she'd thought.

But now, having seen Diane Fleming, she supposed it might be true. Something was consuming the girl. *I need help.*

She thought of her in that interview room, slightly breathless and entrancing. Wanting desperately to be told that nothing was her fault, that her body and brain had conspired against her. The feeling she must have, always, of being in between worlds, the worlds separated only by an impenetrable pane of glass.

It wasn't until two years later that her name came up again, in a stack of applications for summer internships in the Severin Lab. With an appointment to lecture in Grenoble, she knew she wouldn't be there, but she didn't hesitate to give the slot to Diane. She had all the bona fides and Dr. Severin couldn't help but feel sorry for her in some quiet way. She too understood something about the ways people—women—had to isolate themselves to protect themselves. To keep going.

It turned out, however, that there was some trouble in the lab in her absence. Diane hadn't really fit in and hadn't participated in any of the group extracurriculars. And then there was the matter that had to be addressed: the incident report one of the junior lab techs had filed about her treatment of the animals.

"Serge," I say. "That was Serge."

"He couldn't let it go. That's why he was the best."

I look at her.

"Poor Serge." She shakes her head. "He was always burdened by a kind of male rigidity. Black and white, right and wrong. It's harder for men to understand. Some men."

I nod, putting my cigarette out.

"Women have to live so much of their life in the in-betweens."

Serge's incident report was faintly hysterical, but it was Dr. Severin's duty to follow up. She hoped she might talk seriously with Diane. Encourage her to get some kind of treatment. And, if Diane was resistant, perhaps move the report forward to the dean.

But when she arrived at the lab and saw Diane—that soft golden leaf of hair, the delicately blinking eyes, the steady hands as she held the test tube up to the light, studying it—Dr. Severin found herself inexplicably moved.

The girl, she thought, has no one in the world looking out for her.

So she took her to dinner. Diane had a late train that would take her far away, to graduate school on the opposite coast, and so they sat at the station diner and drank coffee and ate hot turkey sandwiches and talked about the work Diane would be doing

next, studying gender differences in parent-child bonding, injecting oxytocin into the brains of voles.

Finally, as she was paying the check, Dr. Severin decided to
ask. Had she ever gotten help for the things she'd been feeling two
years ago? The disordered thoughts?

Diane smiled faintly and said yes.

Leaning forward, she confided she'd had that all taken care of.

Taken care of?

It's all gone.

Gone.

And she confided that she'd had a radical hysterectomy, elec-
tive.

The keyhole surgery, she said. *I used an inheritance and had it all
taken out.*

Just shy of eleven o'clock, they stepped out onto the dusty train plat-
form. Staring up at the sky, Diane said it reminded her of the first
time she ever saw micrographs of astrocytes, those exquisite star-
shaped brain cells, and discovered the strange beauty of science.

*It was astonishing to me to think the human brain has more cells than
there are stars in the Milky Way.*

But as they waited, spotting the train's smoke swirl in the distance, all Dr. Severin could think of was this girl, this young
woman, had chosen to have her womb cut from her body for no
reason at all. Or, at least, no reason that made any sense.

Untimely ripped—the phrase came to her.

The train approaching, whistles and horns screaming, Dr. Severin found herself moving toward her to hear, closer and closer
until their faces were inches apart.

You know I saw you once, Diane said, grabbing for her bags. *I was
just a high-school student, fifteen,* she said, *but you talked to us about*

*women and science. You were showing these brain scans and I knew what
I wanted to do, to be.* The blood is the life, *you said.*

As the train thundered in, enveloping them both in the manner
of a Russian novel, she found herself placing her hand on Diane's
gleaming forehead.

Show them what you've got, she said, *show them what you have in
there.*

She wasn't even sure what it meant.

As Diane stepped onto the train, Dr. Severin was thinking that
the brain was a monstrous and beautiful thing. A ravishing chaos.

Shouting over the chugging train, the brake pipe and conduc-
tor's cry, the crackling intercom, Dr. Severin reached for her arm,
thin as kindling.

*Dr. Severin, do you remember the first time you held one in your
hands? A brain?*

Yes, Dr. Severin said. *Of course.*

How did it make you feel?

Humbled, she said honestly.

A quizzical look came over the girl's face.

Really? Diane replied, just as the train began pulling away. *It
made me feel powerful.*

"Last year, in the hiring pool, her name came up, and then came
up again. A rising star," Dr. Severin says to me. "I don't know. Call
it curiosity, call it something else, something..."

She cleared her throat, hiding her eyes from me.

I don't say anything, still thinking of Diane, her womb plucked
out. Her shorn hair and shorn body. The wormy logic of her
wormy brain.

"It's best," she says, "to think of Diane as a sick person like any
other kind of sick person. She can't help what she is."

What she is. But what was she before?

Or did I already know?

I think about her that first time at camp, before everything with her dad, before her exile at her mother's hands. In the hotel room, how sick she got after all our secrets were told, everyone's but hers, and how I held that hair in my hand, like a fistful of silk, and the way, sleeping in our shared room's bed, our bodies curled, the only time we were ever so close, front of knee to back of knee.

I could feel all her breaths, hoarse and high. I could feel her breaths vibrating through me and not even be sure if they were hers or mine.

My mom always says, you don't have a self until you have a secret.

That girl, that girl. Hurt already a thousand times by fifteen.

"There is something especially hard about mad people who know they are mad," Dr. Severin says, tapping out her cigarette. "If Diane weren't so brilliant, maybe she wouldn't know how mad she is. But she does. And I think that must be a terrible feeling."

I take another cigarette. "Sorry," I say, trying to still my shaking hand. "I'm not going to feel sorry for her."

"Well, Kit," she says, leaning back in her chair, those legs displayed, one shoe slipping off, "that's a shame. But, like I said, you're still so young."

I drop my head and take a breath, not wanting her to see me.

When I lift my head again, her eyes have gone glassy.

They're nearly ready for us.

I have no idea what to expect. Obstruction of justice, at best, and what about the lab? The scandal?

We stand and Dr. Severin smooths her hair, then mine.

"You might think about what draws the three of us together," she says, gathering herself now. "We've all tasted the apple, haven't we? We ate it whole."

As I walk by, I see her seated on one of the rolling chairs in the animal-prep room, the officer with the mustache standing beside her.

"Are they taking me now?" she is saying, looking up at him. "I explained what I did. I explained about Serge and about Alex and about Dad."

I wonder if she can see me.

"We need to wait here a minute," the officer is saying. "Then we're taking you to the station."

Her head lifts, golden under the lights, that Saint Joan face, composed and sure.

"I killed them," she says, eyes skittering toward me. "I killed all of them."

Detective Harper and her partner, the rooster-breasted one, are waiting for me.

"You don't have to be afraid of her any longer," he says. "We got it all in writing."

"Afraid?"

"She told us how she threatened you."

I don't say anything, trying to imagine what she might have said. *Alex and I were fighting. He knew my secret. The glass broke. Kit came in after. She wanted to call 911—I pressured Kit and threatened her into concealing everything.*

Oh, Diane, I think. *I never asked you to do that. I never would.*

Detective Harper tells me he'd be very surprised if the DA bothered with me at all. "You were dealing with a multiple murderer, after all," she says.

"Right."

"Some days," her partner says, handing me some forms, "fortune smiles on you."

"I've always been a lucky girl," I say.

"Or smart enough to make her own luck," says Detective Harper, looking at me.

I see her from a distance.

The two policemen from before are escorting her back through the vivarium to the door. Her back is hunched, head ducked, and she looks so very small.

I start moving toward her.

"Diane," I say, unable to stop myself. "Diane, you didn't have to."

I can hear Dr. Severin behind me, asking the mustachioed officer if we can approach.

"Diane," I say, but she doesn't see me, or won't look at me.

Her arms drop to her sides stiffly as the three of them pass a long lab bench, stainless steel so bright it hurts my eyes, all the gleaming containers of pipettes, scalpels, specimen scissors and knives, capillary tubes, glass septums.

"Diane," I say again. "I'm sorry."

And all I mean is *I'm sorry you're like this. I'm sorry your parents didn't love you enough and I'm sorry no one ever taught you how to be. I'm sorry for all the feelings you had that you never learned how to stop and most of all I'm sorry your brain couldn't work out how to live in this world.*

But she won't look at me, and there's that strange, stilted way she's walking now, one arm hanging in front of her like a broken limb, her sleeve covering her hand.

"Officer," Detective Harper is calling out, "can you escort Dr. Fleming to the squad car?"

Diane raises her head and looks at me, at Dr. Severin, both of us still. The feeling inside of something—

"Kit," she says. "Kit. I fixed it."

Diane's long arm lifts, her hand like a white spider. I see the flash of a specimen knife slipping from her sleeve into her palm.

"Don't, don't!" I shout to anyone at all.

The officer moves quickly, his arms flying up, but Diane is faster than anyone when she wants to be. Because she's already so far ahead before you even begin.

"Diane, no!" Dr. Severin cries out.

Her eyes on me, her face trembling, she throws her head back, that long neck bare and gleaming—

The carotid, you die much faster, she'd said. *So fast.*

—and with one endless sweep she drags the blade forward and across, ear to neck, everything going red.

Her legs falling beneath her, that great burst of blood, bright red, redder than anything I've ever seen.

My mouth opening, I'm running forward, a sprinter always, and never fast enough.

TEN YEARS LATER

"It's the lab you dream of," the young woman says, leaning forward slightly in her chair.

She is so nervous, neck straining, her CV in her lap, her scholarly publications neatly bound. She wants the position. She wants so badly to be on the team.

"It took three years to renovate," I say, "but we made it, thanks to some very generous women's foundations and a little Big Pharma. They're always circling, hoping for a proprietary treatment."

"The biotech center, the mass spectrometry facility—I saw the pictures in *Time* magazine. I mean, you should see the lab I'm coming from at State."

I smile, wanting to pat her on the head. "Well, it turns out there was a lot more money for 'female problems' than anyone thought," I say. But she's too young to think about these things: funding, budgets, the long, slow march of scientific progress. She's just finishing graduate school and has the dewy, wide-eyed look of a fairy-tale virgin.

"There's something about the light here," she says, looking up at the skylights and out into the glass-walled corridors, offices, and laboratories. "It's inspiring."

"All the better to see you with, my dear," I say, tapping my pen. Counting, in my head, all the security cameras on us now. The first steps taken, years ago, after everything. After Diane.

"I never believed any of it," the young woman says, lowering her voice. "All that stuff about the lab's toxic environment."

"The Laboratory of Death," the newspapers called it, way back when. "The Microscope and the Angel of Death." "Madwoman in the Lab: How Far Would She Go to Keep Her Secret?"

"Good for you," I say. Even smarter than her GPA indicates, this one.

"You've worked with Dr. Severin for longer than anyone, right?" she asks.

But my mind is now with Diane. Those photos of her in the paper all those years ago, her lab coat like an angel's wings. I try not to think about her, about all of that, but sometimes it comes back—meeting a transfer student from Lanister, spotting the new lab tech with the pale gamine haircut.

"Yes," I say, finally. "For her, and now with her. She's very loyal." I see the look in the young woman's eyes and remember it well: *When will I get to meet her? What is she really like?* "She travels a lot, but she counts on me here."

Dr. Severin and I, bound forever.

Crimping the edges of her CV, the young woman peers through the glass into the central atrium, the scattering of bodies down below. Like the dark, swarmy backs of mice in a maze.

"And what makes you so interested in our work?" I ask, pulling the CV from her hand.

"Well," she says, her face frozen now, panic dancing across her eyes. Then, a smile emerging, a grin, really. "It's still the dark continent, right?"

I smile and nod. "It is."

*   *   *

After the interview, there is the requisite tour of the shiny new stem-cell unit, the endless security march into the animal unit, the vivarium with its new modular wall system promising "state-of-the-art airflow control for unprecedented employee safety."

"You'll hear from us," I say as I walk her out, her extra CVs curled between her sweaty fingers.

When I return to my office, I see a stack of mail on my desk.

The apple-green envelope stands out, not interoffice, not government mail, not slick research-publication Mylar. It's greeting-card size and sealed with a foil wafer. The return address is Sarasota, Florida. When I open it, I smell perfume, strong and cloying. There's a jolly card with beach umbrellas and, inside, a folded piece of paper on sunny stationery. I open it and begin reading.

Dear Kit:

Do you remember me? If so, I hope it is with fondness. You were very kind to my troubled daughter. May she rest in peace.

You can't imagine my surprise when I sat in my doctor's waiting room, opened up a copy of Time *magazine, and saw the profile of your lab and your important work on behalf of women.*

I shouldn't say "surprise," really. I know I only met you once, Kit, but I feel like I know you. Diane spoke of you so often, with such admiration. After reading the article, I began to think about why things went so right for you and so wrong for Diane. But the truth is, there is no one to blame but Diane for the mess she made of her life. You worked so hard, harder than anyone. And now I hear about all this research you're doing that is definitely going to change women's lives. Is it wrong to say I'm proud of you?

No one ever imagines what it must feel like to have a murderess for a daughter. Every time I tell someone about Diane's crimes, they sympathize, assure me it's not my fault. Even though I know they are right, it pains me. Sometimes I do blame myself. But it is my nature to take on the pain of my children.

You see, Diane always was a demanding, needy child. Her father and I were so young when we had her. We still had so much growing up to do. And he was never a warm person—he never knew how to show me love, I can tell you that. So of course Diane wanted to be with me—all the time, really. But a woman has needs beyond her child, doesn't she? When I found love again with my husband, Steve, Diane was unable to cope. She even conjured some tale of his seduction at the hands of a teenage girl. It is sad to think about now. Perhaps I should have seen it as a cry for help. But, as everyone tells me, there was nothing I could do. Who could understand her sickness?

I'm only glad I didn't believe her deceit (I see it now as a symptom of her illness). And, in the end, it brought Steve and myself closer together.

I can't say, when she moved in with her father, I ever suspected the dark path it would lead her down. It may seem hard to believe now, but a month after his passing, Diane came to me and confessed. I did not believe her. Diane always had strange ideas, even as a small child. Sometimes I wonder if she fell out of the crib as a child or if she suffered some damage all those times she wandered off as a little girl.

Diane, I said, this is just another one of your stories. But she was insistent, hysterical. I told her if anything had really happened, the doctors would know. Still, she would not give up and kept de-

manding I take her straight to the police station. She begged me to make her go. She wanted to drag me down with her, you see? Just as she did to you. Thankfully, we are both stronger than that.

In the end, I told her she was just going to have to live with what she'd done. Next time you want something, I said, make sure you really want it.

My point is, Kit, we did more than anyone could to help Diane. She always said you were the smartest person she ever met. And now, look at all you've achieved. Devoted your career to seeking a balm for the maladies of being a woman.

On behalf of women everywhere, I thank you.

Growing in love and wisdom,
"Mrs. Fleming"
P.S. I enclose a picture of my "new" family from a few summers ago. Got it right this time!

I peer into the envelope and shake loose the photograph inside. A family of four standing on a dock, Diane's mom at the center, tall and blond as ever, her tan skin thickened with time, what my mom used to call banana-boat skin. She has one arm around each of her girls, both long-legged beyond their years, their mouths full of orthodontia. And the husband with the boatman's cap, the big grin, his arm reaching down to rub the drooping liverish belly of a very large bloodhound.

There is something in him that's familiar.

They stand in front of a cabin cruiser, sky blue. Along its side, in flamboyant silver script: THE DREAM CATCHER.

No single guy has a dream catcher in his car.

Who said that? I think, smiling. Then I can nearly picture it, four teenagers huddled on our double beds at the Wheels Inn. Sarina and the other one—was it Shauna?—and Diane. My sordid tale of Stevie Shoes, the sportswear salesman with bloodhounds I used to dog-sit for. Stevie and his fast hands and the dream catcher hanging from his rearview mirror. Purple feathers tickling my chin. Stevie Shoes, who must've been fifteen years older than me, sliding his fingers down my jeans, telling me all his girlfriend problems.

Stevie Shoes.

. . . *my husband, Steve* . . . The feeling comes slowly, and I hold the photo closer, squinting.

And closer, grabbing the arm on my lamp and tilting it.

What, I think, *is Diane's mom doing with Stevie Shoes?*

Because that's who the man in the picture is. Older, a little huskier, but he is Stevie, and he is also apparently Steve, Mrs. Fleming's husband.

The pieces jumble in my head for assembling, before fitting into place: How I told Diane about Stevie that night at camp. How the next time I saw Diane, more than a year later, she'd been ousted from her mom's life. How Diane admitted she'd found something out about her mother's boyfriend and told her. Things that showed the kind of man he was.

Mom, your boyfriend is cheating on you with his fifteen-year-old dog-sitter in the front seat of his car.

Mom, it's true. I know it happened. It's absolutely true.

Mom, you believe me, right?

Mom.

The truth can't be poison, she'd told her mother.

But it was, for Diane. Exiled, banished, expelled from a questionable Eden to the pullout sofa in her father's bachelor apartment. And everything that came after.

*   *   *

I look at the photo again, for a long time. Diane and me, joined together from the start, long before I even knew it.

A professor once described the brain to me as a great silent vault. A dark theater with nothing playing on the screen. Just electrical charges bouncing corner to corner, like lightbulbs flashing off and on.

Science doesn't yet have any idea how everyone's private, personal experience of the world springs from that empty vault. We don't know yet why we sleep or why we dream. What and how we remember.

The world is a fiction the brain constructs. The smell of a fresh peach, the punch of a firefly in the night sky. The lilting *hush-hush* of a first lullaby. The brain fashions it all and we don't know how, or why.

So how could I know about myself, what I am, what Diane is or was before?

What Diane and I are together that we might never have been alone.

THEN

Graduation Day

This is a golden moment. That's what my mom kept saying.

The big Lanister sky made sure I felt it. Was it possible I'd never noticed it before, Barbicide blue and stretching on forever? And how the shaggy buildings of old downtown were winking at me? Even the sensual push of rust-pocked cars in and out of the strip malls struck me that day. All the colors and window-glassed agony of so many sad souls dying, dying, dying to get home or to get back to something like they felt before, long ago, that feeling they had the night of their graduation, drunk and tickle-nosed on Cold Duck and everything smelling of new dresses and blazers and the smack of social performance, a masquerade, and all the adults getting caught up in it, bemoaning their lost innocence when they still had youth but didn't know what to do with it.

I was eager to let mine go, but I also felt feelings I couldn't quite grab hold of. Like maybe the ending of things was the best part, the only time you saw the beauty in anything at all. And you had to honor those moments.

Maybe my dad taught me that, his sudden sorrow at being called on all his bad behavior, crying on our front lawn, begging to be reformed, redeemed at last. It was only at the end that he realized everything *had* mattered after all.

"You may not care, but I care," my mom announced as we drove up to the Hair Cuttery.

"I have to wear the flat hat anyway," I said, trying once more, but it was no use. I was getting my hair done, and my nails too.

"You'll thank me later," she said.

I wanted to tell her it didn't matter, nothing here did. I'd already reserved the $19.99 U-Haul, stockpiling liquor boxes from the Safeway, swiping the good cartons from the Golden Fry. I couldn't move to State until August first and it'd be six weeks of cleaning cages and bagging ferals before then, but in my head, I was already gone.

"I skipped my graduation," she said, pulling into the lot. "Instead, I got drunk on Southern Comfort with your dad and spent the day fishing croakers and silversides off the dock down at Point Cooper. Jet-Puffed marshmallows as bait. Your dad fell and hit his head on a post. I had to hitch us a ride with two meatheads to the urgent care, his head bleeding on my lap all over my Pepto-pink graduation dress. In the ER, they kept calling me Jackie O."

For the first time, I remember thinking that in all my mom's stories about how my dad ruined her life, she made it sound like fun. Like that was the only time she felt like she was really living this life.

That probably was the surest sign that it was time to leave, and fast.

"You'll come home weekends," my mom said, as if reading my mind, "sometimes. It's only six hours on the bus."

And we both pretended I would.

*　　*　　*

"Diane."

I turned, and it was already happening. My mom reaching out to embrace Diane, who was exiting the drugstore. Diane, to whom I hadn't spoken in two months but who was always there, like a ghost, haunting a different school from mine. An empty, silent one. I hadn't spoken to her, so had Diane spoken at all?

"Hi, Mrs. Owens," her voice came, so low and hoarse it was as if she truly hadn't spoken in ages, her words tentative, her head bowed. "Kit."

There was a smell about her, not her usual baby powder and Ivory soap. I spotted a slick of oil in the hair tucked behind her ear.

"You must be excited for today," my mom enthused. Swept up in everything, her purse fat with cash from taking the swear jar to the bank, she put her rubbed-red arms around Diane again.

"We've missed you at the house," she added. "But we'll see you at graduation, right? And your grandpa?"

"Yes," Diane said. "Well, not him. He's in the hospital."

Which I'd heard but wasn't sure was true. That her grandfather had been sick. But based on the look on Diane's face and the way her head ducked lower still, maybe it was worse.

"Oh no, sweetie," my mom said. I saw what was going to happen and I couldn't stop it. "Listen, honey, I have an idea."

The salon door opened, and Rae and Reena and the shampoo girl Taffy all lifted their arms—scissors in hand, curlers, Aqua Net—in celebratory cheers. That's when I saw it was a party—a kind of party, at least. Rae, whom my mom had known all the way back to kindergarten, had run silver streamers across the mirror tops and around the pedestal ashtrays heavy with fresh cigarette butts. A big plastic bowl of slush punch shivered by the perm station, and silver-sprayed mortarboards with tassels balanced on top of every hair-dryer hood.

It was kind of great.

"Happy graduation, superstar genius," Rae said, swathing me in a floral smock. "I could've predicted this when you first caught me shortchanging you at age six!"

"Oh, well, goddamn," my mom said, not quite crying yet. "This is harder than I thought."

Diane's whisper between the shampoo sinks, our heads sloshing in froth.

"Kit, I shouldn't be here. I'm sorry."

"Don't apologize," I said, Taffy's knuckles hard against my scalp.

The sinks were vibrating from the hair dryers and the air was dense with perm solution, hairspray, smoke, heavy perfume.

Squinting to my side, I could see my mom whispering gravely to Reena and Rae, her lips moving, I knew it was *And her granddad in the hospital and Mom nowhere to be seen and did you know her dad died last year? So sudden.*

And Reena and Rae clucking their tongues and Taffy, her hands lifting from the soap, turning to listen, shaking her head sorrowfully.

"Sorry about your grandfather," I said, feeling my eyes pinch from the smells. "Is he going to be okay?"

"I don't think so," Diane said quietly. "He had a pretty bad stroke." Since I couldn't turn my head, since the nozzle was spraying fitfully next to my softening ear, it sounded like her voice had come from inside me.

Neither of us said anything for a few long minutes, Taffy sticking her fingers in my ears through the towel.

"Congratulations on the scholarship," Diane said. "I wanted to tell you."

"Thanks," I said. I felt my mouth filling with perfumes just by speaking. "It's the only way I could've gone to State."

"Kit, I wanted to tell you. It's okay. All of it."

"What?" I said, my head turning, a plash of water on my neck. "What did you say?"

"Ms. Castro, how she looks at me now. I figured it out."

She knows. I shook my head, unable to look at her. Unable to look.

"But Kit, it's okay. It's the right thing, how it should be. Please don't ever feel bad—"

"I never would," I said, angry now. "I never would. You did this—"

"But if you do, just remember what I'm saying now. It was right. And you deserve it."

My eyes, aching, filled quickly. Suddenly, I was crying; all the chemicals were making me cry.

"I don't know what's wrong with you," I blurted out, rising to my feet, my hair dripping. Taffy ran after me with towels.

Because I could feel myself sinking back into it, the feeling of Diane.

Because there we were: Valedictorian, salutatorian. Rising stars one and two. A murderer and a tattletale. Secret-keepers, both.

"Are we going to get this party started or what?" Rae shouted. My mom whisked over to the punch bowl and Taffy turned on the ancient, fuzzy stereo system that piped through every hair station.

Diane and I exchanged sneaky smiles.

The music was loud, Bob Seger, something like that. The door locked, the CLOSED sign hanging, all of us sipping punch, staining our lips magenta, as Rae and Reena hovered over our heads, the clatter of pins, curlers, rods. Taffy dancing, waving a shampoo cape like a tore-ador, when that old Madonna song came on.

Diane couldn't take her eyes off my mom, who was shimmying a little and kept squeezing both our shoulders.

Wielding her comb tail like a sword, Rae talked as she sectioned Diane's hair for curlers, making a pineapple of her head, making all of us laugh.

"Diane, are you sure you trust her?" my mom said, plastic punch ladle in one hand, reaching for Diane's arm with the other.

"Damn," Reena said, already through with my shorter locks, strolling from me to Diane. "Diane has magic hair. Like Cinderella, right?"

"Sleeping Beauty," my mom said, squeezing Diane's fingers. Patting and touching her like she did her rescue pups, her mangy pit bulls.

"Graduation fever," I said to my mom. "That's what you have."

I'd never seen Diane so happy, all these women swirling about her, tending to her as she sat under the hair dryer. Taffy filling her punch cup and Reena buffing her nails and no one saying anything about anything, my mom even making me sit on her lap for a few minutes, bragging to everyone about my scholarship, my honors, the grand future before me.

"She's never coming back, Mama Owens," Rae said, clucking her tongue. "What're you gonna do?"

"I have my dogs!" my mom shouted, raising her glass and laughing and everyone laughing, except then my mom was crying too and Rae and Reena both teased her mercilessly. (*Poor Mommy! "Aw, shit, baby's got a full scholarship and can't stick around for my dog-hair soup!"*)

*　　*　　*

Diane and I kept catching each other's eye. We were circling each other from far out. We were gripped in some kind of energy, wondering about the other. We'd forgotten about blood and dead dads, or I had. Only for today. It wasn't just the punch, not even nearly. It was graduation day and the end of high school and the end of things, and Diane was a red lick of hunger, of desperation.

"Thank you for all this," Diane kept saying, tilting her punch glass to her mouth. Head bobbing tipsily. "I'm very grateful. I never had this."

"Had what, honey?" my mom said, dancing to Sheena Easton and, each time she passed us, brushing stray hairs from our necks and ears.

But Diane couldn't answer, and as we sat in our chairs, too punch-weighted and perfume-drunk to move, I felt like everything I wanted to keep inside was coming to the surface.

"Well, both of you should know how loved you are today," my mom was saying. "And how proud your family is of you."

"Even if your grandpa can't be there," Rae said, "he's with you in spirit."

"And your mom too," Reena said, her hands on Diane's sharp shoulders.

Adults, I thought, had this funny way of forgetting. Because if, earlier today, my mom had forgotten about everything with Diane and her own advice to me on Senior Achievement Night (*You must do for you*), in that moment, she remembered it. Remembered it and turned away, lashes fluttering, something in her eye, something making her busy her hands with filling more plastic cups of clouding punch. My mom feeling my gaze, her face flushing watermelon pink.

"Well, goddamn," Reena said this time.

Rae had spun Diane's chair around, spraying madly, and we all got to see.

Those long blond locks stroked and smooth and coaxed and curled into something like a pin-up girl's, a movie star's, old school.

And Diane smiled in that small way of hers, this time even showing the tiny tips of her pretty white teeth. And her lips dark from the punch, and skin that glowed like radium. Like Marie Curie might.

I guess I never saw anything quite so lovely.

"Now you're ready to graduate," Taffy said, running a hand just above the sheen of Diane's hair, pretending to smooth it like a sheet. "Now you're ready for anything."

They made her look in the mirror, but Diane barely glanced. Instead, she kept looking all around at the women, the twinned bosomy presence of the sisters, Taffy's chirpy energy, and my mom, laughing and wiping a steady stream of tears away with the heel of her hand.

"Like an angel," Taffy said, touching her hair, lifting it high. "Your daddy would be so proud."

That's when Diane looked in the mirror, her hand on her long, long hair like it was suddenly a stolen treasure she didn't deserve. Like it was an affliction.

She looked in the mirror as if hoping it would swallow her.

The music swelled, Taffy swirling the dial on the stereo, the speakers spitting out Fleetwood Mac. Rae and Reena danced, clicking their metal hair clips like castanets, and my mom began dutifully sweeping up the hair, singing along loudly.

As Diane and I sat beside each other, catching our breath, the city hall bell tolled. It was definitely time to go, to graduate, to leave, to never come back. Facing our mirrors, speckled with sprays and potions, our eyes landed on each other and it was me who did it. I was the one, my hand swinging like a bell clapper, reaching for her hand, red and clenched at her side. Reaching for it, pushing it open, making her surrender it to me. Her face didn't change, but her hand gave itself to me, grabbed onto me for dear life. Our fingers locked tight and Diane's face still and blank and everything raging and lamenting inside, and I could forget, I could. We both could.

She was Diane Fleming, and I was never going to see her again.

Acknowledgments

Deepest thanks go, foremost, to Reagan Arthur, the ne plus ultra of editors, for whom I am grateful every writing day.

And to the wondrous Sabrina Callahan and all my heroes at Little, Brown: Craig Young, Ashley Marudas, Katharine Myers, Alyssa Persons, Joseph Lee, and so many more. And my lifesavers, as ever, Peggy Freudenthal and Tracy Roe.

By the same token, I am so grateful for the wise and wonderful Francesca Main, Paul Baggaley, and Emma Bravo at Picador.

To Dan Conaway, as stalwart, steadfast, and true an agent as one could hope for, and to Taylor Templeton, Maja Nikolic and, more largely, to Writers House.

And heartiest thanks are owed to Sylvie Rabineau and Jill Gillett.

To Jessica Malberg, for her invaluable fact-checking and question answering. And to Heather MacLeod, for providing a key early assist.

And personal thanks to my dad, Philip Abbott, who inspires and encourages me with every conversation, and my mom, Patricia Abbott, whose own creative daring is a marvel to behold.

Acknowledgments

To Josh, Julie, and Kevin, whom I treasure and adore, and to the kindhearted Nases: Jeff, Ruth, Steve, Michelle, and little Marley.

To that stalwart and sneaky genius Alison Quinn, and for the eternal friendship and grand company of Darcy Lockman, Lisa Lutz, the FLs, and my beloved Oxford, MS, friends (Jack, Theresa, Ace and Angela, Bill and Katie, and Jimmy) who save my life all the time.